Finally Free

Women of Fossil Ridge Series

Book Two

LYNNE GENTRY

TRAVEL LIGHT PRESS
FANTASY · DRAMA · ADVENTURE

Finally Free (Women of Fossil Ridge Series, Book Two)

Copyright © 2018 Lynne Gentry

Sign up for bonus information at: www.lynnegentry.com

This is a work of fiction. Names, characters, organizations, places, events, and incidents are products of the author's imagination.

Cover photo licensed by Shutterstock©2018

Edited by Gina Calvert

ISBN: 978-0-9986412-5-6

DEDICATION

For my beautiful mother-in-law, Mary Gentry.

I'll treasure your support and unconditional love forever.

Finally Free

Chapter 1

CHARLOTTE

"Family is not always flesh and blood, Charlotte Ann." My mother clutches the porch railing and glares at the senior citizen van lumbering up the lane. "Ira and Teeny belong here…on the Fossil Ridge…with us."

I cast a weary glance at the small U-Haul trailer still hitched to my rental car. Maybe it was a mistake to press a pillow to the face of my dying marriage, pull my daughter away from her friends, and flush my financial stability down the toilet to move home. I wish doing the right thing didn't give me such heartburn. Like it or not, Momma's recent accident and subsequent escape from an assisted living facility proves she can no longer fare for herself. There is no one else to assume her full-time care. I'm it.

This is not the first time I've completely remodeled my life to do right by my mother, to somehow make it up to her for failing to save

1

my sister. My old college roommate and long-time friend Winnie— at least I think we're still friends—says I'm a glutton for punishment. She also says there's really not a sacrifice big enough to make up for not drowning that day.

Winnie's opinions aside, I moved home for three reasons. One, my daughter deserves a shot at a normal family, if the Slocum women can ever be *that* again. And two…

"Charlotte Ann, I want them to stay," Momma repeats.

I can't allow Momma to pile a couple of extra geriatrics on my plate. The added weight would bury the needs of my thirteen-year-old. I'm not shortchanging Aria again. Navigating my mother's descent into dependence and my daughter's ascent toward independence will take everything I've got. I have to draw the line at taking on senile strangers.

And two, I tell myself as I mentally review my list, taking care of my aging mother is the right thing to do.

"Momma," my exhausted sigh pushes out the reprimand I've been holding back for two days. "We've talked about this…several times." Guilt immediately swamps me. Condescension is exactly the opposite of what my mother needs. "The director at The Reserve agreed to let Teeny and Ira *visit* here for a few days, but they can't stay."

"I haven't forgotten what it takes to run a household, Charlotte." Momma shakes her pointer finger at me like the wooden ruler she once used to control her students. "I'm simply asking you to look beyond how this affects you and help my friends."

I'm pleased that my mother is finally asking for my help, but the implication that I've *never* done anything for her before nicks my resolve to do the right thing. "Momma, do you realize that I left a very lucrative career on Capitol Hill, pulled my thirteen-year-old away from her school and friends, and drove a U-Haul half-way across the country so that *you* wouldn't have to spend your last days away from your ranch?"

"My friends shouldn't be punished. I'm the one who planned the entire prison break. I won't let you send them back."

Momma's determined expression reminds me of the disapproval she expressed on my wedding day. "Marrying James McCandless is a mistake," she'd said right before she reluctantly dropped the veil over my face in the stuffy little nursery of the Addisonville First Baptist Church and marched out.

It's been nearly fifteen years since I walked myself down the aisle. Less than a year after the exotic honeymoon my mother-in-law paid for, I caught James and a beautiful woman model in X-rated affection. Momma was right. James McCandless was a mistake. One of many. Making up for my mistakes is the *third* reason I've circled back to this ranch.

I turn and gently clasp my mother's shoulders. "Momma, we got lucky this time. Teeny doesn't have any family left to press charges against you, and Ira's threatened to disinherit his kids if they even think about taking legal action."

"Geez, Mom." Aria sits wedged between Ira and Teeny on the porch swing. "They're sitting right here." She strokes the Siamese cat curled in her arms. "Nana's friends are old, not deaf." Her hostile stare pushes me deeper into what's fast becoming a very lonely corner.

No matter what I do, it's not going to be right for someone. I'm destined to be the bad guy. "Everyone needs to understand the seriousness of this situation." I'm the only one who blinks. "Leaving your assisted living center...in the middle of the night...in a stolen car was...a dangerous thing to do. You're all very fortunate that you eventually found your way here and that no one was hurt." There I go with the reprimands again and, as usual they fall harder on everyone than I intended.

Ira pulls his little lap dogs close to his chest. "How can anyone claim that I stole my own car?"

"When my mother drove your Cadillac off the premises, it was considered stolen," I explain...again.

"Sara only drove because I can't see good no more," Ira points to his thick glasses. "Heck, I gave her the keys and got in...of my own free will."

"And that's the only reason Momma's not in jail." Bless Ira's bald head, the fact that he no longer has a driver's license is obviously a sore spot so I try a different angle. "Ira, your children let you keep your car at The Reserve only—"

"To keep me busy." Ira sets his dogs at his feet then drags a palm over his shiny head. "Tinkering on an old car ain't the same as nurturing the land or watching things grow." His rheumy gaze lights on my mother. "Helping this fine woman fix a few things around here these last few days has been more fun than polishing my whole fleet of antique cars."

"Fun." Teeny's voice is rusty from lack of use. According to Momma, this Yankee wearing a huge pink hairbow on the side of her snowy-white head has become a chatterbox since Momma planted her in Hill Country soil.

"Mom," Aria deposits her cat into Teeny's arms and leaps from the swing. "Nana's right, why can't you pull one of your fancy, lawyer tricks? Become their legal guardian or something?"

My jaws clench at how quickly Aria's loyalty has landed squarely with my mother. Shoring up either relationship is going to be harder than I thought. "How do you know about legal guardianship?"

Aria holds up her phone. "I Googled it."

"Have you Googled how Texas frowns on lawyers practicing law who are not licensed in their fair state?"

"I did." She swipes her screen. "Here's the short version: Until you pass the Texas bar exam, you can get another lawyer to vouch for you." Aria dramatically waves her musically-gifted fingers in the direction of Momma's fellow escapees. "You've got to do something to make money. While you're getting your Texas license, Ira can pay you to live here and to represent him. Right, Ira?"

"I can," he says.

"Ari, let me worry about our finances, okay?"

My daughter's eyes blaze with the same stubborn streak I've seen in the mirror. "If *these* people are part of Nana's family, doesn't that make them part of *our* family?"

"We'll visit Nana's *friends* often." I land hard on the differentiation.

Aria jams her hands on her hips. "How often?"

"As often as we can, okay?"

"More than we used to visit Nana?"

The Reserve's shiny-white-people-mover comes to a stop in front of the porch, but four sets of pleading eyes stay glued on me, waiting for my answer. "I don't know, Ari. There's no set plan. We're going to have to make this up as we go along."

"Teeny and Ira won't be any trouble." Aria's tears are a tow truck wench on my heart. "Nana and I will do everything. You won't even know they're here."

This child has always had a special attachment to her Nana, but her willingness to hatch a secret plan with her grandmother proves that it's grown even stronger in just the few days that we've been here. No question about it, Aria has always brought out the best in my mother—the softer side—the side that I remember but haven't felt or experienced since my older sister Caroline died.

I want my daughter to know *that* woman…the one I lost.

But until this very moment, I hadn't considered the emotional blow my mother's inevitable passing will have on my daughter. I was eighteen when I lost my sister. I know the damage of tragic loss at a young age. Allowing Aria to attach herself to my mother's elderly friends sets my little girl up for two extra heartaches.

The driver pokes his head from the van. "Morning. This the Slocum residence?"

"It is," I turn, smile, and chirp like we're all so excited to see him that we've baked a cake. "I'm Charlotte McCandless."

He steps from the folding door dressed in blue scrubs. "I'm the nurse sent to pick up two wayward Reserve residents."

I don't know why, but the term *wayward* doesn't set well with me. "You'll be transporting Ira Conner and Teeny McElroy. They're lovely people."

"Are they packed and ready?" he asks like that's all he cares about.

"Yes," I say.

"No, they're not." Aria snaps, then rapidly corrects herself after I shoot her a confused scowl. "Ready to go, I mean."

The driver's conflicted gaze jumps between me and my

daughter. "Why don't I get my clipboard...give everyone a minute to say their goodbyes?"

"That would be great," I smile despite the visual daggers being plunged into my back.

His gaze slides toward my mother. "I have a few papers for you to sign, Mrs. Slocum."

Momma crosses her arms and presses her lips into a thin, defiant line.

"She's not signing anything!" Aria shouts.

"Ari!" While the nurse slips back inside the van, I take my daughter aside. "Listen to me." I assume the exact same parental clasp of the shoulders I'd just taken with my mother. "There's twenty minutes of dusty road between the Fossil Ridge Ranch and the nearest milk and bread. What do you think would happen if Ira or Teeny needed emergency medical care?"

Aria rolls her eyes at me as if I'd left all of my brain cells in DC. "We'd do the same thing for them we'd do for Nana. We'd call an ambulance."

"Help could take too long to get here."

"If it's so dangerous, why are we letting Nana live out here?"

"It's her home." I shake off Aria's belligerent glare. "Honey, Ira and Teeny deserve to be in a home where qualified professionals can look after them and get to them immediately."

Momma steps between me and Aria. "Then you might as well

send me back, too."

From the corner of my eye, I see the well-built nurse making his way up the sidewalk. Provoking my mother in front of a muscled, medical professional probably isn't the wisest choice, but for Aria's sake I can't let Momma's ridiculous demand go unchallenged.

"What do you mean send *you* back?" At the strain in my voice, the nurse stops in his tracks. I don't care if this stranger thinks I'm the one who needs a seat on the senile bus, this has to be said. And I'm going to keep saying it until my mother finally hears me, no matter how long I've put off changing from daughter to caretaker. "We're trying to be a family here. Not a retirement village. I can't raise my daughter, take care of you, and babysit two failing geriatrics."

Momma sets her shoulders. Her don't-mess-with-me stare pins me to a porch pillar. "I used to manage twenty-five third graders with varying family lives, IQs, and behavioral issues. And I did it all by myself. I'm more than capable of taking care of two wonderful friends." My mother marches over to the swing and plops down between Ira and Teeny. "Friends are the family you choose, Charlotte Ann." She hooks one arm around Teeny and the other around Ira. "We're a package deal. Take us or leave us."

"Don't tempt me, Momma."

Chapter 2

SARA

Against my better judgment, I concede to Charlotte Ann and allow two of the kindest people I've ever known disappear from my life. I dig my nails into the porch railing to keep from running after them.

It's true that I hadn't thought through all of the ramifications of adding extra bodies to my household. For once in my life, I wanted to veer away from the safe and expected formulas I've always followed:

$A + B = C$.

Time + busyness = relief from grief.

Mother + return of prodigal daughter = one big happy family.

Lauralee, the bent little candy cane who took me under her wing after I arrived at The Reserve, taught me that happiness wasn't dependent upon solvable equations. Healing and happiness are found when you give so much of yourself that you eventually have nothing left to give.

After everyone went to bed last night, I gave Lauralee's theory a go. I begged the Lord to let me keep Ira and Teeny. I've squandered so many opportunities to pour into the lives of others, God's probably a little wary of my real motivation. But having Ira and Teeny around means more to me than simply having someone on my side.

A few days ago, Charlotte and I stood at the river's edge and took our first steps toward each other in twenty-five years. I was excited and hopeful that we could completely close the gap between us when she offered to move home.

And then she got here.

My daughter didn't come back to Texas to reconcile. She moved into my house to escape her life and take over mine.

Granted, I may need help stopping a lawn mower or keeping my medicines straight, but it's up to me to make sure the important things, like Ira and Teeny, do not disappear from my memory. I'm not sure exactly how am I going to do this, especially when I can barely find my way back to the home I've lived in for over forty years.

I'm terrified at how quickly I'm losing my ability to hang on to the memories that matter. I'm afraid my love for Ira and Teeny will sink into the thickening sludge filling my head.

I swipe hot, angry tears from my cheeks and straighten my

shoulders. Without looking at my daughter, I snatch gardening gloves and pruning shears from the galvanized bucket by the steps. "Well, that's that."

Charlotte gently catches my arm, "Momma, please—"

I lift my chin and study this woman trying to mitigate my hurt. Blonde. Early forties. Attractive, even with the worry lines around her beautiful eyes and the sheepish expression on her speechless lips. This hard, heartless woman is nothing at all like the child of my memories. "I thought I knew you, Charlotte Ann. But I was mistaken."

"It's for the best, Momma."

I cram my hand into a stiffened glove. "For whom?"

"Ira and Teeny."

"No, you did what was best for you."

Charlotte throws her hands up in surrender. "Don't shoot me for putting you and Aria first. Momma, we've got a lot to get used to. This ranch needs so much work and..." She stops short of saying our relationship is in desperate need of repair. "I don't think it's too much to ask that we *not* take on extra boarders."

"I'll admit I was wrong to fight you so hard about placing me in that rehab center in Austin." I cram gnarled fingers into the other glove. "The Reserve wasn't so bad after all."

Charlotte laps up the admission with a satisfied smirk on her lips. "Wrong? You?"

"Sweet Moses, I'm not so far gone that I can't learn new things. And I learned something very important in those few weeks."

"Momma, I don't think you're far gone."

"That's why you've come home, isn't it? To see this old woman to her grave."

"Momma, I came home because…because it was time. You're my mother and you need help."

Charlotte's insistence that I accept my decline is a gift I am not yet willing to give. "Do you want to hear about what I've learned or not?"

"I doubt I have a choice," she mutters.

"I'm losing my mind. Not my hearing." I grab the handrail. "Hearts don't stop because they get old, Charlotte Ann. Closed off emotions is what stops hearts." I continue before I lose my courage. "I was wrong earlier."

"Admitting wrong?" Charlotte says this like she's surprised the words had tumbled from her mother's mouth. "For a second time? This *is* a first."

I look my daughter up and down. "I *do* recognize you. You're me."

Leaving Charlotte looking as if I've slapped her hurts me. But leaving her without a comeback, feels smart. Mentally sharp. Like my old self.

I turn and hobble down the steps. "Aria, put that cat in the house," I call over my shoulder and make one last peevish point. "I want to teach you how to properly prune a rosebush and I don't want that shifty-eyed feline getting any ideas about eating one of my birds."

Chapter 3

CHARLOTTE

Living with someone who's difficult is far different from popping in for an occasional visit. According to the book my ex-paralegal gave me on how to care for aging parents, I'll get used to Momma's cranky ways, learn what works for us and what doesn't. Maybe if Loraine were here to run interference, I might stand half a chance of pulling off this new gig. But I can tell, the truce I made with Momma when I agreed to move home has not made us family. That bridge was washed out twenty-five years ago and will have to be rebuilt from the ground up.

Just as I'm about to scream *"I'm going back to DC,"* Aria opens the screen door and carefully sets her beautiful, blue-eyed Siamese inside on the braided rug.

"In you go, Fig." She pats her cat on the head. "Go take a nap."

If I'd ordered Aria to put up her cat, she'd still be arguing. But my daughter's tossing her faithful companion aside as if pruning roses is an adventure.

"Ari." I snag her arm. "I'm sorry that Teeny and Ira couldn't stay. I didn't send them back to upset your Nana."

She shrugs off my explanation and my touch. "And yet..."

I reach for her arm again, as if I can squeeze out the sorrow all of us are feeling. Over the top of my daughter's head, I notice Momma leaning against the thorns of her New Dawn climbers and clipping with a vengeance.

"She'll come around."

"Don't count on it," Aria mutters.

I don't care what that stubborn old woman says, she and I are nothing alike. "Your grandmother hates losing a fight almost as much as she hates cats."

Aria pushes away from me and the distance she's intentionally put between us feels as cold as the Frio on a hot summer's day. "Is this going to get ugly?"

Tucking a blonde curl behind my daughter's ear is my attempt to bridge the gap. "I won't let it, kiddo."

Ari puts me in my place with a firm, "Mom, I'm thirteen."

"And growing up way too fast."

"I love her, Mom."

"And I love *both* of you."

Aria's brows draw together in doubt. "When you love people,

doesn't that mean you do hard things…even things you don't like?"

"I moved us here, didn't I?"

"You moved us here to get me away from my bad friends and…," she hesitates. "and to hide from Dad's bad press."

"Ari—" I bite back the urge to defend my point of view. This is an argument I can't win. These ugly accusations sit squarely on the side of truth. "Coming here was not a decision I made lightly, nor was it easy to send Nana's friends back. I can see how much she adores them, but I'm doing what I think is best for you *and* Nana." I cup my hand on my daughter's cheeks and realize that while I was busy managing my career and my mother's declining health the baby fat had melted away from my little girl's cheekbones and left her with the defined face of a budding adult. "This is hard, sweetheart. Harder than I anticipated."

She removes my hand. "You're not the only one who has to adjust." She turns from me and leans over the porch railing. "Nana, do I need gloves."

"If you don't want to bleed." Momma reaches for another branch and clips without so much as a glance in my direction.

I can stand here feeling hopeless, or I can ignore the frustration of my mother's pout and the sting of my daughter's lack of support.

I opt to get to work putting this family back together. Staying busy is something I know how to do. "While you two are tackling the roses, I think I'll look around and make a list of what needs to be done." Neither Momma nor Aria pay me any mind. "Just holler if you need me."

The quiet of the country swallows the exchange going on between my mother and daughter and shuts me out of their world.

That leaves me on my own to contend with the real world. There are so many projects to tackle in this world my mother is abandoning at breakneck speed, I'm not sure where to begin. It's a toss-up between the mounds of paperwork on her desk or an arm's-length list of repairs on the house, barn, and fences. Despite the heated start to the morning, the temperature has remained remarkably tolerable for August. It would be foolish not to take advantage of the weather and let Momma cool down.

I decide to start prepping the house for paint. The turret is three-stories high and probably better left for a professional, but I'd rather risk breaking my neck than stirring up my mother anymore today. The last time I disregarded Momma's objections to hiring a handyman, she took a water hose and blew Raymond Leck off a ladder.

But when it comes time to patch the tractor-sized hole she made in the side of the barn or repairing the split-rail fencing she hit with her little Ford Escort, I may have to ignore her protests and hire someone.

For now, painting I can do. I love having a reason to be outside and the mindlessness of dragging a brush will give me a chance to think, regroup, and figure out the best way to make this new arrangement work. Without help, I estimate it could take at least two weeks just to scrape away the peeling blue chips. Replacing all the warped siding and shoring up the loose shutters will keep me too busy to worry about the mental steps leading Momma farther and farther away from me.

On my way to my father's woodworking shed, I skirt the flower bed on the side of the house. Momma and Aria are so engrossed in their task that I'm able to eavesdrop.

"Rose gardening in this rocky soil requires a little more thought than it does in other parts of the country." Momma proudly offers Aria a freshly clipped blossom. "That's why I only plant roses with resilience and fortitude."

Aria buries her nose in the delicate pink petals and inhales deeply. "Tough like you, right Nana?"

"You reap what you sow, young lady. Take it from an old lady…you must learn to be careful with what you sow. Do you understand what I mean, Aria?"

"Not really."

"Bad friends corrupt good morals. Don't let anyone pick your flower before you bloom." Momma points at a drooping bud. "Clip right below that thorn."

A smile pushes its way past my earlier frustration. Momma is still a darn good teacher at heart. But how she can make life analogies about roses and not remember the order of the pills she takes is a mystery. It's obvious having Aria around is giving Momma purpose, and that's a good thing. My presence, on the other hand, she treats like a bud she'd rather nip than allow to bloom into something meaningful.

I retreat and head toward Daddy's woodworking shed.

The flimsy metal door is chained shut. Freeing the padlock requires a quick sprint to the house for the keys hanging on a nail by the back door. One of smaller keys fits, but I can't get the rusted lock to turn. I stomp back to the kitchen for the can of WD40 I'd spotted next to the garlic salt in Momma's cabinet above the stove. If I hadn't made spaghetti last night, I'd have never thought to look for an anti-corrosion lubricant in the kitchen. When I asked Momma why she was keeping a can of WD40 in her spice cabinet, she shrugged and said, "To grease things." I don't even want to know how many times she's used WD40 in place of cooking spray.

I swing open the door to the shed. The garage-size space smells of rough cedar logs, rusty lawn equipment, and the piles of saw dust on the floor. Sunlight spills through the crack around the shuttered window. I take a tentative step inside and flip the light switch. The light above my father's workbench does not awaken. I navigate to the waist-high table, reach over all the tools, and pry open the shutter. Sunlight pours over the abandoned sandpaper, drill bits, and a pair of old work gloves.

I run my finger over the curves in the leather left by my father's sweaty hands. The hole in my heart opens up. In an attempt to plug disturbed emotions, I slide a trembling hand inside the right glove and bring the leather to my nose. The dry, dusty smell evokes images I haven't visited in years. Momma calling Daddy to supper. Daddy stomping up to the back door, lowering his head, and running his gloves through his hair to rid his sun-bleached curls of any wood shavings. Me waiting at the table. Daddy lifting his head, putting on a smile, and then barreling into the kitchen. He always swatted Momma on the butt with these gloves. His chuckle when she protested was the music of my life. I couldn't wait for the light pop of his gloves on my head. "Beetle Bug," he said as he took his place at the table. "You're pretty enough to eat and smart enough to make me regret my haste."

I swallow the resentment this memory churns in my gut, yank the glove from my hand, and return it to its resting place.

Behind me, a half-spun wooden bowl is attached to the power lathe. The unfinished art is a gaping reminder of a life half-lived. Now that I know about my father's drinking, I can't blame mother for shutting the door to this painful part of her life. When my father chose to jump off the bluff, he didn't just leave me, he left Momma too. I spin the unfinished bowl attached to the chuck. There are many ways to leave someone. James stayed in our bed but he'd actually left me years ago.

Glancing around the shop, I search for a paint scraper and a ladder among the abandoned tools and stacks of unused wood. I spot the closed door of Daddy's darkroom at the far end. Above it is a caged light bulb. When the red light was on, Caroline and I knew better than to open the door and spoil the magic in Daddy's secret world.

Curiosity pushes me past the band saw and clambering over a pile of scrap lumber. I yank open the door to my father's private sanctuary. The pungent odor of vinegar and sulfur assaults my nostrils. My search for a light switch ends when the string hanging from a single bulb brushes my face. One hard pull and the bulb flickers to life.

No solution shimmers in the trays my father used to develop, bathe, and fix his photos. Above the dried-out trays a wire is strung between two nails. Three black and white photos dangle from clothespins.

A gasp escapes my lips.

My knees are jelly as I step forward and unclip the photo on the left. It is a photo of me...and my sister. Based on the new bikini Caroline was wearing, the one she'd proudly brought home from college and then fought with Momma when she judged it far too skimpy, this shot was taken on the day my sister died. Lina and I are laughing and spinning together on the tire swing.

I don't remember my father having his camera with him that

day. But of course, he did. Photography was his true love. His passion. His ticket to finally being able to provide for his family. If Momma hadn't threatened him with bodily harm if she ever caught him wearing his camera while he was turning a bowl on the power lathe, his camera would have been around his neck every minute of the day.

Why hadn't he shown us these pictures?

Moving on to the next photo, my hand stops mid-reach. Caroline and I are standing opposite each other on the swing and blowing kisses toward the camera. I step closer and let my finger trace my sister's dark hair and then trail across her fierce, impetuous face.

"Oh, Lina. I need you." I unclip the picture, slide the treasure beneath the one in my hand, then eagerly look up to confiscate the last photo.

The breath leaves my lungs. Neither my hands nor my eyes move. I bite back the gut-wrenching scream clawing at my throat.

Daddy must have snapped this picture in that terrible split-second after I jumped off the swing and gave Caroline the push that sent her sailing to her death.

I move closer and study the photo with blurry eyes. Caroline's body is threaded through the hole of the tire. Her toes are pointed in preparation of a splash-free entry into the river. Her shiny black hair is a veil that flows behind her. Above her the loose end of the frayed rope dances like a snake. From the carefree smile on Caroline's face, she's blissfully unaware that in the space of a breath, the rope will fall around her neck and twist into a knot I can't free.

Hot tears drip onto the two photos I hold in my shaky hands. The need to escape is a hammer pounding inside my head. Truth rises to the forefront of my thinking and suddenly clarifies.

I know why Daddy killed himself.

He didn't drown himself because he was drunk the day his eldest daughter drowned. He jumped because he was so wrapped up in capturing the perfect shot of his beautiful daughters that he'd failed to notice the rope stretching thinner and thinner above us. By the time it snapped, it was too late.

Hands trembling, I release the last photo from the line.

Do I show these to Momma and drag her through that terrible day again? Do I let her know that for a year Daddy stood in front of these photos and tried to douse his shame in alcohol? Or do I just tuck them away and pretend putting this family back together is even possible?

I slide the photos into my pocket and close the door.

Chapter 4

ARIA

Fig is curled up on the sill of the bay window that overlooks miles and miles of rocks, twisted trees, and a river I'm never to go near. My cat's tail waves to the rhythm of my fingers plodding across the yellowed keys of Nana's piano. Mom promised she'd have this dinosaur tuned soon. In the meantime, she expects me to pretend the tinny strikes of this console mimic the deep rich tones of the baby grand back home.

My fingers are focused on a minor scale warm-up, but my mind is back in DC. Maybe Mom can act like moving us into her old room will make us one big happy family, but this is not my home.

Don't get me wrong, I love my grandmother. I'm glad moving here has given me time to hang with her. She's a little cuckoo sometimes, like when she can't remember where she put her teeth. I don't know what's more gross: seeing teeth floating in a glass or having to rinse them off and take them to her. Truth is, I'd carry Nana's teeth all the way to town to hear her say *Sweet Moses* right before she gives my Mom what for. Makes me want to grow up to be just like my Nana...except for the false teeth.

Nice as it is to clip roses with Nana, I miss home. Not the fighting. Mom and Dad didn't duke it out in front of me. They're far too civilized for that. They always took their arguments outside, even when the snow was three feet deep on the back deck. Like that stupid Christmas Eve when they had the mother of all their arguments.

My mind drifts back...motion sensors flip on the patio lights. From my upstairs bedroom window, I can see my parents shivering but squared off in the snow. Dad is wearing only his boxers. Mom is barefoot and draped in that ugly robe Dad can't stand. All it takes for me to hear what they're saying is a small lifting of the window pane.

"James, who were you messing with in your studio this time?" Mom jabs her finger into Dad's bare chest.

"Dang, Charlotte. Do we have to do this outside?" Dad crosses his arms and rubs his hands over his biceps. "It's freezing out here."

"Who was she?"

"A client. A model. Okay?"

"For who? Playboy?"

"None of your business."

"It's 2:00 am and I'm just getting in from a long, horrible day in court. Instead of welcoming me home with a bowl of hot soup, you give me a blonde wearing nothing but her coat." Mom's yelling and slapping her palms on his chest. "When *you* and your *clients* can't keep your clothes on in the house we share with our child, it's my business."

Maybe Mom thought I couldn't hear her accusing my dad of all kinds of disgusting things. But I did. Every word. Every time she caught him with a female in his studio. I don't know why I was surprised when my friend Caitlyn showed me the national rag sheet with Dad's picture plastered on the front. A stupid grin on his face and his arm around an NFL cheerleader. In the bottom corner of the front-page spread was a pic of Mom looking all mean and serious. Caption read: Capitol Hill lawyer can't fix this.

Geez, Dad. That skanky cheerleader was barely old enough to drink. The next edition of that same rag quoted Mom saying, "James McCandless can rot in jail." She denies saying that, but I know she didn't bail him out.

Obviously, neither of my parents give a flip about how hard it is for a flat-chested, skinny girl to make friends when they act like idiots.

So, yeah, I sold my soul and fell for the BS the most popular girl in school shoveled my way. Caitlyn said her parents were famous too so she acted all *"oh, I totally get you so maybe we should be friends.*" Like an idiot, I thought Caitlyn and her friends liked me. But when everything hit the fan, the truth came out. All these pretty-girl users want is a photo shoot with my dad. Caitlyn and all of her friends are tools. None of them care about me or my dream to go to Juilliard. At least, for a few weeks during my seventh-grade year, I wasn't alone.

"Your technical ability has improved." I don't know how long Nana's been standing at the piano watching me. "But your fingering is off. That's why it's labored." Faint red lines spider out from her bright red lips. Nana's beautiful, for an old woman. Her white hair, blue eyes, and perfect skin pop with the touch of color she likes to add...on her good days. When Ira and Teeny lived here, she combed her hair and put on makeup every morning. But after Mom sent Nana's friends away, she didn't shower for three days.

Mom got so worried she called LaVera. Nana's pudgy neighbor came over with a whole bag of Avon samples, but none of her creams or lipsticks could snap Nana out of her funk. Nana's red lips are the first positive sign I've seen since the day she and Mom had their big fight about who was going to be in charge. I don't look for either of them to say they're sorry. Forgiveness isn't a Slocum strong suit.

I lift my hands from the piano keys. "I'd like to see you do better."

"Slide over, kiddo." Nana wiggles onto the bench. "Juilliard's audition committee will expect a high level of technical ability as well as your own unique artistry. Watch and learn."

Nana pumps her gnarled fingers a few times and then lightly sets them upon the keys. In an instant, they're flying, pounding out notes that melt into a beautiful song, a song I recognize from the night my mother and I took the train to New York and saw *Les Misérables* on Broadway. Nana's technique is flawless. Her artistic ability amazing. But it's her performance of this difficult piece of music from memory that has me staring slack-jawed. Nana's a rock star. The score of this French musical is way beyond my level. How can this woman remember every note of "One Day More" and forget where she put her teeth?

Crazy. Huh?

Though I'm hungry to scoot close, to channel her talent by letting our shoulders rub, I give her space to work the entire keyboard. I'm mesmerized by her fingers. Long and slender like mine. But unlike mine, Nana's fingers float above the keys delicate and light. She tackles the melody with the same expression I'd heard from the masters Mom had taken me to see in DC. Her pianissimos caress each note as if they're as fragile as one of her roses. She attacks the crescendos with the same force she gives the flyswatter hanging on the pantry door. For the length of her performance, the old piano is no longer tired and sour. And neither is Nana. Her face is serene, her eyes closed, and her head swaying as if the music has carried her away.

When she finishes, I can't help but clap. "Teach me to do that."

Her smile connects our hearts. "I taught your mother, I can teach you."

I point at the silent keys. "Mom can do this?"

"Better than anyone I've ever seen." Nana squeezes my knee. "Now, back to those scales and your fingering, young lady."

Chapter 5

CHARLOTTE

Aria's at the piano again. With a smile, I shoulder the broom and grab hold of the ladder that's leaning against the three-story turret. On my way past the bay windows, I peek in on my daughter toiling away. I hear a distinctive difference in her technique, a connection to the music she's never had before. I suspect the change occurred the day I took a painting break and found Aria and Momma sitting at the piano with their heads pressed together, the metronome ticking, and Momma pointing at the music with a ruler. The sight of my mother doing for my daughter what she'd once done for me floods me with a mixture of gratitude and envy.

"I don't know why you need a broom to paint," Momma's questioning from her position at the ladder's base snaps me back from the land of dreams that could have been, if only...

To avoid a confrontation, I change the subject, "Are you holding

31

the ladder steady?"

"I said I would."

I shimmy up the last few rungs, press my body into the ladder as best I can, then raise the broom and swing for the nest under the second-story eaves.

Barn swallows dive bomb my head in protest. "Your free rent days are over." I wave a broom at the angry pair of birds. They scatter. One bird circles back and swoops close to my ladder. While I'm distracted by his too-close-for-comfort maneuver, the other bird darts in and pecks me on the forehead.

"Ouch." My hand flies to the pain and the broom clatters to the ground. "This means war," I yell, bloody fist raised at the squadron of swallows circling and screeching above.

"I didn't know you were going to wreck the homes of my birds." Momma holds the broom I dropped with one hand and the base of the ladder with the other. "Leave them alone."

From the angry tone of her voice, she's forgotten the real reason she's mad at me—sending her friends away—but she's not forgotten that she's mad. So, everything I do just makes her madder. Which has really been the pattern of our lives. Maybe if I'd been more like Caroline…

"If I don't get a coat of paint on this house before winter, none of us will have a home." I drop my paint brush into the empty paint bucket, unhook it from the ladder, and start inching my way down.

Keeping an eye out for angry birds, I notice a cloud of dust coming up the lane. "You expecting company, Momma?"

"Do I have it written down?" Her rare admission of her increasing need to leave notes all over the house surprises me.

"I haven't seen it posted anywhere."

"Then you must be mistaken."

I shake my head then nod toward the lane. "Better put on your lipstick because someone's kicking up the caliche."

"Probably just Bo bringing LaVera by to deliver my Avon order. She and Aria are the only ones who give a hoot about me since you wouldn't let me keep my other friends."

Obviously, I was a bit hasty to believe my mother had forgotten why she was mad at me. I'm beginning to think Momma suffers from selective-memory rather than dementia. She can remember what she wants to remember. The first thing on my to-do list is to make an appointment with her primary care doctor for some definitive testing. She's not going to hand over the reins of her health care management easily, so I've yet to tell her that I intend to call Benjamin Ellis soon.

"It's not Bo's tow truck." I tent the paintbrush over my eyes. "Who do you know who drives a gold Cadillac?" I back down another rung as I wait for my snarly ladder-holder to answer. But she doesn't. "Momma?" I duck my chin and search the ground. She's nowhere to be seen. "So much for keeping me from breaking my neck!" Which is exactly why she'd protested my climb up the rickety old thing in the first place. "Momma!"

As my foot searches for the next rung, images of Bo Tucker flit through my head. Thank goodness it's not my old boyfriend pulling up to the house. I didn't make the best impression when I met him while trying to put my mother in rehab. It wouldn't lift my esteem in his eyes to be caught wearing a paint-splattered t-shirt and one of Momma's old straw hats. Yep, I've avoided Bo Tucker, his gas station, and his mother's house when I looked good, no way am I going to let him see me now.

Get ahold of yourself, Charlotte.

I have no business thinking about how my life might have turned out had I married my high school sweetheart. Especially, since James McCandless is still a dagger stuck in my heart and a chain around my leg.

My foot sweeps air as it searches for the next rung. The ladder wobbles. "Momma!" I grab hold of the side rails with both hands. "Momma! Put your foot on the bottom rung, please." She doesn't answer. "Momma?"

The sound of the Cadillac rolling to a cautious halt is followed by the immediate and distinctive cock of a shot gun.

My gaze whips from the man climbing out of his car back to the ground ten feet below me. "Momma! What are you doing?"

My mother ignores me. She plasters her raised gun against her left cheek and marches past the ladder with both barrels aimed at the dark-haired driver poking his head over the top of a hard-shell convertible. "Get off my land before I fill you and that Caddy full of holes, young man."

The man's hands fly into the air. "Don't shoot, Mrs. Slocum."

"Momma!" I drop the paint bucket, shimmy down the ladder, and rush to her side. "What on earth are you thinking?"

"I told this sidewinder that if he ever stepped foot on my land again, I'd do more than shoot out his tires." Momma advances a couple of steps, unbent and clearly focused. "Young man, if you don't think I'll pull this trigger just dial my former yard man. Raymond Leck ended up in the hospital because he didn't think I'd do what I said I'd do."

Aria bursts through the screen door, her cat in her arms. "What's going on?"

"I'm shootin' a no-good, lying trespasser," Momma says without lowering her gun.

"Nana's not shooting anybody, Ari," I counter.

"You're not the boss of me, Charlotte Ann." Momma aims a sideways warning at me. "Just because you think you can push me and a couple of old people around a little bit, you don't run the world. This boy nearly cost me my last friend on this earth. If LaVera didn't have such a forgiving spirit, I'd be left with no one." Momma advances with her gun, Dearfoam slippers, and ninety-six pounds of steely grit. "I'll give you to the count of three, and then I better see the red glow of your taillights."

"Mrs. Slocum, I was invited here."

"By whom?" Momma barks at the man no longer cowering behind his car.

The man takes another bold step toward the hood of his Caddy and nods his head in my direction. "By her."

Now I'm mad. "Me?" I reach for Momma's gun with the intent to shoot over the head of the lying trespasser myself, but she swerves out of reach. "I don't know you." I point a finger at him. "Why would I invite a stranger to Fossil Ridge?"

A cocky smile slices his tanned face. "I'm Sam Sparks."

My hand drops. "Sparks? Of Sparks Development?" I'd been so busy, I'd forgotten all about the papers he'd sent me to look over while Mother was rehabbing, and I'd totally forgotten the promises I made to convince Momma to sign the acquisition deal of the Fossil Ridge he was offering.

From Mr. Sparks' brazen steps forward, he obviously had not. "The one and only."

"Go back in the house, Ari." I say.

Aria wraps an arm around a porch pillar. "No way. This is the most excitement we've had around here since the old people's bus hauled off Ira and Teeny."

"Now, Aria!" My order sends her stomping across the porch.

"What's going on, Charlotte Ann?" The weight of the gun is making Momma's arms quiver but her resolve is as steady as I ever seen it.

Sam withdraws a folded piece of paper from his pocket and points it at me. "Unfinished business."

"What business could you possibly have with my daughter?" Momma asks.

"Finalizing the sale of your property."

All of the sudden, I'm the one staring down the double barrel of Momma's shotgun.

Chapter 6

SARA

I push a piece of toast around on my plate.

"Momma, quit dawdling. Eat." Charlotte leans against the sink, shoveling lumpy oatmeal into her mouth when she should be eating crow.

I slowly lick the jelly from my spoon. "What's the hurry?"

"We're going to be late to your doctor's appointment."

"You're the one who swallowed that nasty boy's snake oil, Charlotte Ann." I plunge my spoon into a cooling cup of tea. "I don't see why *I'm* the one who has to submit to a mental evaluation." I wink at my granddaughter who, in an effort to support me, is taking forever to eat a bowl of sugary cereal.

Fatal error.

Charlotte is like a duck on a June bug the second she realizes the two of us are in cahoots to sabotage today's itinerary. "Sam Sparks is not a boy, Momma. He's a very powerful man in this county and *you* held him hostage…at gun point."

"And a trespasser."

"What?"

"You forgot to add that Sammy is also a trespassing fool."

Charlotte scrapes more than half of her lumpy oatmeal into the cat's bowl. Since my daughter's arrival, I've been keeping tabs on her habits. When she sleeps. When she plays. When she eats. Charlotte would probably argue that it's vain foolishness to try and fill in the gaps caused by our twenty-five-year separation. And maybe she's right. Twenty-five years is more than a gap. It's a blooming crater. But I can't shake the hope that if I acquire enough tidbits, eventually I'll have a bridge that can link all of my other disjointed thoughts.

That's why when I hear Charlotte pacing her old room late at night, I know she's not sleeping. She doesn't have to tell me all the reasons behind her insomnia, but knowing she's struggling stirs compassion I thought long dead. When she refuses to take Aria to play in the river, I see in her eyes the same guilt that stares me down. Neither of us will find it easy to ever play again. But what worries me most is this: I haven't seen her eat a full helping of anything. Either my cooking has gone south, or fear has tied her stomach in knots. If I thought another little necklace could give her appetite back, I'd cash in my entire retirement account to get her one. Maybe something with a cross.

No, her fear is bigger than performance anxiety. This fear is shaping who she's becoming. No wonder her body is thin as a walking stick and her tongue as sharp as knife blade.

"You'd be sitting in jail if that shot you fired hadn't missed Sam by a mile." Charlotte drops her bowl in the sink. "What were you thinking, Mother?"

What *was* I thinking? When? Then or now?

The question is a wagon wheel falling into the ruts in my head. Maybe I'm fooling myself to think I can gather enough intel on Charlotte to fill in these holes. Sorting my thoughts into columns that add up sensibly is becoming more and more difficult. If we're talking about fears, my greatest fear of losing my mind before I lose my life is a freight train speeding right toward me and I'm tied to the tracks.

I've wasted so many years trying to keep grief and anger from dulling my mind. But instead of peace, I keep circling back to the same grief and anger. I don't know how much time I have left on this earth. I want this living new arrangement to work out. I want my daughter and granddaughter to become the family I've done without for far too long, and yet I've gone and endangered everything by pulling a gun. My inability to control these illogical impulses might have just given Charlotte the nail she needs to have me declared crazy and then locked away.

40

I raise my tea cup in defiance. "I could have lowered that boy's ears a notch or two if I'd wanted to hurt him." Sloshing liquid forces me to set the cup down with a noticeable tremor. "I scared him good, and that's what matters."

"You scared me *and* your granddaughter."

"I wasn't scared." Aria looks up from her cereal bowl. "Can you teach me to shoot, Nana?"

Charlotte cuts off my reply with a resounding, "No, she can't."

"Why not?" Aria asks. "Nana taught you how to shoot."

"Who told you that?"

"Nana."

"When?"

Aria wipes the milk dribble from her chin with the back of her hand and an apologetic look my way. "While you were locking up the gun."

Charlotte releases a slow, frustrated exhale. "There'll be no more shooting of anything or at anyone from either of you. Is that understood?"

Aria's face sours. "Not even target practice?"

"No."

"Nana says you used to be able to nail a pork n' bean can from fifty yards. Do you think she can still do it, Nana?"

I wrap both of my unsteady hands around the warmth of my tea cup. My eyes search the kitchen for something to deflect the

41

conversation away from my foggy mind. My gaze lights on the empty swing in Polygon's cage. Life was so much easier when I only had a bird to argue with, but it was also much lonelier.

My thoughts are a bird swinging back and forth on a tiny trapeze. "There's lots of things I suspect your mother can still do."

"Like play the piano?" Aria asks.

My granddaughter's impatient touch to the back of my hand is a clarifying poke at the oily film floating in my mind. "Play the piano. Sing like bird. And execute a perfect double backflip dive off the bluff."

"A back flip? Really, Mom?" Instant respect glows in Aria's eyes. "I thought you couldn't swim. At least, that's what you say whenever I try to get you near the water. Can you take me to the river this afternoon and teach me how to dive?"

"No."

"Charlotte doesn't go to the river anymore."

"Mother," Charlotte's cross warning cuts deep. "Enough."

My tongue recoils like a skittish river salamander.

I shouldn't have done it...stomped out Aria's budding admiration of her mother, but in the space of a heartbeat, that wave of anger erupted from this growing fissure inside of me and swept away my good sense. These sudden pivots in emotions are becoming more and more frequent and rapidly increasing in intensity. I'm not mad at Charlotte for sending Ira and Teeny away. She's got plenty on her plate. Besides, Ira calls every day, and while he's hinted that he would rather be with me, he's trying to make peace with his lot in life.

No, this roiling inside me is a red-hot anger, the likes of which I haven't felt since Martin died. Unjustified and uncontrollable.

"Why can't we go to the river?" Aria demands of her mother. "There's nothing else to do here. It's so stinking hot, I don't understand why we can't swim."

Charlotte's frustration cuts through the silence that hangs in the kitchen. "River's too low this time of year."

"You'll have to tell her the truth someday, Charlotte Ann." My hand flies to my mouth but it's too little, too late.

"Tell me what truth?" Aria demands.

Why had I implied Caroline's death was Charlotte's fault when I'd told her the truth? I had told her the truth, right? I wanted to tell Charlotte that her father had been drunk that day. Had I? I can't remember.

Whether I've offered Charlotte absolution or not, I know better than to bring up subjects best left buried, especially in the presence of my impressionable grandchild, a child I wouldn't want to bear the weight of these ancient secrets.

Not trusting my mouth, I pick up my spoon and stir my tea as if concentrating on something I did every single day can slow these uncontrollable urges to hurt somebody.

"Tell me what?" Aria demands again.

Charlotte's brief glance in my direction is one-part reprimand and two-parts warning for me not to say another word. "Ari, you're to stay away from the river and all guns, hear me?" She hands her daughter a dish cloth and nods toward the spilled milk. "Clean that up."

"What if she needs to run someone off her land someday?" I clench the spoon. "And let me be clear, it is still *my* land."

"How many times do I have to apologize, Momma?" Charlotte snatches the dish cloth from Aria and tosses it into the sink. "I only talked to Sam Sparks because *you* were refusing to go to rehab. I was afraid you might never live here again. If you had remained in assisted living, selling the ranch would have been in your best interest."

"Don't try to pawn this off as my best interest."

"How many above-market value offers do you think we could have gotten for your small sliver of Texas hill country?"

"It's on the river, Charlotte. This land is worth something."

"To you."

"To me and your daddy."

"You mean Grandpa?" Worry creases Aria's face. "Why doesn't anybody ever talk about my grandfather?"

I feel the fire inside me sputter. "I meant, your mother had no right to go behind my back."

Charlotte's hands fly up. It's not a gesture of surrender, but more like someone has a gun pointed at her head. "Want to shoot me too, Mother?"

"Of course not." Why must I always attack? Hurting Charlotte, or anyone for that matter, is not what I want. And yet, it keeps happening. "How many times do *I* have to apologize, Charlotte Ann?"

Charlotte's mouth flies open, anger flashing in her eyes. With the agility of someone nearly half my age, she manages to rope her tongue into submission, but not the sigh the sneaks out. "You can't help it, Mother." She wears pity on her wrinkled brow like a scarlet letter.

Pity.

That must be what's setting me off. Pity is what brought Charlotte home and it's pity keeping her here now. Not devotion. And certainly not love.

I hate pity. Had crawled into a hole to escape the pity I'd seen in everyone's eyes after I lost Caroline and Martin. Until Charlotte's return, I'd escaped the pity-filled offers of assistance from my church, my employer, and even my friends.

I'd rather be dead than to allow pity to become my lot in life.

"We're going to be late if we don't get a move on." Charlotte retrieves her keys from the lopsided ceramic bowl she'd made in her third-grade art class. She lets out a long sigh, her silent admission that she doesn't want to fight either. She gently places a hand on my shoulder. "You calm enough to go?"

Charlotte's sympathetic touch riles the multi-headed, fact-gobbling monster growing inside me into a frenzy. I try to wrestle this conversation from his jaws, but the details are already shredded.

All I can do is spit out, "Where did you say we're going?"

Chapter 7

CHARLOTTE

To the doctor, Momma. For a checkup and an assessment." I point to the big calendar on the fridge. "I've told you several times and wrote it on your daily calendar. See?"

Eyes squinted, Momma studies the writing as if the new glasses I bought her when she went to rehab aren't the least bit helpful. She should be able to read the large words with ease. But from the confused expression on her face, either her eyesight is failing or she's can't discern the meaning of *doctor reassessment*.

"Momma, you okay?"

Her eyes refuse to meet mine. She lifts her teacup. "Can't we just sit around and look at each other for a while longer?" Brown liquid sloshes over her trembling hands. "I haven't finished my breakfast." The fight of just a few moments ago is gone...no, it's more like it never existed.

I refuse to waste energy worrying about how I'm going to pay for Momma's long-term care if the medical tests confirm my fears. She's losing it, but I can't. According to the certified letter I received yesterday, I'm going to need every ounce of strength to fight James. My husband is refusing to sign the settlement agreement I proposed. His counter offer claims he is sole owner of all our properties and reduces his child support liability to pennies.

I don't have the time, money, or patience for another crisis. "I'd love to sit, Momma. I haven't sat down since I got here."

Her cup rattles into place on the saucer. "No one is making you paint the house."

I'm strangely relieved to hear the return of her sarcastic wit. "Dr. Ellis was kind enough to work us in. I think it would be rude to make him wait, don't you?"

"Last time I saw that traitor, he sent me away."

Yep, Momma's still in there. I'm determined to find every bit of the medical help that will keep her wits as sharp as possible for as long as possible…no matter how it hurts when she slices me. "You left him no choice." I dig through the stack of papers on the counter. "He tried to get you to cooperate after your hip surgery, but you refused."

"That's because Nana's physical therapist was a sadistic brute." Aria sucks the last of her milk from her upturned bowl then looks up when she realizes I've stopped pawing through paperwork to stare at her with an open mouth.

Aria shrugs. "What?"

"Did you tell her that before or after you told her I play the piano, Momma?" I cast a disbelieving glance at my mother, but she simply shrugs. "We're going to have to set some boundaries." Momma shrugs again, even more nonchalant this time, as if my threats don't scare her. I give Aria a reprimanding tap on the shoulder. "Get Nana's purse and let's go."

Aria doesn't move. "I don't want to meet the principal."

Momma snaps to attention. "You're subjecting *my* granddaughter to Wilma Rayburn? You know she's sadistic."

"Mrs. Rayburn is not sadistic, Momma. She's a cutting-edge administrator who's turned Addisonville's little country school into a modern, exemplary school. And why are we suddenly so fond of the word sadistic?"

"Those ratings are subject to interpretation," Momma growls. "I don't see the point in subjecting my granddaughter to that woman and her unproven methods."

"I'm not subjecting *my* daughter to anyone," I say. "We're merely dropping by the school for a tour and a counselor visit. Aria's never attended a school that has Pre-K through 12th grade on the same campus. School starts in a couple of weeks and I want her to know her way around."

"It's not hard," Momma says. "Go through the front doors. Turn left for the elementary classrooms. Turn right for the high school classrooms. Or go straight ahead for the Junior High."

"I know navigating the campus is not hard, but coming early might give Ari a chance to meet some of the students."

"There are only three hundred students in the whole place. She'll know them all and everything about them within a week. And they'll know everything about her as well. You remember how it is in a small school? How hard it is to keep your private life private."

I graduated from Addisonville ISD just a few days before Caroline died. I didn't come home the next summer. The excuse I used was that I had a job at a coffee shop near the college, but the truth was I couldn't bear running into people who knew me before I lost my sister. But then Daddy killed himself a year to the day that Caroline died and I ended up having to come home. I returned for the funeral then ran from everything Addisonville.

I was so traumatized by those two back-to-back events, I'd never considered how tough it was for Momma to continue to live in the same community, work with the same colleagues, and walk the familiar halls knowing everyone knew everything about the catastrophic changes in her life.

"Why can't Nana homeschool me?" Aria looks to her grandmother for reinforcement and I get the distinct feeling these two have had this conversation behind my back. "She's already helping me get ready for Juilliard."

"Nana's retired." I grab a stack of papers and start flipping. "She deserves a break."

"She doesn't want a break," Aria argues. "Breaks are for quitters. Right, Nana?"

Momma's gaze rotates between me and Aria like the conversation is a tennis match too-close-to-call, so she remains silent.

"Homeschooling you would be too much for her," I counter.

"If you taught my English and music theory courses, Nana would only have to tutor me in math and science." Aria's well-articulated logic doesn't mask the real issue. She's terrified. And it's my fault. I'm the one who yanked her away from her home and friends.

Guilt steers me headlong into a conversation I'd really hoped to avoid. "Ari, I'm not going to let you hide out. You're going to school." I cup my hands around her angry face. "And you're going to make new friends."

Her face turns to stone in my grasp. "Because you say so?"

"No, because you're brave, smart, and—"

"And you say so," she challenges.

"Yeah. I'm your mother." I remove my hands. "It's my job to say so, whether you like what I say or not."

"You were right, Nana." Aria shoves back from the table. "Mom thinks she's the boss of the whole world. She shouldn't boss you, and she can't boss me forever." She stomps from the kitchen.

"Put Fig in your room then get in the car, Ari," I call after her then I wheel on my mother. "I'm glad you and Aria are becoming so close, but she's *my* daughter and I wish you wouldn't undermine the decisions *I* have to make for her."

Momma sets her teacup in the saucer and quietly says, "I can teach her more than the piano scales and theory I taught you, you know."

"I didn't say you couldn't, Momma."

"Not out loud."

"Momma—"

"Whether *you* like it or not, Charlotte Ann, Aria is already learning a thing or two from you. Parents are a child's primary teacher."

It's not a compliment she's offered. But if I really wanted to fight over every single thing, I'd bring up some of the uglier things I've learned from her. Silence. Long-held grudges. Withholding love until someone is perfect.

I force the frustration to whoosh from me in a long, exhausted sigh. "Every eighth-grade girl needs friends." I slid into Aria's empty seat and do what I always do: try to put a Band-Aid on the wound I have inflicted. "Remember the big slumber party Caroline wanted when she turned twelve?"

"It's my idea," Momma pushes her tea saucer away.

"Was it?"

"Was? No is."

I overlook her verb confusion and say, "You said Caroline could have her Little House on the Prairie party if I could be included."

Momma's gaze drifts beyond me. A tiny smile tugs at the corners of her mouth. "Your father and I have hauled hay to the barn loft all week. You and Caroline will catch your death sleeping in that old outbuilding, but Martin says it's my fault for insisting that you two read Wilder's entire series before puberty."

It's not just Momma's gaze that has drifted past me, but it sounds like somehow her mind has left the present and is now wandering around in that long-ago weekend like it has yet to happen.

I experiment with trying to join her in those old memories and change my voice to that of a ten-year-old girl. "Will you make sourdough bread, Johnny-cakes, and homemade maple syrup, Momma?"

She chuckles and looks at me with so much love I actually feel like a little girl again. "I draw the line at making a black bird pie."

The sensation of having the mother I once knew is so deliciously overwhelming, I'm tempted to ignore the ache of being a turkey wishbone pulled in opposite directions. I want to snuggle up beside her and stay in the fantasy. But Aria's footsteps on the stairs tug me toward all of the adult responsibilities of today.

To keep my heart from snapping, I say, "You and your blasted birds, Momma." I reach for her hand and give it a light squeeze.

She ignores my nudge to return to the present. "Caroline loves my birds."

I can't dwell in the presence of the dead any longer, so I change the subject. "You did so many things right. I want to be the kind of mother who'd haul hay for a week if it will make my daughter as happy as that party made me and Caroline."

My mention of my sister yanks Momma back to the present. Her face scrunches in an effort to say something. I can't help but lean in, my heart hoping for a breakthrough in this cold war of ours.

"Where did you say we were going?" she whispers.

I swallow my disappointment and pat her hand. "To the doctor." I stand. "The nurse told me to bring the list of all your current medications. Where do you keep it?"

"On the counter. Behind the sugar cannister."

"I've looked through this mess." I wave toward the disheveled papers on the counter. "The list is not there."

"It's always there."

"Maybe you moved the piece of paper, put it in your recipe drawer or something?"

"When would I have had the time? I've been too busy cooking for twenty pre-teen girls who've giggled and laughed all night in the hayloft."

"That was thirty years ago, Momma."

Her eyes dart from the calendar to me. My frustration sends her gaze flying back to the calendar again. She stares intensely at the numbered boxes then simply says, "Oh."

"Don't worry," I say with an edge of guilt. "We'll find your medication list and then I'll transfer everything to my phone so we won't have this problem again."

"I'm not daft, Charlotte Ann." She pushes back from the table. "It's here somewhere." She pads to the sugar cannister and begins her own search. "You're just like your father. He can't find the nose on his face."

Picking my battles carefully, I decide her present tense reference of my deceased father is not worth the effort it would take to correct her thinking and tackle the issues keeping us from heading out the door. "Momma, where are your shoes?"

She continues rifling through the papers. "Where they always are...on my feet."

"No." I point at her thick, yellowed toenails. "They're not."

She drops the electric bill in her hand and glances down. She studies her feet then frowns as if the big bunion on the side of her left foot belongs to someone else. "I want my Dearfoams."

"Your Easy Spirits are by the back door."

"I must wear my slippers."

My jaw clenches. "Aria!" My call summons my angry teen to

55

the kitchen.

Aria tromps into the room with her nose glued to her phone. "What?" she snaps without looking up.

"Can you put your phone down for a minute and help us find Nana's slippers?"

Aria glares at me then slaps her phone down on the table. "I'm helping Nana, not you."

For the next twenty minutes the three of us tear the house apart searching for slippers and the sheet of paper with Momma's medications.

By the time we uncover the prescription list buried under a stack of magazines, sweat drips from my face. We have yet to find the slippers. "I'm having central air installed next week, and I don't want any arguments." I march to the refrigerator for a bottle of water. "Oh. My. Goodness." I reach in and pull out a pair of grass-stained Dearfoams wedged between two egg cartons. "Why are your slippers in the fridge, Momma?"

Momma looks to Aria.

"I didn't do it, Nana."

Momma's gaze flies to me.

I hold them out to her. "I sure didn't put them there."

Momma's chin lifts. "I put them there so I wouldn't forget to take LaVera her eggs." She snatches the slippers then drops into the nearest chair. "Besides, chilled slippers are good for bunions."

I clamp a hand over my mouth to keep from laughing and flash a look to Aria to do the same. Embarrassing Momma further is not going to increase her cooperation. If I have any hope of stopping the unwieldy beast devouring my mother's memory, I need her to be truthful during the doctor's exam. Spewing the answers she thinks we want to hear won't help her. Even though I've Googled the heck out of dementia and read every depressing research article I can find, I'm clinging to the hope that there's some drug that will help. If there's not, I don't know what I'll do because I can't stand the hurt in Aria's eyes as she watches her Nana deal with her confusion.

"Aria, can you get the eggs?" I dig the keys from my purse as Momma wrestles her feet into the Dearfoams. "We'll drop them at LaVera's on our way to town."

Once Momma has her slippers on, she lifts her head. "There, that's better." Pride has completely replaced her earlier bewilderment. "Where are we going, Charlotte Ann?" She seems almost excited about the prospect of taking an unknown adventure.

"To the doctor," I repeat for the millionth time.

Chapter 8

SARA

Charlotte pumps the gas on my sweet little Ford Escort for the second time. "We'll have to drop the eggs by LaVera's on our way home from the doctor."

"They're fresh now." I clasp my hands tightly. Pushing Charlotte from behind the wheel won't stop her from hauling me in for another round of humiliation. I can't remember to take my meds, so why can't I forget the real reason Charlotte came home? It's bad enough she believes me no longer fit to live on my own. Must she have these totally bogus ideas medically documented as well? "I don't want two dozen of my best eggs to spoil."

"There's plenty of ice in the cooler, Momma." Charlotte looks at her phone and huffs. "We're already ten minutes late."

Gasoline fumes drift through the open windows. "Smells like you've flooded her."

"Mother, I know how to start a car." Charlotte hunches over the wheel and cranks the key again. The engine grinds but fails to ignite. Angry barn swallows swoop out of the carport to escape the increasing gas fumes. "Soon as I get my finances untangled, I'm buying us something more reliable."

I can't remember where Charlotte is in the process of severing her ties to that sorry husband of hers and I don't want to ask. I've already humiliated myself enough today by letting the doctor's appointment slip my mind. "I told LaVera we were on our way."

I love having Charlotte and Aria around, but I miss the company of people my age. People who understand the irritation of being treated like a child simply because you're growing old. Neither LaVera's very attentive son nor her bag full of fancy potions and creams have stopped her slide down the slippery slope. Maybe LaVera's face doesn't look a day over fifty and her mind doesn't run off on tangents of its own, but LaVera's body is letting her down almost as fast as my brain is failing me. After my nursing home escape caper and my accidental stumble back to Fossil Ridge, I was so relieved to find LaVera waiting on the porch. Her initial welcome was spry enough, but later, I noticed quite a bit of huffing and puffing as my old friend scurried around the kitchen to scramble some eggs and burn a few pieces of toast.

"You can use my phone and call LaVera when we get to Dr. Ellis's office." Charlotte's annoyed, but I'm not sure if she's annoyed with me or everything that has to do with me. It's all the same, I guess. "That way you can ask if we can bring her anything from town. We'll drop by with the eggs this afternoon."

"She made a cake."

"We'll have some this afternoon."

"It'll be so dry by then, we won't be able to cut it with a hacksaw." My desperation isn't helping my case. "I don't want to hurt her feelings."

"I've heard you tell LaVera to her face that she can't cook. You've never worried about LaVera's feelings before. Why are you so worried now?"

"She set out her Avon samples for Aria to look through."

Charlotte jiggles the key in the ignition. "We don't have time for cake or digging through old cosmetics."

"You and Caroline always enjoyed playing in LaVera's makeup bag."

Charlotte's hand drops from the key and comes to rest on my bony knee. "Tell you what, Momma, on the way home, I'll drop you and Ari at LaVera's and you can hack off pieces of dry cake and show off your granddaughter for as long as you'd like, okay?"

Outside, I give a nonchalant shrug. Inside, I'm celebrating. After the cold slipper humiliation, I wasn't sure I could successfully rally my wits again. "You're in the driver's seat."

Charlotte pats my leg the same way I used to placate a struggling child. "Only because you don't have a driver's license, remember?"

"Let's skip the doctor and go straight to the DMV," I say.

"You haven't passed the eye test in three years."

"I've got new glasses now."

"True, but..." Charlotte fiddles with the keys. "I noticed you seemed to be having trouble reading the calendar."

"You're worried I'll get lost again, aren't you?"

"It's not that. I can put a tracker on the car or get you a cell phone I can track."

"I'd rather wear a big cow bell around my neck," I huff for emphasis. "What's the real reason you don't want me to drive?"

"Let's get your eyes tested again. If you can pass the driver's eye test and the tests Dr. Ellis will have for you today, we'll see about you driving." Charlotte's answer is not reassuring.

"Are you taking my keys away from me?"

"Momma, nobody's taking anything away—"

"You've taken everything."

"Don't worry about driving, Nana." Aria leans forward. "I can get a hardship license at fifteen. I'll drive you to LaVera's and all the way to Austin to see Ira if that's what you want."

Charlotte's head is a Lazy Susan spinning around on her shoulders. Surprise has made her pop-eyed. "What makes you think you can drive at fifteen?"

"I Googled it." Aria thrusts her phone between the bucket seats.

"At fourteen I can start driver's ed. When I'm fifteen, I can apply for a learner's permit. After that, all I've got to do is pass a test, provide proof of Texas residency, and explain why it's a hardship on my family if I don't drive. But that should be easy."

"And why is that?" Charlotte's sarcastic tone doesn't faze Aria.

"Look at the dust on this car." Aria drags her finger along the console. "I live in the boonies with a gun-toting looney, right Nana?"

I can't help laughing at Aria's willingness to judge my little dust up with that sneaky real estate developer in the lighthearted vein it deserves. If only Charlotte were willing to do the same, we could spend this lovely morning getting reacquainted instead of wasting a perfectly good day waiting on a doctor to tell us what we already know: The remaining days of Sara Slocum's sanity are too precious to waste.

"Brilliant idea, Aria." Initiative is something I believe deserves to be nurtured. "I've always wanted a musically gifted chauffeur."

Charlotte shoots me the fish eye, then lasers an equal amount of disapproval on Aria. "You're only thirteen, Ari."

"Just until September." Aria pulls back her phone and gives it a couple of those magic taps. "I've already checked into taking Driver's Ed next summer. Lots of kids around here must do it because they only had a couple of slots left. So, I went ahead and signed up." She turns the screen of information toward her mother.

"See?"

"You signed up? Without asking me?"

"Geez, Mom. Don't freak. It's not like they've charged the fee to your credit card yet."

"Yet?" Charlotte's voice raises a notch.

"They'll hold my spot for a couple of weeks."

"Ari, we haven't even talked about this."

"That's why we're talking about it now. I can't apply for my hardship license until I pass the driver's ed test. And I'm going to pass that test. All you have to do is sign off. Dad will pay the fee."

"How do you know?"

"Because I asked him."

The hair on the back of Charlotte's neck stands straight out. "You've already talked to your father about driver's ed?"

"You've been busy."

With the enviable agility of youth, Charlotte slaps her hand across her mouth. It is worth the price of admission to watch her work at holding back the lecture she believes Aria deserves for going behind her back. I don't sympathize with Charlotte even a little. Martin was always Charlotte's first choice when she wanted something.

"Let me pay for the driving class, Charlotte," I say.

Charlotte ignores my offer. "Ari, I thought you wanted to audition for a spot in Juilliard's summer program next year."

"Maybe she can do both." Normally, these are the kinds of battles where I back out and let the parents fight it out with their child, but Charlotte's making a mess. She needs my help. "Juilliard's summer programs are usually only four to five weeks long."

Aria pops her head between us again. "How do you know so much about Juilliard, Nana?"

"I remember when—"

"Enough, Mother." Charlotte straightens in the seat and places her hand on the key. "None of us are going anywhere if I can't get this car started."

"You remember what, Nana?" Aria isn't going to let this one drop. "Nana?"

I can't believe my tongue had become so unhinged. Slocums are tight-lipped. But there are so many things Charlotte doesn't want discussed in front of Aria that I need a cheat-sheet to keep them straight. Charlotte's childhood plans and dreams are off limits. Caroline's death is taboo. And I might as well commit my own suicide if I ever dare to mention Martin's decision to take his own life.

What's left to talk about? Aria's obsession with her phone? Charlotte's obsession with restoring the ranch? My obsession with this mental battle raging in my head? The latter subject won't take more than a couple of seconds to cover. I intend to win my personal health war and hang on to my mind as long as I can. End of story.

I pretend not to hear Aria's pleas and pat the dash. "Third time is always a charm with this one." I hold up crossed fingers and nod to Charlotte to crank the Escort again. "She's temperamental."

"Like me?" The car sputters to life, sparing me the need to answer. Charlotte drops the shifter into reverse. The engine screeches. "What on earth?"

"My cat!" Aria claps her hands over her ears and shouts, "Stop, Mom! Fig's caught under the hood."

I grab Aria before she can scramble out. "That's just the serpentine belt," I holler over the high-pitched squeal.

"You sure, Nana?"

I nod. "Give her time to warm up."

"It's a hundred degrees out here." Charlotte pumps the gas. "The engine is warm." She drops the shifter into drive. An ear-piercing sound shakes the entire vehicle. "How long has it been since you've had your car serviced?"

"I haven't driven since before you put me in old people's prison."

"The Reserve was hardly a prison, Mother."

"Bo's my mechanic. When we get to town we can stop at his service station." I yank the seatbelt from the ceiling latch. "He'll spray it with something and she'll purr as contented as Aria's cat."

"Not funny, Nana." Aria slumps into the back seat.

Charlotte taps the gas and the car lurches forward. "I hope we make it to town."

The belt squeals as we motor down the lane, past LaVera's drive, and over the trestle bridge that spans the Frio. By the time we putter into the city limits, Charlotte's knuckles are white and my head's throbbing. I'll have to work extra hard to scrape my brain cells together if I'm going to ace this round of cognitive tests.

"You missed Bo's station," I point at the orange and green sign on the corner of Tucker's Towing and Gas Station.

"We're late." Charlotte tightens her grip on the wheel. "We'll have to stop on our way out of town."

I turn in my seat and study my daughter carefully. "You saw Winnie's VW parked under the canopy and decided to blow on by, didn't you?"

"Momma, I wish Winnie and Bo nothing but the best."

From the twitch in Charlotte's clenched jaw, I doubt that's completely true. "Then why are we still screeching down the road?"

"Because it's more important to me to know what can be done for *you* than what can be done for this old car."

"*For* me or *to* me?"

Charlotte starts to say something, changes her mind, then whips the Escort into one of the many open parking slots in the abandoned strip-mall parking lot. Fluorescent lights glow in only one of the storefronts, the other four commercial spaces are deserted and dark.

Below a humming window air conditioning unit, someone has painted: *Dr. Benjamin Ellis.*

"I can't believe it's come to this." I stare at the sign, unable to make myself get out of the car. "Benjamin showed such exceptional promise in third grade."

"What's that supposed to mean?"

"Coming home to practice medicine in a deserted shopping center has to be a... disappointment."

Charlotte cuts the engine and the screeching comes to a blessed halt. "Is that true for lawyers who come home to paint old farm houses?"

"Nobody's making you paint *my* house, Charlotte Ann." I open the door and do what I can to put a spring in my step, because dragging into Benjamin's office won't do any of us any good.

Bodies of all shapes and sizes fill most of the plastic chairs crammed into the small, dowdy waiting area. The chugging window unit spits out very little cool. In the sticky heat, I detect traces of ink and toner leftover from the days when the Dixon family operated an office supply store in this space.

"Aria, could you please grab a seat for Nana?" Charlotte takes me by the elbow. "Let's get you checked in, Momma." Charlotte knocks on the opaque, sliding glass window. When no one answers, she sticks her finger in the little notch and slides the panel back herself. The chair behind the desk is empty. "Hello, anyone here?"

67

"Don't get your panties in a wad." Some tall brunette with her hair twisted up and held in place by a plastic clip bustles in from the hall. She looks familiar, but I can't immediately place her. "I'll be with you when I get to you." She drops into the rolling desk chair behind the counter.

"Corina?" Charlotte's leaning in for a better look. "Corina Klump?"

The woman lowers the red-framed glasses perched on the top of her head. "It's Corina Miller now." Dark lashes frame the enormous green eyes studying Charlotte the same way a cat studies a canary before it pounces. "Do I know you?"

"Charlotte Slocum...McCandless now." Charlotte's cheesy smile screams *remember me*? "Caroline Slocum's little sister."

Corina's striking features furrow like she doesn't believe Charlotte's claim. "You've changed."

Charlotte gives that short-sheeted laugh, the one I can't stand because it belies her nerves and makes her seem weak. "You look exactly like you did when you captained the cheerleading squad."

"Caroline was the captain," Corina corrects. "She beat me by one vote." A deadly smile lifts the corners of the ex-cheerleader's mouth. "I always thought it was you who cast that deciding ballot."

"Me? Why would—"

"That's enough, Corina." I push between Charlotte and the glass panel and stick my head through the opening. "No wonder Raymond

Leck bit you, Corina."

"What?" she says.

"You were a spiteful little thing in third grade, and when I pointed out this character flaw to your mother, she said you'd eventually outgrow it. I suspect your mother now wishes she would have heeded my counsel." I mercifully leave out the part that she's also the mother of two of the worst-behaved kids to ever come through the elementary school doors.

"Momma!" Charlotte hauls me from the window. "I'm sorry, Corina. She's just anxious about her appointment."

"Well, she'll just have to wait," Corina nods toward the full waiting room. "As you can see, Dr. Ellis is extremely busy."

"Never too busy for my favorite teacher." Dr. Ellis appears in the doorway behind the steaming ex-cheerleader. "Send them on back, Corina."

Corina's pink cheeks turn an eat-crow shade of crimson. "Certainly, Doctor."

I know I shouldn't, but I can't help reaching around Charlotte and waving with every ounce of sweetness I can muster, "Morning, Benjamin."

"Morning, Mrs. Slocum. Meet me at the hall door and I'll usher you to an exam room myself."

"You heard him." Corina reaches up to shut the sliding glass divider.

I thrust my hand in time to stop the glass from closing. "If you're still keeping score, you should also blame Charlotte for Caroline's election as homecoming queen, president of your senior class, and Miss Addisonville. My Charlotte's quite the go-getter when she sets her mind to it."

"Momma, what's gotten into you?" Charlotte's grip pinches nearly clean through my elbow as she leads me to the open door on the opposite side of the waiting room. "Corina is not worth it."

"But your self-esteem is," I huff. "You teach people how to treat you, Charlotte Ann and Aria is watching."

"Over here, Mrs. Slocum." Dr. Ellis holds the door open with his backside and leans in to the waiting room with a friendly smile. "I'll be with y'all shortly," he tells the perturbed patients eyeing us. "This woman is a legend."

"See?" I whisper to Charlotte as I wave off his praise. "Just his third-grade teacher." Inside, I'm soaking up the admiration. "Mind if my daughter and granddaughter join us, Benjamin?"

"Not if you don't." His smile whips right on past me and lands squarely on Charlotte. I couldn't have chosen a more perfect place for my favorite student's attention to park. "Hello, Charlotte."

The attractive, deep timbre of his greeting clearly rattles Charlotte's bones because she sputters, "Itty...I mean, Benjamin."

"Itty's fine," Benjamin says with a grin. "In fact, I miss my old nickname...almost as much as I've missed marching band."

70

"You still play?" Charlotte drags the tiny gold treble clef back and forth on the chain around her neck. She is turning all different shades of red and stammering as if her tongue is swollen to twice its normal size, but at least she doesn't emit a single peep of that short-sheeted laugh of hers.

That's something. Exactly what, I'm not quite sure, but something.

"Yep, some of the church's worship band members put together a little jazz ensemble and asked me to join them." Benjamin motions for us to step into the inside hall, but instead of following me, he just stands there...staring at Charlotte. "We could use someone who rocks the keys. You interested?"

"She doesn't swim anymore." Aria breaks right into the middle of Charlotte and Benjamin's awkward stare. "And she hasn't touched a piano in years, according to Nana."

Benjamin's gaze drops to the small blonde with her hands jammed on her hips and her chin raised like she's looking for a fight. A wide grin breaks on his face. "Charlotte, there's no denying that this little firecracker belongs to you."

Aria rolls her eyes but I'm smiling like a cat who's just been handed a bowl of cream.

"Momma says she's a chip off the old block." Charlotte's hands cup Aria's shoulders. "Ari, this is Itty...I mean, Dr. Ellis. I've known him a long time. He's one of the best trumpet players you'll

71

Lynne Gentry

ever meet."

Chapter 9

CHARLOTTE

To keep myself from pacing the yellowed tiles of the windowless exam room, I lean against the small sink and whip the music charm back and forth on the chain. The longer I watch my mother struggle to draw a clock face, the tighter the noose grows around my neck.

"Benjamin." Momma sits beside Itty at a small desk. Though they have their heads together and their backs to me, I can hear him gently coaxing her to move forward with her assignment. Instead of knocking out the simple task, she continues to hold a pencil above a blank piece of paper and fire off questions. "Do you want the clock numbered in Roman numerals or Arabic?"

Encouraged by the brilliant wit in her latest attempt to clarify exactly what's expected of her, I'm hopeful Itty's tests will reveal another reason for her increasing lapses in memory and judgment. A treatable and reversible cause. According to my internet research, there's a long list of things that can cause or mimic Alzheimer's symptoms. Perhaps Momma's medications need adjustment. Or maybe she needs some dietary changes. Or possibly more brain stimulating activities. I'm willing to try anything because moving here to increase her human interactions has not reversed her mental atrophy.

Itty smiles. "Whatever suits you, Mrs. Slocum." His exceptionally large hand swallows Momma's shoulder in an encouraging squeeze. "Like I said, take your time. It doesn't have to be a work of art."

Momma points her sharpened pencil at him. "Benjamin, anything worth doing…"

"You caught me." Itty's rich, deep chuckle fills everything but the bottomless hole I've dug in my head. "Anything worth doing is worth doing well."

"Promise you won't forget that, young man."

"I promise, Mrs. Slocum."

What am I going to do if my mother has Alzheimer's? Totally losing her mind is different than wrecking a lawn mower or putting a dent in her car and not telling me about it. How am I going to deal with the increasing lack of judgment that's sure to come? Already her impulsive behavior has cost me a total change to my life and several thousand dollars. Paying off a yard man is nothing compared to what Sam Sparks might demand. If that real estate developer dares to ask for river access again, I don't want to be responsible for the damage Momma's unpredictable mood swings might inflict.

I don't want to be solely responsible for my mother.

The thought hits me hard.

There is no one else.

Walking away from Momma would have dire consequences. Not just for her, but for the relationship I long to have with my own daughter. Aria is watching me and I don't mean just during this exam. She's watching my every move, listening to every irritable word, and looking for love in every gesture I make toward my mother. I'm so afraid of the impact shirking my responsibility to my mother would have on the shaky relationship I have with Aria that I can't even consider placing Momma in a home and going back to my old life. No matter how difficult all of this might become, I'm not walking away. My father did that to me and I've never been the same. The only way to teach my daughter how to love someone who doesn't deserve it is to show her.

Momma jabs the name embroidered above the pocket of Itty's white coat with her pencil eraser. "Say it, young man."

"Anything worth doing is worth doing well." Itty finishes with a blinding white smile framed by a thick mahogany beard. "Now, quit stalling and get to work, young lady."

Mother pinches his cheek. "You always were one of my favorites."

"Don't try to butter me up." Itty rises from the rolling stool and slowly removes from Momma's sight a small silver tray with the three objects he'd asked her to identify and remember when he first began her exam. She'd easily named the scissors and cotton ball. The tongue depressor had her stumped for a moment. It was as if the word was on the tip of her tongue but ironically being held in place by a plank of wood.

The flash of terror I'd seen in her eyes, sent a shudder straight through me. But no one was more relieved than Momma when she'd finally found the word. Aria had cheered for her when she repeated *scissors*, *cotton ball*, and *tongue depressor* three times in a row without the least bit of hesitation. Itty explained that he wanted her to remember these items so that she could name them at the end of her exam.

Itty reaches around me and sets the tray inside the small sink I'm leaning against. Our shoulders brush. My worried gaze shoots up to his.

"It'll be all right," he mouths.

Because Itty is at least a head taller than me, his breath warms my forehead. It's hard not to call him by the silly nickname pinned on the skinny boy forced to lug a tuba because Addisonville's band already had too many trumpets. Momma was incensed at the injustice. Her favorites were not to be deprived of opportunities to further their talents. By the start of our senior year, she'd finally worn the band director down. Trumpet in hand, Itty quickly proved his natural ear. I can't help but wonder why Itty, who's no longer bitty, took up medicine instead of music.

Shifting away from a sudden longing to tickle a keyboard, I mouth back, "Should Aria and I step outside?"

"You're fine," Itty whispers. "Let's see how well she concentrates with distraction close at hand." He turns and leans against the counter with me.

Shoulder to shoulder, we watch Momma start to write, then stop. I've not had someone solid to lean against in so long, I hope Itty's keen ear isn't picking up the panic pounding in my chest.

Itty tilts his head toward me and whispers, "So, you're painting the house?"

The randomness of this question works like a speed bump that slows my racing worry. "How did you know?" I whisper back.

"White paint in your hair." His arm wraps around behind me and he pulls a paint-splattered strand from my head.

My hand flies to my head. "Ouch."

"Diagnostics are my specialty." The toe of Itty's shoe hits the lever on the trash can. The lid pops open and he drops in a white hair, then dusts his hands with a satisfied smirk. "You're stressed."

"What makes you think that?" I whisper between clenched teeth.

He crosses his arms over his broad chest. "House painting is about as far from lawyering as it gets."

Mother taps her pencil on the table. "Is this part of the test, Benjamin?"

Itty rips his intense gaze away from me. "Ma'am?"

Momma's frustration drills us both. "I don't think anyone could concentrate with all this blatant flirting going on not three feet away?"

Heat speeds up my core and spreads to my face. "We were just catching up, Momma." I inch left until Itty and I are no longer touching.

Mother lifts her pencil over the blank sheet of paper. "How big do you want the numbers, Benjamin?"

I can't help but worry that the tiniest of distraction has hindered her concentration, so I make a silent pledge to ignore my crazy desire to confide anything more to Itty. No matter how spot-on his deductions are about me, I don't want my mother's doctor making an erroneous diagnosis because he was distracted.

"Well, the goal is to number the circle like a clock," Benjamin repeats kindly.

Mother looks down at the paper then back at us. "What circle?"

"The one the doctor asked you to draw." Aria's empathy for her grandmother sounds more like disapproval of my comfort with Itty. "A clock. Like the one on your kitchen wall."

It's all I can do not to jump in and defend my right to have a friend. "Ari, let's all try to give Nana a quiet moment, okay?"

"I'm not the one chatting up the doc." Aria pulls out her cell, turns her back to me, and frantically begins typing with both thumbs.

Momma hunches over her project and finally lowers her pencil to the paper. She's scrapes the lead along the paper so hard it snaps. She stops and calmly says, "They don't make pencils like they used to."

"Here," Itty pulls the pen from his pocket and clicks it on. "Try this, Mrs. Slocum."

Momma lets out a long, slow breath. "I have my own pen. Is there a rule against using one's own pen when one's future is being tested?"

"No, ma'am."

"Good." Momma motions for Aria to hand over her purse. She digs through its contents until she finds a pen, then sets the purse on the small desk to block our ability to see her paper. "Keep your eyes on your own work," she says, as if we are taking the same test and might be trying to cheat by getting a peek at her answers. A few clicks of the pen and she finally sets to work.

I hold my breath. Aria clutches her phone to her chest like she's trying to hold herself back. Benjamin casts a supportive nod my way. I'm grateful, but there's nothing he can do to take away the pounding in my chest.

Minutes tick by at a snail's pace.

"There." With a smile, Momma holds up her answer sheet. "The student has failed to trip up the teacher."

I can't move. I can't blink. I can't believe what I'm seeing.

Not only is the circle horribly lopsided, twelve odd-sized numbers are written in three shaky rows of four, and most of the numbers are out of numerical order. The woman who used to solve complicated algebraic equations in her head cannot properly number a clock.

Aria lowers her phone. "Oh, Nana."

Momma's gaze surveys our stunned expressions. The smile slides from her lips. She places the paper face down on the desk. "Go ahead and say what we all know. I'm losing it, aren't I?"

Itty comes to our rescue. "Let's finish up the test before we start handing out grades. Okay, Mrs. Slocum?" He plops onto the rolling stool and wheels up beside her. "Remember the tray I showed you earlier?"

Momma's bottom lip is quivering and her rapid blinking tells me she fighting tears. "Yes."

"Can you name the three objects on the tray?"

Her hands search the surface of the tiny desk. "Where is it?"

"Take your time," Itty reassured. "Think about what was *on* the tray. I'm going to give you a clue."

"No!" Momma snaps. "A clue would be cheating." She pulls her hands into her lap and makes a clenched fist. "I've never been a cheater and I'm not going to cheat what's happening inside my head now, am I?"

It's Itty who finally breaks the deadly silence. "Remember how you used to give me a little help whenever I got stuck on a multiplication fact?"

"That was different."

"How?"

"You didn't really *need* my help," Momma conceded.

Itty gently places his hand over Momma's clasped ones. "The items on the tray were all things you'd find in a doctor's office."

Momma looks around the room, as if she's hoping to spot what's missing.

"Geez, Mom," Aria says. "If you're not going to help her, let me."

I grab Aria's arm and shake my head. "She has to do this."

Momma's gaze travels from Aria to me. At my encouraging nod, defiance fills her eyes. She withdraws her hands from Itty's grasp. "Charlotte's obsessed with painting. You really should let her paint this place, Benjamin." Momma snatches her purse from the table. "Her efforts to gloss over things is as unproductive as subjecting me to these ridiculous tests." She threads her arms through the stiff straps. "I may not be able to draw a clock, but I've never been late and don't intend to start now. My granddaughter and I have an appointment with the infallible Wilma Rayburn."

Lynne Gentry

Chapter 10

SARA

I let my gaze dart in and out of the honeycomb of empty storefronts on Main Street as Charlotte passes the stack of my new prescriptions to the gray-haired woman working the drive-thru window at Penny's Pharmacy. This drug store has been on the corner of Main and Third for fifty years.

When the founder, Ezra Penny, died behind the cash register, his daughter Gertrude took over management of the family-owned business. Even in her younger days, Gert was never much to look at. Thirty years of standing behind the drug counter has dragged her bosoms to her waist and flattened her feet. From the scowl on her face, it has also stomped out her hope. If she died with a half-filled pill bottle in her hand, there would be no heir to cry at her funeral or carry on the family legacy.

I cut a sideways glance at Charlotte. Life has snatched so much from me. It's only a matter of time before it takes this daughter. Since I don't have a piece of paper to record the blessing of having her and Aria with me now, all I can do is pray silently that I never forget them.

Several vacant doors down from Penny's is the office of the Addisonville Herald. Mitty Stringer is the only employee left at the county newspaper. A few years ago, he started working from home. His office lights are only on one day a month, the day he fires up the small press. Across the street, at the Addison National Bank—the one my father started and my older brother Burl, Jr. inherited—all of the lights blaze. Junior wants everyone to believe money is not a problem, but his new pickup is the only vehicle parked out front. When the big-box store popped up in the next county, Burl Jr. did nothing to help the local businesses survive the economic blow. In fact, most everybody in this town believes he made a tidy profit selling the land upon which the store was built. Except for me, everyone in this town has a long memory. Maybe the good thing about losing my mind is that someday I might forget what Burl Jr. did to me.

If what Benjamin says is true, my brain is like Main Street. Something's attacking my once thriving mental real estate. It is creating small holes in my memory's economic flow. As information travels along the cracked neuro sidewalks in my head, it falls into these tiny caverns. Once a thought disappears, it is as impossible to retrieve as a small town's viability.

Eventually, my entire brain will become a honeycomb, darker than Addisonville's struggling Main Street. The malevolent gene moving in is a big box store hell-bent on starving me out. It is only a matter of time before I have to close up shop.

Anger stiffens my spine. I've been a fool to trust medical advice dispensed from a deserted strip mall. These unsettling lapses in my thinking are from having too much to think about. Not dementia or early-onset Alzheimer's. I can prove it.

While Gertrude and Charlotte exchange pleasantries, I study each of the three remaining downtown businesses. I mentally repeat their names, then shut my eyes tight. A black and white imprint of the two-block heart of the city appears on the backside of my eyelids. But upon making a closer examination of the picture I see not the decrepit Addisonville of today, but the vibrant hometown of my childhood.

It's summer and I'm clutching the dime my father gave me before he shooed me from his office and sent me to buy a root beer float at the pharmacy. His wink told me he was only acting cross for his customer's sake. In truth, he swelled with pride when I correctly compounded loan interest in my head and spit out the answer a full five seconds before the adding machine.

That memory I can see clear as a bell. I can even taste the fizzy ice cream and hear the honk of cars as I dart across the street with the heat of August burning my skin. My new memory, the one I'd just entered in my mind, is gone.

I squeeze my eyes tighter. My mind mentally wanders the street in search of what I'd asked my brain to do. But it's like walking down the hallways of the school long after the janitor has turned off the lights for the day. Familiar, yet totally unsettling.

Gert Penny's unusually thick southern drawl snatches me from the past and drops me smack dab in the seat of my struggling Ford Escort.

"I'd heard you'd moved home, Charlotte." Gert shouts over the squeal coming from under the hood of the Escort. The scowl deepens on her brow as she shuffles the pile of prescriptions. "I can see why."

Charlotte's everything's-fine smile appears so fast I wonder if she'd been anticipating questions about my health. "Mother's just feeling a little run down," comes out of her mouth, but the worry on her face tells the truth. She believes Benjamin. And she is scared. Maybe as frightened as she was the day her sister died. The day everything changed. And now, just when she's remodeled her life once again, Alzheimer's has changed everything. "How long will this take?"

Gert's brows rise above her half-glasses. "I'll need an hour."

"We can stop by after we tour the school." Charlotte drops the shifter into drive, lurches forward, then slams on the brake. She throws her arm over the seat and backs up until she's once again even with the window. "Oh, LaVera asked if we could pick up the order she called in?"

"Bo usually picks up whatever his mother needs."

"LaVera asked us to help because Bo has the engine of Winnie's VW scattered all over his shop. Her tummy's a little upset and I think she doesn't want to wait until this evening to get an Alka-Seltzer."

"Should I send someone out to check on her?" Gert asks.

"That's up to you, but our next errand won't take long." Charlotte cranks the window back up. "What's the matter, Momma?"

"Wilma Rayburn will know I'm on crazy meds before we get to the school."

"Gert knows better than to breach a patient's privacy."

"And yet, somehow, everyone in town knew Cora Jenkins was losing it long before Cora's kids put her away and forgot about her."

"Momma, everyone knew Cora was losing it when she rode a bicycle through town stark naked."

I turn to my daughter. Worry lines pinch Charlotte's brow. This is going to be hard on her, which is exactly why I have hidden my concerns for so long. I don't want Charlotte ignoring her own problems to assume my burdens. Charlotte deserves her own life. A happier life.

But if she isn't going to live her own life, at the very least, she deserves support. A family to help her navigate the potholes in her mother's brain. I hadn't thought it possible for anyone to miss Caroline more than I, but Charlotte's face tells me I am wrong. There's nothing to do but accept that Caroline hadn't meant to die and leave all of this on Charlotte. But Martin...now that is a different story entirely. His decision to dump his family obligations was a great selfishness I can't forgive.

I will not be guilty of thinking only of myself, and that's exactly what asking Charlotte to care for me would be. "Get me some gaudy snowflake earrings and put me in the room next to Cora. She can teach me to crochet afghans."

"Are we still talking about Cora Jenkins?"

"Do you know another Cora?"

"Momma, Cora Jenkins has been dead for thirty years."

My insides jump high as a frightened jack rabbit. "Promise you won't let me parade my problems down Main Street, Charlotte Ann."

Charlotte grabs my hand and squeezes. "That's why I'm here." She pulls out from under the drive-thru awning. "I can reschedule Aria's school tour if you'd rather go home."

Facing a classroom filled with slothful Raymond Lecks sounds way better than being subjected to the smirk of my former principal. Wilma played innocent when I waylaid her in the administration's parking lot after the school board meeting, but it was Wilma who'd been collecting complaints, tallying test scores, and making surprise classroom visits. It was Wilma who'd stood up in that school board meeting and read off a detailed list of all my shortcomings. And it was Wilma who'd delivered the exaggerated report of the student whom I'd sent home with a regurgitated peanut butter and jelly sandwich in his lunchbox.

The lunchroom story was the ugly nail the board used to declare me no longer fit to teach. It wasn't like sending the nasty lunchbox home had unnecessarily traumatized the child. Especially when all twenty-three of my students, including that little boy, went home that day well taught. Rinsing out a soiled lunchbox had simply slipped my mind. It could have happened to someone far younger.

Forty years of loyal service and I'd been fired for forgetting to clean up after a child who was tired of PB&Js and wanted his mother to know.

"We've got to kill an hour." I open the visor mirror and check my lipstick. Senility has yet to abolish my vanity. "Making Wilma look me in the face after what she did is more likely to kill her than me."

"I can park in the shade and you can wait in the car."

"And let that sadist sell you a bill of goods? I don't think so."

"Momma, I know this has been a very upsetting morning, but could you please stop using that word in front of Aria."

"Very well. Vindictive backstabber. That better?"

Charlotte rolls her eyes like what's the point. "We're going to get to the bottom of what's going on with you, Momma."

My daughter will need support. What I need is a piece of paper to write down the things I want set in order before I completely lose it. For now, I'll have to settle for repeating things again and again in hopes of retaining some of the information whirring about in my head.

"If one of my students couldn't draw a proper clock, I would think that child suffered some sort of cognitive impairment," I say.

"*Possible* impairment."

"Splitting hairs is a waste of time."

"Itty's not sure it's Alzheimer's, Momma. Let's wait until he gets the blood work-ups and scans before we start acting like we have a definitive diagnosis, okay?"

"I have brain agility loss, Charlotte Ann. Not hearing loss. I heard Benjamin's entire spiel."

Charlotte's brow scrunches in that way it does whenever she's thinking on something she isn't sharing. "We're going to figure this out, okay?"

"Why do you keep using the word *we*?" It's a sane and legitimate question. "I'm the one losing the ability to solve problems, control my emotions, and eventually even the ability to feed or dress myself."

"There are treatments."

What did Charlotte want me to say? Would it comfort her to know that she's not the only one scared to death? Who wants to lose their mind before their body gives out? Terrifying as it is to think of my brain as a bowl of mush, my insides shake at the possibility I've waited too long to retrieve all the good memories I've tucked away. There are hundreds of recollections I've shoved deep and avoided on purpose. My faith in the trite adage that time heals all wounds is thin, but I've been counting on those old memories to ferment to a vintage that will comfort me in old age. I have stacks of memories I want to enjoy...Caroline's tiny fingers wrapped around mine, the tinkle of Charlotte mastering her piano scales, and Martin's laughter whenever the two of us sneaked to the river for a midnight swim.

I'd rather choke on my overwhelming emotions than suck Charlotte down with me. "Benjamin has always been a smart one."

Aria reaches over the seat. "It's going to be all right, Nana."

Maybe I hadn't sounded as brave as I'd intended. I can barely nod, but for Aria's sake I bob my head a couple of times. I will not fail my granddaughter the way I've failed Charlotte. "Yes, yes, it is, my dear."

Red lights scroll out a message on the new digital Addisonville ISD sign flashing up ahead.

Back to school registration now open.

The Escort bounces over a couple of pot holes at the parking lot entrance. Only a smattering of cars bake in the morning sun. The nandina bushes I'd helped the janitor plant around the campus seem a little bigger and the three-pronged, single-story hill country stone building seems a little smaller. Is the discrepancy the result of time or Alzheimer's?

I sneak a quick sideways peek at my daughter. Charlotte's jaw is set and her knuckles white. Returning to the place where she'd lived in her older sister's shadow isn't any easier for her than it is for me. Charlotte doesn't need me along to show Aria around her second childhood home. She knows every inch of this campus. Every summer, she and her sister rode their bikes in the halls, practiced their piano scales on the old upright in the music room, and spent hours playing hide and seek while I worked on my classroom. Charlotte planned this tour to coincide with my doctor appointment because she needs me along for moral support.

Needed. I haven't felt truly needed since Caroline died and Charlotte pushed me away.

Longing spins my gut into a ball. Perhaps not being able to remember the mistakes of my life won't be so bad after all.

"Is this it?" Aria's poking her head between us. "How many kids did you say go here?"

"Between three hundred and fifty to four hundred." Charlotte is so busy taking everything in that the car has slowed to a crawl. "The teacher/student ratio is great. You'll probably have the fine arts teacher all to yourself."

"Fine arts?" Aria scoffs. "A box of crayons does not a fine arts department make."

Charlotte's jaw clenches. "Ari, give it chance, okay? Mrs. Kirk is an excellent musician. She taught me music from kindergarten to twelfth grade."

"Yeah, and look how you turned out." Aria throws herself against the backseat. "They probably don't even have internet access."

"I loved helping your Nana get her classroom ready." Charlotte shoots me a sideways plea for support. "Remember, Momma?"

"I do." The ease of accessing this information bolsters my spirits. "One year, your mother cut out a hundred paper bunnies for my math bulletin board."

"A hundred?" Aria asks.

Charlotte chuckles. "I can't see cottontail to this day without thinking about our *multiply like a bunny* slogan."

"Wilma thought it was so catchy, she used it the next year." Bitterness curdles my tongue. "But then the only thing original about Wilma Rayburn is her creative ability to stab you in the back."

"Momma, that was seven years ago."

I can't tell if Charlotte's marveling at my ability to recall this incident or my inability to let it go. I point at the empty space beside the *Principal Parking Only* sign. "Wilma's come up in the world."

"Momma," Charlotte warns. "This is important."

"My career was as important to me as yours is to you." I pop the door hard with my shoulder and it creaks open. "Come on, Aria. I want to show you the corner administration office that should have been mine."

Chapter 11

CHARLOTTE

The cinderblock halls of the old school building smell of freshly waxed floors and newly-applied off-white paint. With only two weeks until school starts, I'd expected the place to be crawling with teachers, but it's deathly quiet in the empty corridors.

I'm worried that keeping this appointment is just too much for all of us. I, for one, could use a few minutes to process all that Benjamin said and didn't say about protecting what was left of Momma's working memory.

"You girls okay?" I whisper over the squeak of Momma's non-skid slippers.

"Right as rain," Momma chirps quickly, way too quickly.

Is her attempt to fake it for Aria's sake or has she already entered into the next stage of mental decline? Benjamin warned me that not being able to remember something that was said ten minutes

95

earlier was a sign. What if she's really right as rain because at this very moment she can't remember how much she hates the school that cast her aside after forty years of dedicated service? What if she really can't remember the furious injustice she'd felt when she demanded I file an age discrimination lawsuit accusing Wilma Rayburn, the very woman we were about to face?

As much as I'd love to believe Momma needs me close to keep her from leaving the flame burning under a pan of grease, evidence is stacking up to support the very real possibility that she might not have as much sane time left as Itty had implied. This gut punch puts a big dent in the excitement I'd had about showing my daughter where I'd grown up. A quick glance at Aria's wrinkled nose stomps out the last remaining hopes of my child loving this place as much as I had.

"I can reschedule." My offer echoes off the cold cement walls.

"Slocums never back down." Momma takes Aria's hand. "This way."

Sometimes backing down is the best way to win. I need time to think. To sort through how I'm feeling. To come up with a plan that stops the Slocum dysfunction: Momma denies anything's wrong, then shoves me aside. I feel guilty and try to change up my whole life to please everyone. And Aria clams up.

None of these approaches will change what's really happening.

My mother has Alzheimer's.

According to Benjamin, the first phase is trouble with short-term memory and rational decision making. This stage can last up to two years. I'm not sure when the clock started on this phase, but I feel Momma's already suffering from an inability to make good decisions. The time has most likely been ticking on this stage for quite a while. I knew something was wrong at least a year ago. It's not normal for someone to drive a riding lawn mower straight into a tree or to blow a man off a ladder with a garden hose. How many months have I wasted justifying Momma's crazy actions?

"The elementary wing is down the hall to your left." Momma's dragging Aria along as if she's delivering a naughty child to the principal.

"Can I see your old classroom, Nana?" Aria asks.

The question trips Momma up and slows her down. "I suppose it won't hurt to take a peek at it before we leave."

"Is the high school wing still the hallway to the right, Momma?" I ask.

"Unless Wilma got a wild hair and flipped everything around."

"Then the middle school must be straight ahead." Aria's eyes are huge and I suddenly remember how hard it is to be thirteen.

"Want to see my old locker?" I ask.

"Aren't we late?" Momma points at the letters on the frosted glass of the principal's office. "Don't give Wilma any more ammunition against the Slocums."

I push the door open and we step into a chilly waiting area. Even though no one is working the neat and tidy secretary's desk, I still feel the need to defend my tardiness. Across the room is an open office door. The metal plate is engraved with the single word that can still strike fear in me.

Principal.

"Wait here." I leave Momma and Aria still holding hands and hurry to the threshold of the principal's office. Not sure whether to knock or clear my throat, I just stand there, staring. Seated behind a large wooden desk is a frosted-blonde woman who could pass as the slightly younger doppelganger of the stunning actress Glenn Close. "Mrs. Rayburn?"

Wilma looks up from the stacks of papers piled on her desk and smiles. "Charlotte Slocum." Her genuine pleasure activates an equally pleased grin from me.

Feeling like a traitor to Momma, I dial my smile back a notch. "Good to see you, Mrs. Rayburn."

"You haven't changed a bit."

If she only knew how far that was from the truth. "Things seem pretty much the same here, too."

"Progress is a tough row to hoe in Addisonville." She pushes back her chair, strides confidently around the desk wearing white linen pants, a tangerine top and hemp-colored espadrilles. Wilma is only a year younger than mother, a fact I discovered when I researched her age in order to shut down Mother's age discrimination suit. If I hadn't seen a copy of her birth certificate, I'd guess her to be in her early fifties. "Are you alone?" Her furtive gaze shoots past me and I wonder if she's been expecting a Slocum ambush.

"Aria's in the waiting room." I don't know why I don't tell her that Momma's with me, too. Maybe I want Momma to have the advantage for once.

"I've looked over her transfer records," Wilma says. "It appears Aria's very bright."

"And a little nervous. This is all very different from the metro schools I've had her enrolled in."

"Well, let's see if we can put your daughter at ease, shall we?"

Almost as if Wilma's leery of being set up, she puts on a tight-lipped smile and motions for me to step into the waiting area ahead of her. Momma and Aria stand across the room. Wilma follows after me. I step aside, giving these two warring women their first face-to-face in five years. The temperature in the room drops thirty degrees.

Wilma's smile doesn't abandon her but her voice goes AWOL for a split second. She blinks and recovers. "Sara." Wilma wouldn't have beaten my mother to the kill-them-with-kindness punch two years ago, maybe not even yesterday. But today, the fully cognizant school principal obviously has the mental upper hand. "Is this the beautiful granddaughter you were always going on about?"

"Wilma," Momma's tone is laced with the old hostilities she ironically can't seem to forget. "She's as brilliant as her mother and just as gifted."

"If you've said it once, you've said it a million times, your daughter is exceptional."

I don't know what's more surprising: that Momma believes me brilliant and gifted or that she's actually bragged on me to a woman she once considered a friend?

"Some things are worth repeating," Momma's reference to the reason she was dismissed is a shot fired straight at Wilma for leading the school board's charge against her.

From the slanting of Wilma's body away from her accuser, I can see that she still holds to her complete innocence in the whole sordid affair.

In an attempt to get this glacier moving, I say, "Maybe we could start with the music room?" I know I'm talking too fast, but I'm determined to get through this tour without any more of Momma's potshots. "Aria's preparing for Juilliard and she's excited to meet her fine arts teacher."

"Let's save that until last, shall we?" Wilma motions toward the middle school wing. "This will be your hall, Aria."

My daughter's head rotates slowly as she takes in six classroom doors. "This is it?"

"Here in Addisonville, we believe the older students have a great deal to offer the younger. Our middle schoolers spend quite a bit of time in the elementary halls and classrooms. And each of our high school students is expected to mentor a middle schooler."

Aria crosses her arms. "I don't need a babysitter."

"Good, then you'll really enjoy making a new friend." Wilma walks past my fence-post stiff child and opens the first classroom door. "Mrs. Rogers teaches sixth, seventh, and eighth grade English. She's travels the world during the summer and loves bringing a new perspective to the required reading."

I take in the room where I'd trudged through the pain of diagramming sentences, but devoured Little Women and To Kill a Mockingbird. I slid into a nearby desk. "This was my seat."

"I'm not sitting on the front row," Aria wheels and storms into the hall.

Maybe it's better I keep my mouth shut, let Aria have her own experiences. After all, I know all too well how it feels to live in someone's shadow. I wiggle out from the tight squeeze of the desk and hurry to catch up.

"Sorry, Ari," I whisper into her ear. "You've got this."

She storms ahead.

Without my comments, the tour moves along quickly. It only takes a few minutes to see all six rooms, learn the respective teacher's name, and get a quick rundown on the curriculum.

"Any questions, Aria?" Wilma asks as she closes the science

room door. Aria shakes her head and I can see that her sullenness flies all over Momma as much as it does me. "Very well. You're welcome in my office any time if you need answers. Now, let's investigate the common areas. We'll start with the gym."

Wilma stops us outside double doors. "Wait here while I flip on the lights."

The moment she disappears behind the swinging doors, Aria grabs my arm and begs, "Mom, let's go. Please."

"You haven't seen the music department."

"I don't need to. I don't like it here."

A quick glance at Momma tells me I'm on my own. "Everybody in town comes to the basketball games. The gym literally rocks with school spirit."

The buzz of fluorescents warming up sends a sliver of light under the swinging doors. When it brightens to a blue glow, I figure it's safe to enter. "Come on, Momma. Let's show her where Caroline once did backflips the entire length of the court."

Momma shakes her head. "I'm fine here."

I could kick myself for bringing up Caroline. Being here now, I'm starting to wonder. Was Momma's unorthodox behavior in the classroom caused by early onset dementia or working in the halls haunted by Caroline's ghost?

I take Aria's hand. "This will only take a second."

The gym floor is twenty bleacher rows below us. Five 1A State

Basketball Championship banners hang from the exposed metal rafters. A new coat of wax on the hardwood court can't conceal the faint odor of socks, popcorn, and fierce competition. I close my eyes and hear the throb of the crowd during the 1992 playoff game between Addisonville and Leakey. Caroline's a senior. I'm a sophomore, shy and awkwardly chewing my nails on the very top bleacher plank. Our team is down two points with only a minute left to play. A time out is called. Bo's the team captain. He leads our players to the bench to regroup. Caroline rushes to the end of the court.

Without asking anyone's permission, my big sister raises her hands above her head. She claps twice, then begins to do cartwheels. Her form is as perfect as it is mesmerizing as she flips the entire length of the gym. Her pleated cheerleading skirt is a roulette wheel that spins the crowd into a frenzy. I'm cheering for her, more than anyone. My sister. The brave one. The bold one. The one who didn't give a rat's behind about what anyone thought of her. She was something special. More than I could or will ever be.

"Ouch, Mom." Aria tugs her hand from my vise grip. "We're going to the lunchroom."

I can't let my eyes meet Momma's as we exit the gym. She was there the night my sister led the charge that rallied the home-team win. How I wish Caroline was here to cheer us on now. I've been doing emotional backflips for the last two years, but our little team refuses to gel. Winning seems impossible.

Nothing Wilma has pointed out on the way to the lunchroom has changed the hard set of Aria's expressions. "If you're a reader, Aria, you'll love the library."

"May I see the music room, please?" Aria's use of the manners I've drilled into over the years is some consolation.

"Of course." Wilma heads for the auditorium. "How about I show you the grand piano first?" Wilma chatters about the impressive test scores and college scholarships twelve of last year's twenty graduating seniors received.

"She's gained weight," Momma whispers to me as we follow the slight waddle of Wilma's behind.

I give Momma the signal to zip her lip, but I notice Aria's wearing a small smile for the first time since we pulled into the parking lot.

"Here we are." Wilma leads us inside a dark auditorium where we're quickly enveloped with the smell of dusty curtains and dry oak stage decking.

My heart sinks. If this is the extent of the music department, nothing has changed since I picked around on the school's only decent piano.

"Stay here until I find the lights." Wilma slips behind the stage curtain. A loud crash is followed by a curse and an "I'm okay." Stage lights flicker on. The same glossy black grand piano I used to play takes up nearly half the stage.

Aria doesn't say a word. She simply hoists herself up on the stage, walks to the piano, pulls out the bench, and starts to play Chopin's Nocturne. Momma and I slip into the front row's wooden seats.

The buzzing lights create a halo atop Aria's head.

"She plays like an angel." Wilma drops into the seat beside me. "That piano hasn't sounded this good since you left, Charlotte."

I don't want anyone to know how much I'm itching to sit at that piano. Not to play so much, but to recapture the intoxication of pursuing dreams instead of obligations. "That was a long time ago."

"I remember how your playing would fill these halls in the summer. I enjoyed having my fourth-grade classroom so close. Your music made the drudgery of cutting out construction paper bunnies go so much faster."

I laugh and smile again when I see that even Momma found the humor in that unknowing confession.

Wilma's brows knit. "Did I say something funny?"

Momma deserves this moment of gloating, but I don't want her to say anything that will cause a fight so I change the subject. "I can't wait for Aria to meet Maida Kirk."

"We're currently in search of a new music teacher."

Momma leans around me. "You don't have a music teacher, *Wilma?*"

"Not right now, *Sara*," Mrs. Rayburn says. "And I won't be hiring a music teacher specifically. If I could even find someone to fill the position, budget cuts will require this new teacher to handle the entire fine arts department. Theater, chorus, band, plus social studies."

"There's no music teacher?" Aria has stopped playing. "What happened to Mrs. Kirk? Mom says she's wonderful."

"She was, but she retired five years ago and moved to California to be near her children," Wilma's glance Momma's way implies Momma should have done the same.

Aria strides to the edge of the stage with her fists balled on her hips. "Geez, Mom. Why don't you just drop me on a deserted island?"

My people-pleasing brain is scrambling for a solution. Private lessons? Where? I was counting on Mrs. Kirk. Now, we'll probably have to drive clear to Austin or San Antonio. Both are over two hours away.

I rush to the stage like I'm afraid my daughter will make a run for it. "We'll think of something, Ari."

"Will you be practicing law in Texas, Charlotte?"

I wheel and flash her a that's-none-of-your-business look.

Wilma shrugs. "I Googled you."

Momma joins me at the stage and, for once, it's three against one…almost like we're a Slocum team or something. "What does it matter to you what my daughter does for a living?"

I stay mother's hand. Curious as to where this conversation is going, I ask, "Why?"

Wilma puts her hands on her knees. They pop as she stands, the first sign that she, too, is aging. "Have you heard of the Texas emergency teacher certification program, Charlotte?"

"No."

"Again, why are you badgering my daughter?" Mother asks.

Wilma ignores Momma and looks directly at me. "Now that you're home, Charlotte, I was wondering if *you* might consider becoming our fine arts instructor?"

"Me?"

"You're more than qualified."

"How do you know?"

"You doubled-majored in law and music, did you not?"

I owe Momma an apology. Sadistic *is* a very accurate description of this woman. Offering me a job in front of a woman she'd fired is just plain cruel.

"Mrs. Rayburn, I'm not a teacher."

Wilma's gaze slides toward Momma. "That's never stopped some of us from trying."

"My daughter will never work for a sadist." Momma holds up her hand and indicates Aria should jump from the stage. "Let's go, Aria. Homeschooling is a far superior option."

Lynne Gentry

Chapter 12

SARA

According to Benjamin, I shouldn't be able to remember what I had for lunch. But after our visit with the school principal, I'm convinced my furry-faced doctor friend must have misdiagnosed me. I will *never* forget Wilma Rayburn's Cheshire-Cat smile when she offered *my* Charlotte a job.

A job! At the very school that fired me...by the very woman who made it her mission in life to end my forty-year teaching career in disgrace.

The nerve of that sadistic woman. She can't have my Charlotte. If it hadn't been for Aria's impressionable presence, I wouldn't have stood by as long as I did while that woman tried to sink her fangs into my daughter. I should have chopped off that viper's head the moment she poked it out of the office I was meant to occupy.

"Please tell me you're not going to take the job, Mom." Aria leans between the seats.

Charlotte suddenly has to check the positions of every mirror in the car. "You were begging me to teach you this morning."

"That's different...it'd be weird having my mom at school."

"I grew up with my mother at school." Charlotte clicks in her seat belt.

"That's different." Aria argues.

"How so?"

"Nana's cool."

"Fasten your seat belt, Ari." Charlotte's such a pleaser she'd teach dog sledding in the Texas heat if she thought it would make somebody happy. "I don't have to decide today."

"If you're going to quit law to teach,"—Aria continues with a tenacity I haven't seen since Caroline— "then spare me the humiliation and homeschool me."

"Homeschooling doesn't pay." Charlotte jabs the key into the ignition.

"So?" Aria asks.

"So, we need the money."

Finally, the truth.

Aria pounces on the admission as fast as a cat after a ball of yarn. "Since when do we need money?"

"Since your father..."

Charlotte's unfinished accusation dangles as big and foreboding as the bunch of carrots Wilma has just offered. Same vacation and holiday calendar as your daughter. Small class size. Only one school-wide talent show a year. And best of all, Master's level teacher's pay. It doesn't take a rocket scientist to interpret Charlotte's biting tone...James McCandless has done something underhanded...again. Charlotte's desperation, no matter how unsettling, is a pinprick to my anger.

Suddenly too tired to fight but still unwilling to concede, I slump against the Escort's warm fake-leather upholstery. "Wilma Rayburn cannot be trusted. Promise me you'll at least listen to my side."

"Momma, it's been a long morning." Charlotte cranks the car. "I promise we'll talk about this when we get home." She throws the car into gear and the belt's screeching starts immediately. "We've still got to swing back by the drugstore and stop at Bo's station."

I've worked up a pretty good mad by the time we arrive at the drugstore.

Gert Penny sticks her head through the drive-thru window. "I need another ten minutes to package up all the pills Benjamin prescribed. You might want to come inside and cool off."

Charlotte lets out a long, exhausted sigh. "This is the day that is never going to end."

"Somewhere it's ending for someone." I shrug off Charlotte's disapproval of my maudlin mood. "That's how it goes. Even the best of days eventually come to an end." I climb out of the car and follow the last remaining proof that I'd ever had good days.

Ancient ceiling fans stir the medicinal-tinged air of the pharmacy.

"I need some...mascara," Aria announces, phone in one hand, neck craning to take in the contents of the drugstore.

"Don't go far," Charlotte warns.

"How far could I go in this store...or this town?" Aria disappears down one of the narrow aisles, her nose now glued to her phone.

Charlotte takes my elbow. "Let me buy you a drink at the soda counter, Momma."

I sense she's trying to make peace, to smooth the feathers this day has ruffled. "Can you afford it?"

"If I take your old boss up on her offer, I'll be flush with cash." Her attempt at humor is not funny.

"Judas probably thought the same thing." I carefully hoist a hip onto a swivel bar stool.

"Good one, Momma." Charlotte parks herself on the stool beside me and clears her throat to get the attention of the girl behind the counter. "Excuse me."

Ember Miller, of the you-don't-ever-want-a-Miller-in-your-class Miller family, turns to face us with a wary look on her face and an ice cream scoop in her hand. "Can I help you, ladies?" Last time I saw Ember, she was a first grader with a sprinkling of freckles across her nose and two missing front teeth. Time had ripened her to a beautiful peach.

"A couple of root beer floats, please," Charlotte says.

Further study of the striking brunette scooping ice cream and pulling soda levers reveals that Ember has the same slow burn I'd seen in her older brother's beady eyes when he was in my third-grade class. Evan is probably a sophomore by now. Addisonville ISD is so small I'd hate to think of my sweet Aria crossing paths with that little devil. Unfortunately, if Evan is a sophomore, that means Ember, who I remember to be a couple of years younger than her brother, is probably close to Aria's age. The girls might have some classes together.

I search the pharmacy. No boxes are stacked in front of the back exit. I'm about to hop off my stool, grab my granddaughter, and slip out before she's exposed to another Miller when Charlotte pokes me.

"Momma?"

I jump. "What?"

"The clerk's asking you a question."

I catch a glimpse of a face in the huge mirror behind the counter. It's the blank, confused face of an old woman I don't know. What was I thinking about? I can't remember.

"Two scoops or one?" Ember repeats patiently. "Mrs. Slocum?"

Her manners are a surprise, especially in comparison to the

spiteful way her mother Corina dealt with us this morning. "Excuse me?"

"Do you want one scoop of vanilla ice cream or two in your float?" Charlotte peels the paper from her straw and slides it into the frosty glass before her. "You used to always get two."

Did I? I can't even remember liking root beer floats. "One is plenty."

While Charlotte is slurping ice cream and moaning about how much she's missed Penny Pharmacy floats, Ember whips up another frothy drink. She places it on the napkin she's set before me. "Enjoy, Mrs. Slocum." Then, like the very capable soda jerk that she is, Ember turns to the sink and quietly rinses ice cream scoops.

With the surprise of an unexpected summer storm, my previous thoughts on the Miller children blow in. I feel a little foolish assuming Ember's like her brother. It's not fair. I know better. My girls are nothing alike. *Were.* The pain is a kick to my chest I don't think I'll ever get used to.

"Where do we checkout?" Aria hefts an armload of bottles and workbooks onto the soda counter. "They don't have ginkgo biloba."

"What?" I ask, confused once again.

"A supplement that…" Aria notices Ember staring at us and clams up.

Ember peers at Aria's selections. "We have so many old…uh…elderly people around here that we can't keep that stuff in stock. You'll have to order ginkgo online." She holds out a frosty float glass to Aria the same way children hold out the offer of friendship on the playground. "Want one?"

"One what?" Aria's discreetly trying to scoop up the items she's dumped on the counter, but bottles of Vitamin D and E fall to the floor.

Charlotte launches into her typical save-the-day mode and scrambles after the vitamins.

"A root beer float." Ember's remarkable poise isn't fazed a bit. She acts like she's used to people purchasing things they don't want anyone to see…and so she doesn't.

Aria stops scooping and relaxes a little. "I've never had one."

"Then I guess this is your lucky day," Ember smiles. "Root beer floats and ginkgo are about as exciting as it gets around here."

"I'm Aria." My granddaughter juggles her load to one arm then thrusts her hand across the counter.

Ember looks at me. "Slocum?"

"McCandless," Aria and Charlotte say at the same time.

Ember drags her wet hand over her apron, then clasps Aria's hand. "Ember Miller. My friends call me Em."

"Do you go to Addisonville's one-room school?" Aria asks.

"Yep." Ember's lack of excitement is so disappointingly Miller-like. "Haven't seen you before."

Aria shrugs. "I'm new."

"Too bad."

The girls exchange understanding smiles and shake their heads.

"Sweet Moses, do something Charlotte," I mutter to my daughter.

Good as Ember obviously is since she has a job at thirteen and can conduct herself in such a professional manner, she's not completely clear of her heritage. Since Charlotte's sitting there with a pleased grin on her face, I feel the need to step in here, to steer Aria away from the bond I see forming. Years of watching good children take up with bad influences has left me with a sixth sense. Colluding with Millers is not the direction I want my granddaughter to go.

"What's all this?" I thump one the crossword books in Aria's overloaded arms.

"Ummm, just a little something to get me ready for school," Aria's lying, which is not like her and totally congruent with my theory of how easily bad influences can corrupt good morals. "I'm going to take it to the checkout. Nice meeting you, Em. Mom, I think I heard the pharmacist say our prescriptions are ready."

Once we're back in the car and screeching down Main toward Bo's gas station, I'm the one, not Aria's mother, who musters the courage to ask about the elephant in the car. "Vitamins. Sudoku books and crossword puzzles. Ginkgo." I swivel in my shoulder harness and glare at Aria's mound of white shopping bags. "Who are those things for?"

"This sack is for LaVera."

"I know that. I'm asking if you felt the need to stock up on vitamins and brain games for my sake?"

Aria squirms, but only for a second. "I know that crazy doctor gave you a buttload of meds, Nana, but will it hurt to try some natural methods?"

"How did you know what to buy?" Charlotte asks as she wheels the car across a long black hose that dings the bell inside Bo's station.

"I Googled it."

I swivel back in my seat and cross my arms. "School will be a good distraction from that phone of yours." I'm not sure if I should be angry or grateful for Aria's worry. It's not every day someone goes to such lengths for me. "Promise me you'll stay away from the Millers."

"Momma!" Charlotte pulls up to the station's open repair bay. A multi-colored VW bug is suspended high on the rack. "We want Aria to have friends, right?"

"Someone has to monitor her *choice* of friends."

"Momma!"

Bo Tucker's loud rap on Charlotte's window stops my daughter from knocking my head off. She silences me with a daggered stare and growls, "We'll settle this later, Momma." Then she plasters on the Slocum everything's-fine smile, turns to the handsome face outside her door, and cranks the window lever hard. "Hey, Bo."

Bo wipes his greasy hands on a rag. "Sounds like that serpentine belt is on its last leg."

"Looks like you're way too busy for that today." Charlotte nods toward the VW's owner who's drifting our way like the insidious smoke of an incense stick. "Momma says you can spray the belt with something."

Bo lifts his UT baseball cap and wipes his brow with his forearm. "It's only a temporary fix."

"But it'll get us home, right?"

"Probably. But sooner or later it's going to break, then your engine will overheat pretty fast. Y'all will be lookin' at some serious costs. Might be cheaper to think about retiring the Escort and getting Miss Sara something more reliable."

"Momma doesn't part with things easily." Thankfully, Charlotte's not interested in telling her old boyfriend about the state of her finances or the sorry mess James McCandless has made of her life.

If putting the blame on me will help her sleep at night, then she can blame me for everything.

"Hey, C." Winnie's face appears in the open window. Damp strands of curly shoulder-length hair frame her tan face. She'd look almost lovely if she wasn't wearing a tie-dyed t-shirt tucked inside the waist of her broom skirt like some sort of gypsy.

Aria leans over the seat. "Hi, Aunt Win."

It pains me that Aria's chosen to make Winnie Moretti part of this family but saying so makes my earlier declaration of who is and who is not family seem hypocritical. I keep my mouth shut...for now.

"Hey, Ari." Winnie's arm wraps Bo's toned middle as easily as that blasted alley cat of hers wraps its tail around my leg. "I didn't know you and your mom were back." Winnie's unusually attractive glow does not come from one LaVera's creams, I can tell you that. "Why didn't y'all call?"

"I told Mom we should, but—"

Charlotte cuts Aria off. "We've been busy." Her white-knuckled grip of the steering wheel tells me I'm not the only one who's noticed how fast the relationship between Charlotte's best friend and her old boyfriend has progressed. "Not quite settled yet."

"Beauregard and I would love to help you unpack." Winnie squeezes Bo a little tighter.

"Winifred's right," Bo says. "Happy to make you feel at home."

"We're good," Charlotte's hands strangle the wheel at ten and two. "We've got eggs in the cooler and an order of Alka Seltzer for your mother, so we need to get going."

"Thanks for checking on Mom. Her cooking probably got the best of her again." Bo nods toward the Escort's hood. "Keep 'er running and pop the lid, Charlotte." Bo pecks Winnie on the cheek. "I'll give that belt a squirt of WD40 and get you on your way." He saunters to the tool bench in the garage.

Winnie leans in, all smiles and flush with love. "The three of us need to catch up over a glass of wine soon."

Charlotte releases the hood latch. "Momma doesn't drink."

"I meant you, me, and Beauregard." Winnie may want everyone to believe she's got nothing between the ears, but she's pressing this invitation because she can tell Charlotte's miffed about something. "Hope your lawyering days aren't over."

Charlotte and I both perk up at this bit of randomness.

"Why?" Charlotte asks.

Winnie rests her elbows on the open window sash and waits until Charlotte finally looks her in the eye. "I've heard the Wootens are having a moving sale. Sam Sparks bought their property and the word at last week's council meeting was that he still has his eyes on yours."

"Sam Sparks will be missing an eye once I find the key to the gun safe," I shout over the screech of the belt.

"Momma!"

Winnie leans in closer. "Hey, Mrs. Slocum. Sorry, didn't mean to ignore you. How are you feeling?"

That everyone is so willing to drop the danger that is Sam Sparks and make such a big deal over something as benign as my possible failing mental health irritates me almost as much as watching Bo make a fool of himself over this flower child. I've had my car serviced at Tucker's station since before Bo was big enough to wash my windshield while his daddy filled my tank. Never once did either of the Tucker man inquire about my health. Now that Winnie has her claws in Bo, excuse me—Beauregard—maybe she's thinking she doesn't want to live in the apartment above the gas station's repair bay. Maybe she wants more and that's why she's taking it upon herself to increase Bo's business by marketing this one-car garage and two-pump station as a full-service automobile emporium.

"My mail's been a bit later than usual, *Winnie*." I smile to camouflage my attempt to throw her off. "Are *you* not feeling well?" Smoke that in your incense burner, you, nosy hippie.

"Couldn't be better," Winnie's smile is irritatingly genuine. "I'm glad you're dropping by LaVera's. She's been going through Alka Seltzer like candy."

I cross my arms. "Bo used to drop everything to see to his mother."

"I told him he could go, but his assistant is on vacation so Beauregard's the only mechanic in town. If I don't get Bella back on the road, no telling how long the mail will be held up. Sorry about the delays, Mrs. Slocum, but hopefully Bella's new radiator will get her back up to speed."

"LaVera's sick?" I ask. "Why didn't anyone tell me?"

A shadow crosses Charlotte's face. "It's what we've been talking about, Momma." She squeezes my knee. "Remember, LaVera asked you to pick up her order from Gert?"

"Of course." I'm not sure what I said that was wrong, but from Charlotte's gentle reprimand, I was supposed to have known about LaVera. But nobody told me. I'm sure of it. I try to replay the conversations we had in the pharmacy, but I can't. "If LaVera's sick, why are we wasting time at the gas station?"

"Bo has to fix your car, remember?" Charlotte pats my knee and I see her pass Winnie a look. Not sure of its meaning because I can't see Charlotte's face full-on, but from the side, her brows are raised and her mouth seems to form a plea for help.

The screeching suddenly stops and all of us breathe easier.

"Finally," Aria says from the backseat.

Bo slams the hood. "Hope that takes you down the road a piece."

"Thank you, Bo." Charlotte's digging in her purse. "How much do I owe you?"

Bo waves her off. "Tell Mom to take her Alka Seltzer but not to worry about supper. Winifred's made some soup and I'll run it out after I close up."

"You're always so good to your momma, Bo Tucker," I say. "She won't forget it." I give Winnie the fish eye as we drive off. Soup? Next thing you know Winnie will be fixing all of LaVera's meals and she and Bo will be sitting around LaVera's table and...I can't remember why this makes me so mad. The tears that have been building all day suddenly seep out. I paw through my pocketbook and find a tissue.

"Momma, you okay?"

When the good days come to an end, how long will the bad days last? The math is more than I can bear. "Right as rain."

Chapter 13

CHARLOTTE

Now that the serpentine belt has been tamed, I can finally hear myself think as we zip along the country roads, windows down and the wind whipping through our hair. Momma's not speaking to me and neither is Aria. My daughter's earbuds are jammed in and her nose is glued to her phone—the universal teen signal to *leave me alone*. Normally, I'd try to relieve the tension by fiddling with the radio. Music is the one thing we last remaining Slocums can agree upon.

But trying to suit my mother and daughter would require me to act like the things bothering them are not bothering me. Which is not true. The list is so long I can barely breathe.

Wilma's job offer is tempting. Far less money than what I'm used to making, but now that Aria and I are staying rent-free in Momma's house, our cost of living has been drastically reduced. I might be able to swing our day-to-day expenses. Not sure how I'll cover Juilliard camp or any other extras, but I'll worry about that when the time comes.

Then there's Bo...and Winnie. They're obviously a couple...a happy couple. I don't know why it bothers me to see them together. Winnie deserves every bit of happiness she can carve from the ruins of her life. Bo, well, he's one of the finest guys I've ever known. He would have made an excellent husband and father, but that's water under the bridge. Letting go of pubescent feelings I once had for the boy next door is the only way I'm going to be able to keep my friend Winnie close. And right now, I could use a friend. Someone with two healthy brain cells to rub together. Someone who can help me think through my options.

Finally, but always pushing its way to the top of my list of woes: Momma's diagnosis.

I mentally beat down the anxiety the word Alzheimer's brings to mind and chance another glance at the woman I scarcely know anymore. We'd talked about LaVera's upset stomach with the pharmacist, Bo and Winnie. Momma knows better than anyone that LaVera struggles with indigestion, yet all of the sudden it's news to her. But Momma forgetting isn't what scared me. It was the panic in her eyes when she realized she had no idea what she'd gotten wrong. I tried not to sound alarmed, but when it dawned on her that I was explaining things again, she retreated into herself and hasn't looked at me since.

According to Benjamin, the distance between us is only going to grow. A few weeks ago, I wouldn't have believed it possible for us to be any further apart emotionally, but now that I'm daily in her presence, I feel like I'm standing at the edge of a small crack in the ground. The earth is rumbling beneath my feet and the crevice is growing wider and wider by the second. Sooner or later, one of us is going to topple in.

I steal another glance at my mother. Thankfully, she's quit crying. I'm hoping that she's either forgotten why she was upset or that her tears were simply the result of today's stressors: A definitive mental diagnosis. A prickly encounter with her arch enemy. Confusion about her best friend's health.

When I add them all together, it's enough to make me cry.

Considering how much everything is going to change, Momma deserves to shed a few tears.

We all do.

The Escort bounces across the cattle guard at the end of LaVera's drive. I'm immediately struck by how well-cared-for this ranch appears to be, especially compared to the decay that's eating away at Fossil Ridge. The parallel fence rows are in good repair and freshly mowed. LaVera's two-story house sparkles with a fresh coat of lemony-yellow paint. Her huge yard is neat, trimmed, and well-watered. Even the abandoned chicken coop, hay barn, and empty pole shed are in pristine shape. LaVera's home place is a testament to what loving attention can accomplish. Obviously, Bo Tucker is a much better son than I am a daughter. Another reason I shouldn't have cast him aside and taken off.

I throw the car into park. "I'll get the eggs out of the cooler if you and Aria want to go on."

Momma turns in her seat. "Aria, if LaVera offers you a slice of angel food cake, smile and say thank you. But don't take a bite. It won't be fit to eat."

"What am I supposed to do with it?" Aria asks.

"I have a fairly effective system," Momma says. "Ask for a tube of Berry Nice lipstick. She keeps all of those samples for herself, but she'll share if she smells a sale. While she's off searching for her favorite shade, drop your cake into my pocketbook."

"Momma!" I don't know whether to be appalled or impressed. "You used to make me choke down every dry crumb."

"Everyone knows I love my granddaughter more than you." Momma shrugs. "I'm teasing, Charlotte Ann."

Although I'm not so sure she's teasing, her quick, easy humor has made so few appearances these past twenty-five years, I'm taken off guard. For this enjoyable relic of her personality to suddenly appear today, after all that she's been through, is an unexpected sliver of light for which I am grateful. I admit finding that part of Momma again was one of the main forces driving me back to Texas.

I want to hang on to this moment. Savor the return of my positive, funny mother and the way she used to look at life…and me. Store it up for the day Benjamin says is coming. The day that mother—the good and bad sides of her—slips beyond the point of no return.

"I can't fault you, Aria's a keeper." I give her a conspiratorial wink and to my delight Momma winks back.

With a pleased-at-herself smile, Momma gathers her handbag. "LaVera's eyesight has deteriorated to the point that she often mistakes sugar for salt or vice versa. Eating anything this woman cooks should be considered hazardous to your health."

"No wonder she needs Alka Seltzer," Aria says from the backseat.

"This is just between us, Aria." Momma opens her door. "Grab the pharmacy bag for LaVera." Momma clambers out.

Arm in arm, she and Aria make their way to the front door. For a second, it is as if I'm watching Momma and Caroline walk to the door. It won't be long before Aria will pass Momma in height. I marvel at how much they're alike. Bold, bossy, beautiful…just like Caroline.

Momma knocks on the emerald green screen door. "LaVera!" She leans close to Aria and says, "LaVera claims her hearing is supersonic because her eyesight is so pitiful, but her hearing is going too." Momma raps loudly on the door this time. "LaVera! It's Sara and Aria."

"Maybe she's resting," I suggest as I open the trunk to get to the eggs.

"She doesn't believe in napping." Momma steps inside and Aria follows. "LaVera!"

"Mrs. Tucker," Aria calls. "It's your neighbors."

They disappear into the house. I dig two egg cartons out of the cooler, close the trunk with my elbow, then start up the steps. Right when I reach the screen door, a blood-chilling scream echoes in the house.

Eggs splatter at my feet. "Aria!" I rip the screen door open. Even though I haven't been inside this house in nearly thirty years, I don't need time to get my bearings. I race straight to the stairs. "Aria!"

"Mom!" Aria's at the top waving me up. "Come quick. I think something's wrong with Mrs. Tucker." Aria wheels and disappears into the master bedroom.

Taking the stairs two at a time, I fly into LaVera's bedroom. It smells of talcum powder, perfume, and something sour. Momma and Aria flank a body clad in an old terry cloth robe and slumped in front of a Hollywood-style dressing table. Lights are blazing on the three-mirrored vanity where Caroline and I experimented with the makeup samples in LaVera's Avon bag.

"LaVera!" I shout, but even as I stride to her, I know it's useless. The one person who always heard me can't anymore. For a brief second, the world shudders on its axis.

The old woman's forehead is pressed against the vanity's glass top. Her ample arms hang limp. Bottles of cream and lotions are scattered across the floor. Under the broken vials, wet circles of sickly-sweet perfume are eating through the varnish on the wooden floor.

"Mom?" Aria's small, terrified voice breaks through the rumble inside of me.

Taking my daughter by the shoulders, I refuse to crumble. "Aria, I need you to go downstairs and call 911." I give my daughter a little shake and force her wide eyes to focus on me. "Aria. Do it now!"

Aria stutters like she's been under water and I've pushed her up for air. "Should I call Bo or Winnie?"

"No!" My heart breaks at the way Momma is stroking LaVera's hair. "I'll do it." Clarity breaks through my muddy thoughts and I realize my daughter is trembling. I pull her to me, hug her tight, then kiss the top of her head. "Do this for Nana, okay?"

Aria's eyes cut to her grandmother. When she sees what I see, her breath shortens to ragged snatches. Momma has a purple hair brush in her hand. She's gently brushing LaVera's hair and whispering, "I promise you'll be presentable before anyone sees."

"Aria, go! And stay downstairs. Understand?"

My daughter nods and dashes from the room. I wait until I no longer hear her terrified feet scrambling down the stairs. "Momma," I say softly. "Let's wait for the ambulance."

"LaVera's dead. Not sick." Momma continues gently brushing LaVera's snowy white strands. "I can't find her lipstick."

"Momma," I reach for the hairbrush. "Let me take you downstairs."

She jerks the brush away. "LaVera wouldn't want her son to see her like this." She waves the brush over the mess on the floor. "Help me find the tube marked Berry Nice. I always thought the shade was too pink for her, but she likes it and I want her to look nice when Bo sees her."

"What?"

"Her lipstick," Momma's teary eyes seek mine. "Please, help me."

"Momma."

"Help is what family does, Charlotte Ann."

I swallow and nod, then drop to my hands and knees. There are probably twenty or more sample lipstick tubes strewn about. While I'm crawling around, flipping over each tiny cylinder, and trying to read the label through the tears swimming in my eyes, Momma's walks to the closet and retrieves a soft pink robe.

"I found it!" I hold up a tiny white lipstick cylinder. "Berry Nice."

"Good." Momma spreads the robe on the bed. "First, we'll change her dressing gown. Help me move her."

I shake my head and struggle to my feet. "That's illegal."

"Don't you wish you would have done this for Caroline?"

But I hadn't. By the time she was pulled from the water, her terrified face looked nothing like my sister. I couldn't even make myself look at her in the casket.

"All right." I slip the lipstick into my pocket and swipe away tears. "I'll get her arms. You grab her feet." As I move into position behind LaVera, I notice a small saucer sitting beside LaVera's head. A single bite has been taken out of a piece of dried up angel food cake.

Momma notices the remnants of LaVera's cake addiction, too. Had LaVera poisoned herself? Accidentally mixed something dangerous into her cake batter? After all, Momma keeps WD40 in her kitchen cabinets. Did LaVera have something equally as deadly in hers?

Across the body of a dead woman our gazes lock. A memory erupts from deep inside me. It's so old and dusty, I have to blink several times, but the picture eventually comes into focus. I'm six years old and so frightened I've soiled myself. Momma is squatting before me and trying to coax me out from under the kitchen table.

"He's gone." She scoots away pieces of the broken plate with her shoe. "You can come out now."

I take her hand and let her pull me to her. "Why was Daddy yelling?"

She shakes her head. "He's disappointed."

"With me?"

"Never." Momma takes my face in her hands and looks deep into my eyes. "With himself."

Truth is a jolting slap I can actually feel burning my face. Momma wasn't the only one who knew my father was a failure. I knew it too. I knew Daddy drank to fill that hole. And deep down inside of me, I knew he was drinking the day we went to the river and I went without saying a word.

Momma and I are once again two women with a secret, bound by the complexities of life and the promise to never tell another living soul.

Nausea bubbles up. I have to turn away from LaVera, swallow hard, and suck in deep breaths.

"Lift with your knees," Momma says with a calm reminiscent of the moments after Daddy destroyed the kitchen, gave her a black eye, and stormed from the house. "LaVera's had more cake than an old woman ever should."

I manage a weak nod, slide my shaky hands under LaVera's stiff, heavy arms, and look to Momma. I want to ask her why she stayed, why we never talked about Daddy's propensity to rage, why she let him destroy our family, but instead I say, "Ready?" A quick heave and my back immediately regrets letting Momma talk me into this. "Grab her ankles. She's dead weight."

"I can see that, Charlotte Ann." Momma slaps a hand around

each of LaVera's ankles. "Only a few feet to the bed."

Backing over lipstick tubes and broken perfume bottles while carrying a dead woman and the overwhelming weight of my family's dysfunction has me struggling to keep my balance. Doing my best to use my foot to clear a path, I can only hope that for once Aria obeys me and remains downstairs. Halfway to the bed, Momma lets go of LaVera's left leg. The sudden shift of weight almost brings me to my knees. "Momma!"

"Sorry." Her bones creak as she bends to retrieve LaVera's stiff, swollen ankle. "We're almost there. Hoist your end up first."

"She's too heavy. We'll have to do both ends on three," I argue. "Think you can do that?"

"Still count to three…or lift?"

"You know what I mean."

Momma wraps her hands around LaVera's ankles and counts, defiantly. "One. Two. Three."

With a grunt and a heave, we swing LaVera up and she lands with a dull thud in the middle of the bed. The arms and tail of the robe float up around the dead woman like an aromatic pink cloud. LaVera's forehead has a dark bruise from where it had been pressed against the vanity for who knows how long.

"I hear sirens." I'm relieved and terrified at the same time. I point at LaVera's forehead. "How are we going to explain this?"

"We're not," Momma says. "Help me get her changed."

"Momma!"

"Charlotte Ann, LaVera loved you."

"What does that have to do with tampering with a body?"

"LaVera never went anywhere without having her face completely done. She said it was a smart business decision. Personally, I think her vanity played into it as well, but she had a point. Who would ever buy beauty products from someone who's face looked as if those products didn't work? LaVera spent her life making others believe that they too could be beautiful. I'm not sending her off to heaven looking anything less than how she lived on this earth. Going out with the dignity by which we lived is all any of us want."

Somehow, I feel this point is not just about LaVera. That it is my mother's attempt to tell me how she's been feeling…to teach me how to treat her both now and when her time comes. I raise my hands in surrender. "Okay. You win."

Together, Momma and I wrestle LaVera out of her old robe and into the beautiful pink silk robe. The scream of the volunteer fire truck has turned off the main road and is now hurtling up the long lane.

We're still huffing from the exertion when Momma holds out her hand and wiggles her fingers impatiently at me. "The lipstick."

"I don't think we should put lipstick on a dead woman."

"I'm putting lipstick on my *sister*."

I fish the tube out of my pocket and plop it on her flattened palm. "LaVera was not your sister."

Flashing lights and blaring sirens now throb beneath the open bedroom window.

"She was the sister I never had but always wanted. That's family in my book."

Momma has just finished the pinking of LaVera's blue lips when the first volunteer fire fighter thunders through the front door. We can hear Aria telling him that we're upstairs.

"Stall him, Charlotte." Before I can think of a sane way to do what she's just asked, Momma rushes to the vanity, snatches the piece of cake, drops it in the handbag still hanging from her arm. I'm at a loss for words, but Momma's face is a study in calm as she turns to the burly man bursting into the room. "Stay right where you are, Ezra." Momma's teacher's voice freezes her former student in his tracks. "There's nothing you can do for LaVera now."

"Mrs. Slocum, I need to get to her. See if she needs CPR."

"She's well past having you pump her chest."

"Momma, it's his job."

My mother looks at me like I've grown three heads then her gaze slowly drifts to LaVera. "As you can see, Ezra, this dear woman has always been a natural beauty. And I intend for her to stay that way. You'll go get your stretcher and handle her with the utmost of care." Her gaze whips back to the fire fighter. "Am I clear?"

Chapter 14

CHARLOTTE

Momma clutches the ruby-glass cake pedestal upon which she's carefully placed her impressive three-layer hummingbird cake. The dessert is a masterpiece of overripe bananas, pineapple, and love. Each swirl of the rich, cream cheese frosting is evenly spaced, as if measured with the ruler my mother used to maintain order in her classroom. Stoic faced, Momma holds out her gift like she's one of the magi bringing frankincense or myrrh to LaVera's funeral potluck. Momma's been cooking for the past three days. Our kitchen is full of enough pies and casseroles to feed the entire county. Winnie says Momma's cooking binge is her way of dealing with the pain of losing her best friend. I say, death has never made much of a dent in this steely woman.

For my contribution to LaVera's Celebration of Life service, I've picked up BBQ ribs from the Shake Shack. They're so fresh off the smoker that the foil pan is burning my hands. "Aria, can you get the door for us, please?"

Last night, Aria and I met Winnie at the fellowship hall. I helped Winnie drape several round tables with the church's tea-stained white cloths while Aria filled milk-glass bud vases with New Dawn roses she'd clipped from Momma's garden.

I steel myself for Momma's opinion of our work as I follow her inside the fellowship hall.

The distinctive scent of southern faith hits me square in the face. Brewing coffee. Worn carpets. A couple of crock pots filled with roast and potatoes. And several stacks of dusty, old Bibles.

"LaVera would love all this fuss." Momma's pleased nod nearly trips me up. It's hard not to read too much into the small smile curling her lips, but I can't help but hope it's the first sign of a possible thaw between us. "When my time comes, keep it simple." Just like that, the smile is gone and winter is back. "Meat goes in the kitchen." She places her cake in the center of the dessert table and spins the pedestal until she's satisfied that the best side faces outward.

I trudge to the kitchen where two women Momma's age are organizing the plastic forks and paper plates. I recognize them but can't recall their names. With sympathetic smiles, they take my offering and put it between the mound of fried chicken and bowls of Jell-O salad. Tempting as it is to say something about the heat from the ribs melting the gelatin, I keep my mouth shut and dutifully return to my mother.

Momma is giving the room a careful going over. "LaVera couldn't grow a rose any better than she could bake a cake, but she knew exactly what shade of lipstick would bring out the color in someone's eyes." Momma critical gaze sends chills down my back. "She always said you should stay away from coral, Charlotte Ann."

I bite my tongue. "Ready, Momma?"

"Do I have a choice?" She takes off toward the sanctuary where we're to join Bo and Winnie in the church nursery in order to be seated with the family.

Momma nods at the early arrivals beginning to fill the pews as she marches toward the nursery at back of the sanctuary. The small room is empty except for two rocking chairs and a rickety changing table. I pick up an old bulletin that's been left on one of the rockers and try to convince Momma to sit. Her resistance to every kindness I've tried to show her finally crumbles and she drops into the rocker. I want to comfort her, but I've never really known how.

I bury my nose in the sick list of the three-months-out-of-date bulletin. The effort to distract myself does nothing to assuage my guilt for refusing to comply with my mother's desire to deliver LaVera's eggs *before* we went to town. Even in her confusion over what we were going to do that day, Momma kept bringing up the need to drop by her neighbor's while the eggs were fresh. I'd dismissed her suggestion as a stall tactic. Had I not been in such a hurry to put a medical label on my mother's strange behavior, LaVera might still be alive.

At the light rap on the nursery door, I stop pacing and prepare to face Bo for the first time since we found his mother. Winnie says Bo doesn't blame me, but I don't know what he'd think if he ever found out that I'd helped Momma move and spiff up his mother's body.

"Sara?" Ira's bald head pokes around the door. "Mind if I offer you my condolences?"

"Sweet Moses!" Momma is out of the rocker with the agility of a woman who's never broken her hip. She flings her arms around the old man's neck and hugs him tight. If I didn't know better, I'd say she was in love. After what seems like forever, she pulls back, tears streaming down her cheeks. "What on earth are you doing here, Ira Conner?"

Tears shed for Ira's arrival and not a single tear for LaVera's departure? Now I'm the one feeling confused.

"Come in." Momma drags Ira into the nursery.

Trailing behind him is Teeny, a huge black bow sitting squarely on the top of her white hair. "Sara." When the big-boned woman steps into the nursery and opens her arms wide, the room seems to shrink.

"And Teeny!" All ninety-six-pounds of Momma is swallowed up in Teeny's embrace. It's such a heart-felt reunion, I'm crying right along with everyone else.

Momma pulls out the tissue she keeps tucked in her sleeve and dabs at her eyes. "How on earth did you two get here?"

"Trixie." Ira's cloudy eyes swim with his own tears. "But before you commence with that lecture sitting on the end of your tongue, my daughter did the driving." Ira turns to the open door and waves in a stout, red-faced woman who seems like she would be far more comfortable working sheep than wearing a faded Sunday dress and low-slung Rockports. "Esther is my oldest."

Hard to believe Momma's claim that Ira's children have made millions from his natural gas wells. I don't mean to judge Esther like she's some kind of threat, but old habits die hard. Before I know it, I'm giving her the head-to-toe, once-over, size-up of a legal rival. I really have no basis for this behavior. Esther's been nothing but gracious and cooperative in all of our phone dealings. She was forgiving of Momma's assisted living escape plan and subsequent use of Ira's car. She was very generous to allow Ira to stay for a few days at the Fossil Ridge once Momma finally found her way home. And when I phoned her to ask her to tell Ira about Momma losing LaVera, it was Esther who'd offered to bring her father.

Momma waves her hand over the mismatched rockers and insists Ira and Teeny make themselves at home.

Ira shakes his head. "Surely you don't think I'm the kind of man who'd take a chair from a lady?"

Momma's smile is so warm it nearly melts the prickles right off the cactus she's been lately. "Always the gentleman." She stands close to Ira, her hand threaded through his arm. Together, they watch Teeny settle, then Ira escorts Momma to the other rocker like he's protecting a queen. Once Momma's seated she asks Ira, "How did you even know about LaVera?"

"Your daughter called mine." Ira flashes a smile my way. "You've got a good girl there, Sara."

Before Momma can respond, Winnie sticks her head in the nursery. "Time to start."

It seems the whole town has turned out to celebrate the passing of Addisonville's favorite Avon lady. Hymns, scriptures, and a rather funny video Winnie put together cap the service. Now comes the hard part. Going to the cemetery for the lowering of LaVera's casket into the ground. I thought I'd never breathe again as the wenches lowered Caroline into the grave. And then Daddy…

"Mom," Aria tugs at the sleeve of my dress. "Winnie says we're supposed to ride to the cemetery in the limo. There's plenty of room for Ira and Teeny and Ira's daughter too."

When I try to beg off, Momma glares at me like I'm trying to make Bo's already bad day even worse. With a sigh, I pile in behind Momma and her friends.

No one is saying much on the drive and I'm glad.

But Ira breaks our silence. "Sara, I'd love to hear your favorite memory of LaVera."

I don't know if it's Ira's encouragement or his interest, but I've never seen a simple statement open Momma's well-guarded gates.

Her face lights up and she launches into the time LaVera convinced her to try the latest Avon mask. "LaVera caked my face with a green thick mud."

"I'll set the timer for ten minutes," she promised. "Once it dries, you'll wash years away." Momma shakes her head. "That mud dried as hard as my river bluff," she chuckles. "LaVera handed me a pink wash cloth. I scrubbed until I thought my skin would bleed, but the effort didn't even make a dent."

"Let's try a warm compress," LaVera said.

"After ten minutes of feeling like I'm in a sauna, my face was still green. LaVera filled her kitchen sink with water and held my head under until I started flailing. At one point she threatened to use a sledgehammer to break away the crusty stuff. We finally picked off all the green one tiny piece at a time. When I was finally free, LaVera dragged her palm over my cheek and said, 'Told you it was good. Your face is as soft as a baby's butt.'"

Even Bo is laughing by the time we reach the small cemetery on the edge of town where LaVera is to be laid to rest beside her husband. I'm mesmerized. The charming side of Momma has been buried so long, I feel like the disciples must have felt when Jesus rose from the dead...not wanting the moment to end. But when the limo rolls to a stop, so does the levity…but only for a moment.

I exit first, intending to help Momma pick her way across the crunchy brown grass, but she waves me off and rushes to sandwich herself between Ira and Teeny. She's so giddy she's almost skipping toward the tent the mortuary set up over LaVera's grave. I don't know if this inappropriate behavior is part of Momma's dementia or a defense mechanism, but it's left me unable to move away from the limo.

Esther spills out of the limo. "They seem to bring out the best in each other, don't they?" She's standing behind me, a gentle hand on my shoulder. "Dad talks about Sara Slocum non-stop."

"Funny, she never mentions him." I immediately regret taking out my embarrassment, horror, terror…I'm not sure what it is…on Esther. Dropping into damage control mode, I add, "But I haven't seen Momma talk that much in a long time. Silence is how we Slocums handle things…not skipping around headstones."

Esther's expression offers more comfort than I deserve. "It's not easy taking care of a parent." She pats my arm then leaves me standing at the limo.

"Your mother is handling this better than I expected." The male voice coming from behind me catches me off guard.

I whirl to find Benjamin leaning against the limo. "Or she's drunk."

His chuckle rumbles deep in his broad chest. "More likely

blissfully unable to properly register the extent of this loss. Don't be surprised if you have to remind her again and again that LaVera is dead."

"Not sure I'm up to watching her relive that over and over."

"You don't have to do this alone, you know?"

"Are you offering to let her move in with you?"

"She's one of my favorites." Benjamin gently takes my elbow. "I missed the funeral. Miss Sara will never forgive me if I miss the graveside."

"True. Holding on to a grudge is one thing I'm pretty sure Momma will never forget how to do."

My heels sink into the cracks in the dried earth. Leaning on Benjamin is all that is keeping me from getting sucked under.

Chapter 15

CHARLOTTE

Mother has dallied so long over her funeral lunch plate that her baked beans are swimming in slimy green Jell-O. I know she's not ready for Ira and Teeny to leave, but Esther is looking at her watch. Ira's daughter has been exceptionally patient. Hopefully, Momma will be grateful and gracious.

"Ira's a good man," Winnie slides into the empty chair beside me. "Teeny's a...unique woman."

I watch Teeny shovel in her third helping of fried chicken. "Momma hasn't been this happy since those two spent a week at Fossil Ridge."

"Maybe you can rent them for a few days."

"If I thought I could manage three geriatrics, I would."

"Never easy doing the right thing, is it?" Something about Winnie has changed, softened, become even more beautiful.

147

I follow her gaze and finally admit the truth to myself. Winnie's in love…and I'm glad. "How's Bo holding up?"

"He's always been close to his mother." Winnie's attention is sitting squarely on Bo who's standing across the room visiting with the Wootens. "He's going to miss her."

"Winnie." The truth is a lump I'm unwilling to continue to choke upon. The only way to breathe easy again is to come clean. "I know we didn't part on the best of terms when I went back to DC, but I just want you to know that I think Bo's a lucky man to have you in his corner." I communicate my sincerity by offering my hand. "Forgive me?"

Winnie ignores my offered hand and wraps me in an incense-scented hug. "Nothing to forgive, friend."

Clinging to each other, it's like we're Momma and LaVera. Two old friends who can fight like cats and dogs, but love each other in the end. Although Winnie will never show up with a new tube of lipstick, all is forgiven and forgotten.

What will Momma do without LaVera? Friends are a treasure. And Momma has so few treasures left.

"Looks like Esther's ready to go," I say, stomach clenching.

"Better follow them out."

"You know I suck at picking up the pieces, right?"

Winnie gathers the paper plates. "It's a dirty job, but somebody's got to do it."

I follow Momma and her guests outside. In the shade of a large live oak, Esther waits beside Trixie, Ira's beautiful old turquoise Cadillac. Momma is in the process of hugging Teeny when Sam Sparks pulls into the church parking lot.

Any hope that Momma may not remember Sam's car is quickly dashed when she shouts, "Charlotte, get my gun!"

Ira turns to see what has Momma in such a stir. "Sara, who is that?"

"A buzzard." Momma shakes her finger at the finely-suited man carrying flowers and striding toward the church doors. "Sam Sparks," Momma yells. "What do you think you're doing here?"

He stops, wheels our direction, and smiles. "Not that it's any of your business, Mrs. Slocum, but I've come to pay my respects."

Momma's fists are clenched as she stomps across the parking lot, the rest of us scrambling to keep up. "LaVera's not even cold in the grave and here you are trying to pick apart the bones of her estate."

"Now, Mrs. Slocum—"

"Don't now Mrs. Slocum me, Sam Sparks!" She marches to within spitting distance, and for a second it appears that's exactly what she intends to do. "What's the real reason you're darkening church house doors?"

Sam juggles a potted plant in one hand and fiddles with the knot of his tie with the other. "Mrs. Tucker was a...friend."

"Liar!" Momma lunges for him.

"Sara, no." Ira pulls her back.

"Momma!" I grab her swinging arm. "Sam, I don't think anybody's up to talking business today."

"Bo's never going to talk business with you." Momma's back is stiff. "He loved his mother and he loves her homeplace as much as she did."

"Now, now, Sara," Ira says. "Try to calm down."

Sam's dark eyes slide from me to Momma. "The only business Mrs. Tucker and I ever discussed was her skin care line for men." Although stunned by his admission, none of us can argue with his assertion. Sam's skin radiates meticulous care. "Now, if you'll excuse me, I'd like to make my apologies for missing the service and offer my condolences to Mrs. Tucker's son." He wheels and leaves all of us with nothing left to say.

Esther's the one who realizes we can't stand out here in the heat waiting on the dust to settle. "Dad, we really need to get going,"

Ira's sober face tells me living at the mercy of others isn't any easier for him than it is for my mother. "I'll call and check on you tomorrow, Sara."

Momma nods. "Take care, Ira. And limit Teeny's trips to the buffet."

"Momma!" I feel the need to apologize for her lack of a filter, but I don't have it in me.

We walk them back to the shade of the live oak.

Overcome by the support Esther and her father have shown today, I hug them both. "Thank you for making the drive today. It meant a lot to Momma."

As I watch Trixie disappear in a swirl of caliche dust, I choke on the loneliness settling on me as heavy as the fine white particles coating the leaves of the live oaks.

Who was I kidding?

The support of these strangers meant the world to me.

Chapter 16

ARIA

Aria, get a picture of that cross-stitch LaVera's mother gave her on her wedding day." Nana points at a wooden frame hanging on the wall in her best friend's kitchen.

I hold up my phone and click. "It's ugly."

"One woman's trash is another woman's treasure." Nana straightens the frame. "LaVera always told me she'd run through a fire to save this gift. I hope Bo's not planning to let it go in the estate sale." Nana licks her lips like she's a guppy needing air. "You think you know people. I never would have pegged Bo to let bargain hunters pick over his mother's things like vultures on carrion." Nana looks at me, but it feels like she's seeing someone else. "I probably won't even be cooled off good before you and your mother sell off Fossil Ridge. Lock, stock, and barrel."

Nana's been mean since LaVera died. Mom says she been mean

for twenty-five years. Just when I was getting used to having my grandmother around, now she acts like I'm getting on her nerves. I've tried everything to cheer her up…even memorized the hardest part of "One Day More" to surprise her with a piano duet. Nothing's working.

Until we moved to Texas, I didn't understand why Nana and Mom fought all the time. I just thought that maybe bickering is normal for Slocums. Mom and I seem to be doing our share of fighting, especially now that she's going to work at my school. I still can't believe she took the music teacher job.

Geez. I can't catch a break.

Mom I can deal with…will deal with. But this change in Nana scares me. I may not understand all the secrets in this house, but I know Nana hasn't always licked her lips. I think it's a side effect from one of her new medications. When I googled some of the stuff she's taking, dry mouth is definitely something we should be watching for. Mom told me not to worry about Nana's chapped her lips and to please quit looking up side effects and/or natural solutions. I'll quit sticking my nose where it doesn't belong when Mom pulls her head out of the sand.

Nana's losing it.

Why am I the only one who's worried that my grandmother has worn the same dress for five days? That she hasn't combed her hair or brushed her dentures since we got home from LaVera's funeral?

I snap a couple more pics of LaVera's hideous wall art. "Mom says if Bo and Winnie get married they wouldn't have room to swing a mouse in all of this junk."

"Married." Nana licks her lips again. "If that bohemian communist moves into LaVera's home, she'll turn over in her grave for sure."

I don't want to think about what the woman I saw slumped over her vanity is or is not doing in her casket. That's just weird. But Nana's stuck on LaVera. Obsessed with her death.

"Keep up, girl." Nana yanks me along on the next stop on this photo safari. We climb the stairs and stop outside LaVera's master bedroom.

"I don't really want to go in there, Nana."

Instead of looking at me like the loser that I am, she points at my phone. "Is that thing hard to use?"

"Not really."

"Show me how to take a picture."

Mom says I'm never to let anyone touch my phone, that we can't afford to replace it if something should happen, but I really don't want to go back into LaVera's bedroom.

"Okay, but be careful with it, okay?" I demonstrate the point-the-phone-see-the-object-on-the-screen-push-the-button method.

"Show me again."

"Point the phone." I click to camera mode and demonstrate

again. "See how the object I want to photograph shows up in the screen?"

"Yes."

"Hold the phone steady, then push the white button."

"So, I…what do I do first?"

Then it dawns on me. Nana's not getting it. The woman who can play the entire score of *Les Misérables* without music can't point a phone camera and push the button.

"What's this button here?" She asks again.

I'm tempted to roll my eyes, but I don't want Nana to see how worried I am. "That's the one you push to take a picture."

"I've got it." She leaves me alone in the hall alone and steps inside the room where her friend died. I think I'm closer than anyone to understanding what she's feeling. LaVera's dead. Ira and Teeny had to go back to that old folks' home. Wilma Rayburn would just as soon never see my grandmother again.

Nana is alone.

Not having a friend sucks.

I have to start a new school on Monday. New girl in town. No friends. A music geek with skinny legs and braces who lives with her crazy grandma and uptight mother.

Maybe I shouldn't blame Mom for this mess, but I do. She wouldn't stop by LaVera's on the way to town. She wouldn't let Ira and Teeny live at Fossil Ridge. She wouldn't let me live with Dad.

And she says she's done it all for *our good*, mine and Nana's. Ha!

If Mom thinks becoming my music teacher is going to make the transition easier, she's crazier than Nana will ever be. So what if she'll be only a few doors away...*should I need her*. I've needed her for years. The woman lives on the moon when it comes to "being there" for me. Don't get me wrong, I know she thinks she tries. Claims she wants to be a better mother than...that's where I stop her.

I don't want to hear smack about my grandmother.

Nana is awesome. A little confused...but awesome.

I don't know what happened to my Aunt Caroline or my grandfather. Nobody tells me anything. It's ancient history everyone thinks I'm too young to understand. But I'm not stupid. I googled it. Yep, accessed archived articles from the Addisonville Herald. The drowning of my aunt and the subsequent drowning of my grandfather one year later in the very same river, the river that runs right behind Nana's house, was big news.

I'm not going to lie, I cried when I thought about my mother losing her sister at eighteen. Explains why Mom keeps everyone at arm's length. Getting close to someone hurts. At least Mom had a sister to get close to. I'm an only child who probably won't see much of her dad or his parents any more. Mom and Nana are the only family I have left. I wish the two of them could let this feud go. We've got bigger fish to fry...so to speak...Nana's slipping.

According to that hairy-faced doc, "Y'all don't have much time left."

I can't believe how quickly I've started sounding like a Texan.

I don't even text my friend Caitlyn anymore. And not because Mom threatened me to within an inch of my life if she scrolled through my messages and caught me talking to "that delinquent." I don't text Caitlyn anymore because she laughed at me when I texted, "What y'all doin' tonight?"

Here's the thing: I won't be eighteen for five more years. If I don't want to spend these next few years staring at a river I can't swim in or scrolling social media, then I've got to do what I can to save my Nana. It won't be the first time I did something that made my mother wonder where she failed.

Chapter 17

CHARLOTTE

Aria stomps onto the porch wearing the first-day-of-school outfit we ordered online. Life was so much easier when she had to wear a uniform. Thank goodness, Addisonville has a dress code or I would have had to let her wear a halter top and booty shorts to get her in the car today.

"I think those jeans were a great choice."

"I look like a freak." She storms past me, tosses her new backpack on the front seat of the Escort, then throws herself into the back seat and slams the car door.

"Our first day of school is going well, don't you think?" I say to Momma who is sitting on the porch swing, glassy-eyed and devoid of emotion.

For the sixth consecutive day, she's wearing the fuzzy winter housecoat LaVera gave her ten years ago. Even though she must be melting under the robe's matted pile, nothing I say persuades her to change.

I stand on the porch steps in sensible heels, a pencil-straight skirt, a blouse that will allow me the freedom to play the entire keyboard of the school's baby grand, and holding a piece of dry toast. The satchel I carry, the one that my paralegal Loraine used to stuff with legal briefs, bulges with worksheets I've designed to inspire a love of music. My stomach quivers at the prospect of resurrecting a very old dream. My heart, on the other hand, beats with the guilt and angst of leaving Momma for a few hours.

"Winnie." Gratitude for my friend's willingness to pop in to check on Momma now that she and Bo have moved into LaVera's house sticks in my throat. "Momma hasn't eaten and I don't have time to fight with her." I hand Winnie a piece of dry toast. "I can't get her to comb her hair either."

"Bo says his mother used to say, I'm heading to Sara's for a cup of tea and a few kind words. How about I fix Sara a cup of steaming brew and see if I can't get her to talk?"

"She doesn't like you, you know."

Winnie's brows raise. "I'm not the one going to work for the enemy."

"Wilma Rayburn is taking a huge chance on me."

"Not really. According to Aria, you're some kind of musical prodigy. How come I never knew this about you?"

"Do I know everything about you?"

"I'm an open book. You, on the other hand, are a mystery yet to be solved."

"I'm not that complicated. I came home to do the right thing. End of story."

"Your story's just beginning."

Hoisting the satchel strap over my shoulder, I watch Momma rock herself back and forth. "I don't think our story's going to have a happy ending. She doesn't want my love."

"She does."

I shake my head. "It's like she doesn't think she deserves it and, frankly, when I think about the way she's pushed me away since Charlotte and Daddy died, maybe she doesn't."

"Who does deserve unconditional love?"

"Bo."

Mentioning Winnie's new husband's name brings a smile to her face. "Are you still pining for your old boyfriend?" she teases.

"You know I'm not," I say. "According to Momma, Bo Tucker is a perfect child...well, he *was* until he emptied LaVera's house and let a communist and her cats move in."

Winnie shrugs. "Nobody's perfect, C. Not even, Beauregard."

Aria honks the horn and yells out the window. "I'm not walking in late holding my mother's hand."

"Coming." I nod toward Momma's flattened bed-hair and flatter-still expression. "Winnie, I don't know what to do. It's almost like Caroline has died all over. Momma won't eat. She's not sleeping. She's hardly said two words. All she does is play the piano. I hate leaving her alone."

"I've got a couple of hours before I have to start my route. I'll pop in around noon when I deliver her mail. She'll only be on her own a couple of hours a day."

Visions of LaVera slumped over her vanity flash through my head. "A lot can happen in a couple of hours."

"She's grieving her friend. She's grieved worse and come out the other side. We'll help her through this."

"What if we can't? What if this is the beginning of the end?"

"Today's got enough trouble of its own." Winnie turns me toward the car. "You're already behind the curve with Aria, you don't want to get off on the wrong foot with Wilma."

"Bye, Momma." I rush to the swing and kiss her papery cheek. "Any advice?"

Momma's vacant gaze remains fixed on the horizon, but there's a slight clearing of her throat. "Don't smile until Christmas."

It's a small olive branch, Momma bestowing her teaching motto upon me, but I grab hold like she's tossed a drowning person a rope. "Thank you, Momma."

She rocks the swing with a gentle push of her foot and says nothing more.

Lynne Gentry

Chapter 18

ARIA

We're not to the end of the drive when Mom says, "You can sit up front, you know."

"I'm good."

Mom sighs. "Well, would you mind turning down your music? I need to call Nana's doctor."

"She's getting worse, isn't she?"

Mom's eyes find mine in the rearview mirror. "Let me talk to Ben…I mean Dr. Ellis. He'll know what to do."

She's crazy if she thinks I'm going to let her keep me in the dark. "We shouldn't leave her."

"Winnie's going to drop by when she can."

"Mom, Nana's brain is going to dry up if we don't find something to get her going again."

"I've tried."

"You've bullied her. Like you do me."

"What's that supposed to mean?"

"You say she needs to go work in her roses, but you don't offer to go with her."

"In case you haven't noticed, I've been a little busy trying to get ready to start a new job."

"Okay, then let me do stuff with her, before she disappears forever."

"What kind of stuff?"

"Brain games, switch her to an organic diet, supplements, and—"

"Ari, nobody knows more than me how hard it is to watch the Sara Slocum we all knew and loved slowly disappear." Mom lets out an exasperated sigh. "You can't fix this, sweetheart."

"Whatever."

I make a big show of unwinding the cord on my earphones. Instead of shoving them deep into my head and cranking my music, I leave space so that I can eavesdrop. Nose locked on my phone screen, I search dementia blogsites. I can read up on what Mom *should* be doing for my grandmother while I'm listening to her trying to shove Nana off on the doc. Perfecting my intel gathering method is how I knew about Dad long before Mom and I had 'the talk' about the painful damage of adultery.

"I've upped her meds," Mom tells the country doctor who gave her his cell number. What kind of doctor wears jeans and plaid shirts and gives out his cell number? "I'm not seeing any improvement." Mom sounds scared, which I have to admit, makes me even more nervous. "Maybe I should bring her in, let you…you know…check her over."

I can't hear what the doc is saying so I take a chance that Mom's so preoccupied that she's not keeping tabs on me and pry one earbud free. The big red-head's booming voice is easy to make out. He does his usual telling Mom not to worry. He goes on to say that caring for someone with declining mental capacity can be emotional—a stressful roller coaster. Then he asks, "You're taking care of yourself, right?"

The hair on the back of my neck stands up.

Mom has a ton of stuff on her plate. I'm not blind. But something about the way he said, *right*, like if she wasn't taking care of herself he'd love to swoop in and fix it for her, makes me…I don't know what it makes me. I jam the earbud so deep into my ear canal that it hurts. I type *brain games* in the search bar. Not for Nana. For me. To give me something else to think about before I go insane.

I don't know how long I've been pecking around on my phone before Mom finally gets my attention.

I yank my earbuds from my ears.

"Want me to let you out at the door?"

"Geez, no!" I lean over the seat and grab my backpack. "Park in a far corner. Wait five minutes after I get out before you walk in."

"But we have our first class together. We could, you know, cheer each other on. Make things easier for both of us."

Making it easier for Mom to sell out Nana is the last thing I want to do…well, not last. Last on my list is having to pretend I don't mind being the new girl at this one-room-country-school. "I'm good."

"You can have a two-minute head start."

"I'm not the one who made us late."

"Ari," Mom says as she pulls into a slot that is as far from the building as you can get in this little parking lot filled with dusty pickup trucks and old cars. "We're going to be okay."

"Because you're taking care of yourself, right?" I get out of the car and slam the door before she can let me have it for eavesdropping and hurting her feelings.

I'm hoofing it across the parking lot, trying to look as inconspicuous as I can in new shoes and new jeans, when I hear someone call my name. I think it's Mom so I keep walking.

"Hey!" Ember runs up beside me. She's slaying it in her ripped jeans, knotted t-shirt, and scuffed cowboy boots. "It's Aria McCandless, right?" She tucks a strand of shiny black hair behind her ear.

"Yeah." I sling my new backpack onto my shoulder. "So?"

"I'm Ember. From the pharmacy. Remember?"

"Yeah."

"Is your mom the new music teacher?"

Since there's not a nearby hole I can crawl into, I stop and let her know I won't be played by the popular girls again. "Why?"

"I'm taking choir," Ember's smile is as genuine as it was over a root beer float. "My schedule says Mrs. McCandless is the teacher." She ignores a group of really pretty girls hanging around the door and calling for her to catch up. "Are you taking music from your mom?"

"No way."

Chapter 19

CHARLOTTE

I use the two-minute lead time I'd given Aria to silently rehearse my what-to-expect-in-my-class welcome speech. My daughter's not the only one who stands to be humiliated today. I haven't touched a piano in years. What if I can't play a simple warm-up scale anymore? Once I'd accepted Wilma's job offer, I'd intended to limber up my fingers. But Momma's been keeping Aria at the keys for hours. Music is the only thing that has interested her. I've been so worried about what will happen once Aria goes to school that I didn't have the heart to push them off the piano bench so I could practice the scales I used to be able to do in my sleep.

Hopefully, Winnie's right. Once I sit down to the keyboard, it'll be like riding a bike. Everything I ever learned, practiced or dreamed will come back to me. I mean, after all, if a woman slipping into dementia can pull the score to *Les Mis* out of the muck, then someone with marginally healthy brain cells should be able to pull up a few scales…right?

Right now, I'd rather face an angry Senate committee than the keyboard, an experienced faculty, and classes filled with new faces. Guilt clenches my stomach. Instead of reassuring my daughter who is probably feeling a similar angst this morning, I'd spent that prime travel time on the phone with my mother's doctor.

I check to see if Aria's far enough ahead to safely exit Momma's Escort.

To my surprise, she has stopped and to talk to someone. I squint over the steering wheel. Aria's shoulders are squared and she's looking the girl from the pharmacy, Ember Miller, straight in the face.

My thirteen-year-old is so like my sister…even when Caroline was scared to death on the inside, she looked fearless on the outside.

"Pull yourself together," I mutter as I snatch up my satchel. "You can do this."

Mrs. Rayburn is waiting at the door, greeting students and teachers as I enter the building. She offers her outstretched hand. "Mrs. McCandless. Glad to have you on board."

"Thanks."

"Nervous?"

"Yes."

"Your mother used to say *don't smile until Christmas*." A cloud comes over her face as she studies my face. "But perhaps today will go a little easier for you if you try to smile."

A tall, good-looking boy bumps my satchel. The strap slides from my shoulder and my carefully organized files spill across the floor.

"Evan Miller," Mrs. Rayburn calls after him. "Come back right this moment."

He wheels, sees the mess, but doesn't move. "Why?"

"A gentleman says 'excuse me' then helps the lady he's caused distress."

"I'm good." I bend and snatch up papers.

Evan saunters over, drops into a crouch at my level, and hands me several papers. "Sorry."

"No problem." I jam everything in my bag and stand. "Thanks."

He gives me a two-fingered salute then ambles off with the air of a senior who knows he owns the joint.

Mrs. Rayburn whispers, "Don't let that one give you trouble."

A bell sounds. "I better get to class."

"I've turned on the auditorium lights for you today. I'll come in after school and show you how to switch everything off."

My fingers tighten on the strap over my shoulder. "Thanks."

"You can do this, Mrs. McCandless." Mrs. Rayburn gives a nod to my bulging satchel. "Teaching is in your blood."

I can't help but smile at the unexpected olive branch. "I guess we'll see if that's true."

The hall leading toward the auditorium buzzes with kids excited to see each other again. I fight the urge to locate Aria and step inside the double doors. A couple of girls are pounding out Chopsticks on the piano. Poorly, I might add.

"Good morning." They scramble to gather their belongings while I take the stage. "I'm Mrs. McCandless. Do you have first period choir with me?"

"We do." The short one, a redhead with freckles, is giving me the once-over. "We're seniors."

"Then you know not to touch the baby grand." I try to soften the tone my mother would have used with a smile. "Unless you'd like to take lessons."

They shrug. "Maybe."

"Good. See me after school."

The bell rings and they amble to the back row of the chairs arranged on the stage in the shape of a rainbow.

Suddenly, the auditorium doors burst open and the place comes alive with the sounds of kids made wild by summer. They're laughing and pushing each other...until they see me standing behind the director's podium. Quiet descends. They stand in the aisles looking me over, sizing up the new music teacher.

I replace Momma's I-mean-business expression with a smile. "Good morning. Come to the stage and take a seat." One by one, fifteen students file past me.

Ember, the girl I recognize from the pharmacy, is flanked by two pretty girls. "Grab soprano seats," she tells them then stops at the podium. "Good morning, Mrs. McCandless. My mother says you can really sing and play the piano."

"We'll see." I'm surprised Corina would say anything positive about me. "Have you seen Aria?"

"In the parking lot. Why?"

I don't want my daughter to feel anymore self-conscious than having her mother as her choir teacher will make her feel but I'm worried she's having difficulty locating the auditorium. "No reason."

Five minutes after the bell, I've introduced myself, taken roll, and handed out my class-expectations sheet. The time has come to actually teach the music I used to love.

"All right everyone. To your feet for warm-ups."

Students groan. Chairs scrape the floor. My stomach clenches.

"Keep your feet flat on the floor." I step from behind the podium and demonstrate. "Shoulder width apart. Balance equally on both legs." Threading myself through my students, I correct a few sagging postures. They size me up much like I used to size up opposing counsel. "Now place one palm on your stomach. This is so you can check yourself to make sure you're breathing from your diaphragm. Keep your shoulders low and your chest relaxed. If you're holding yourself correctly it's easier to breathe and if you can breathe, it's easier to hit those notes in the high register." I glance over my class. Where is Aria? If she thinks I'll let her get away with tardiness she has another thing coming.

I slide onto the piano bench. Deep breath. I search for middle C and place my fingers upon the keys. They feel foreign and familiar at the same time. "Breathe in," I say as much to myself as to my students. "And here we go."

My thumb strikes middle C. "Ahhhh." The sound climbs out of my throat, a bit rusty, but on pitch. I hold the note until everyone is attempting to match the tone. A smile curls my lips and I nod encouragement. Eyes on my students, my voice follows the slow climb of my fingers and then the descent of the five notes of the major scale. Without missing a beat, I take us through the changing keys, pushing until we've climbed an octave. "Think you can go higher?" I issue the challenge, holding the last note until they're nearly blue.

Heads nod. I grab a breath and charge on.

Winnie is right. Releasing music that comes from the soul, no matter how long it has been stuffed, is like riding a bike. My fingers have a life of their own, propelling me back to childhood dreams.

I've come home.

Chapter 20

CHARLOTTE

Thirty minutes after the last period bell, I'm physically tired but emotionally pumped. The two girls who'd given me grief when I chastised them for pounding on the piano had dropped by the auditorium for extra help. By the time I'd finished taking them through some upper level warm-ups, they were eating out of my hand. Both have lovely voices and the short redhead can play the piano a little. With some extra tutoring, these two might give Addisonville's music department a shot at a State duet medal. And both of Corina Miller's kids can sing. Evan might even have a future on the stage…if I can coax him from the back row.

Possibilities swimming in my head, I straighten the chairs on the stage.

Teaching is more fun than I'd ever dreamed. I love the kids. I love music. Social studies and theater are going to challenge me, but if I can make those subjects come alive for me, the students might enjoy them as well.

I'm humming while gathering worksheets when Mrs. Rayburn enters the auditorium. Heels clicking on the tiled floor, she's smiling as she makes her way to the stage. "I've heard nothing but rave reviews about the new music teacher."

"Anyone can pull a few tricks out of their hat for a day." I stuff completed worksheets into my satchel. "But can I do it for forty years?"

Mrs. Rayburn's pleased smile slides. Before I can correct my unintentional reference to my mother she says, "I hope you know, Charlotte, that I think your mother was one of the best teachers this school has ever employed."

For the first time in months, I'd not had time to worry about Momma. One whole day without worrying what sort of danger she'd put herself in. It felt good, liberating, and very wrong. What kind of daughter so easily pushes her responsibilities aside? What if Momma forgot her lunchtime meds, or burned down the house, or wandered off to the river? She was in a bad state this morning and I'd left her.

I fasten the buckles on my bag. "Momma loved teaching."

"She'd still be teaching if she'd not become a danger to the students."

Lips pursed, I can't give Mrs. Rayburn a pass. I can say Momma is a danger...I *have* said it...to Winnie, to Benjamin, to my old paralegal, to myself. But I'm not going to stand by and let someone else besmirch Momma's character. Momma and Wilma were friends. Surely, Wilma could have worked out a more graceful and far less painful way to ease Momma out. If she thought giving me a job made up for...

"Charlotte, was Aria ill today?"

Wilma's interruption of my mental tirade stops my breath. What kind of mother forgets to check on her daughter? I'd meant to, the moment first period was over, but then in a flash it was time for second period theater. Before I knew it, the whole day had passed. Is this how Momma ended up traveling a road she never intended to go down...one forgetful step at a time?

"No. Why?" Checking my watch confirms my failure to set up an after-school-meet-up plan as well.

"She's missed every class...including your first period choir, right?"

"She hasn't been here all day?"

Wilma holds out an attendance sheet. "I've doubled checked with all of Aria's teachers. She didn't show in any class."

My knees buckle. "Where is she?"

"I was hoping you could tell me." Wilma takes the paper from my shaky hands. "Ember Miller told me she saw her in the parking lot. When she asked Aria if she was taking your class, she said no."

I grabbed my satchel. "I've got to go."

"Do I need to call the sheriff?"

"No!" I fly down the stage steps. "Yes!"

I'm running to the parking lot and dialing home at the same time. Ten rings later, Aria answers the phone. "Slocum residence."

Heart pounding in my chest, I scream, "Aria, what are you doing at home?"

"Your job."

Chapter 21

ARIA

Once the sheriff finishes grilling me, Mom banishes me to Aunt Caroline's room. Mom never says a word about how crazy it is for my dead aunt to still *have a room* after all these years, but she feels free to go on and on about the stupidity of me trying to walk ten miles in the Texas heat.

"If Winnie hadn't come along, you would be dehydrated or lying in a ditch," she'd sobbed as she flew up the porch steps, ripped me out of the swing, and hugged the breath from my lungs. "I might never have found you."

I'm not as stupid as she thinks.

Aunt Winnie didn't just *come along.* I texted her when I made it to Bo's station. I was hot and tired and my new shoes had rubbed a blister on my heel. Bo bought me a canned drink while I waited for Winnie's car to putter under the awning. Winnie and Bo argued over whether or not she should take me back to school. The second I realized my flimsy excuses for not going back weren't going to fly, I turned on the tears. I hate that I had to do that to them, but they weren't listening. I was going home to check on Nana…even if I had to walk the rest of the way.

What Winnie and I found when we drove up the lane of Fossil Ridge is the pimple Mom doesn't want to pop. It makes her feel too guilty to hear about Nana wandering around the front yard in that ratty robe and those nasty slippers. At noon, my grandmother still had bed-head hair and no makeup…not even her lipstick. But here's the kicker, the part I don't even like thinking about: When I jumped out of Winnie's car and ran up to her, she called me Caroline.

Caroline.

I've seen my aunt's picture sitting on the mantel in my Nana's bedroom. I know I kind of look like her, but it shook me bad to be called a dead girl.

Winnie and I both tried to explain who I was, but Nana just didn't get it. That's when Winnie caved and said it was probably best if I stayed home, on the condition we let Mom know.

But Mom never checked her messages. So, when she gets home, she gives me what-for then lights into Aunt Winnie. "I can't believe you aided and abetted Aria's truancy."

"Check your phone, C."

Mom's face turned red as her toe nail polish. Winnie and I had blown up her inbox with text messages that she never bothered to answer. I almost felt bad for her when her shoulders slumped. "Wilma won't let us have our phones on during school hours."

Winnie wasn't buying Mom's explanation. "Wilma's just going to have to make an exception. Your mother is ill."

From Aunt Caroline's bedroom window, I watch the sheriff's car mosey down the drive and listen to Mom's heavy footsteps on the stairs. I take a deep breath and wait for Mom's knock on the closed bedroom door.

"Aria, we need to talk." Whenever Mom calls me by my full name, it can't be good, especially when her voice is strained and tired. "Can I come in?"

"Whatever."

Hinges creak. Nana keeps WD40 in the kitchen cabinets, but I know Mom refuses to oil my bedroom door on purpose. She's using the noise like a secret alarm system. If I try to sneak out in the middle of the night, she wants to be able to nail me. I'm not stupid. There's a window that opens onto the porch roof. If I really wanted to get out of here, I could scamper down one of the porch pillars faster than my cat. But if I leave, who's left to give a flip about Nana?

"Aria..." Something about the sad look on Mom's face makes me feel like she's wishing she'd found her sister standing next to the lacy pink curtains instead of me. "You hungry?"

I shake my head.

She sinks onto the foot of the bed. "Me neither. Too tired, I guess."

It's the first time since Mom came barreling up the drive in Nana's old Escort that I've noticed she's still wearing her I-want-to-look-like-a-teacher skirt and heels. She lets out a long sigh as her gaze dusts the trophies and posters my aunt left behind. She gets hung up on the framed newspaper clipping I've memorized. It's an article about my aunt. Caroline Slocum's impressive display of back flips across the gym floor led Addisonville to a State basketball championship. Apparently, my mom's older sister was like some sort of one-girl wonder. Why we can't ever talk about her is something I don't understand.

"Why didn't you tell me you were leaving school today?"

"Would you have let me go without losing it?"

"You didn't trust me, so now we'll never know, will we?"

"I'm sorry I made you worry, Mom." I cross my arms. "But I'm not sorry I came back to check on Nana."

Mom runs her hand over the bumpy bedspread. "When Caroline was your age, she begged Momma to order this bedspread from the Sears catalog. I remember her standing in the middle of this very room arguing that chenille was so durable Momma would never have to replace it. 'It'll probably outlast me,' was her closing argument. I guess she was right."

Although I'm dying to know more about this ghost girl who haunts us all, I'm already in enough trouble. "What's a catalog?"

Mom gives me that half-laugh of hers. "Catalogs are to online shopping what land lines are to mobile phones." Then she turns toward me. Tears glitter in her eyes. "Ari, if you hadn't come back to check on your grandmother today, who knows what might have happened."

I brace myself for the punishment lurking behind this statement. "*But?*"

"Hear me out, okay?" Mom reaches for my hand. "You and I have to go to school, *but* I believe you're right. Nana might benefit from some extra mental stimulation."

"Really?"

"It can't hurt. She always seems a little better on the days you can convince her to play the piano. Maybe you can sweet talk her into trying a few memory games."

"She loves math."

"Sounds like the place to start then." Mom pats the bed and I sit beside her. "Tell me what you need and I'll order it tomorrow during my planning period."

"I can pull up an interactive YouTube video for her tonight."

"After you lay out everything you need for school tomorrow, right?"

"But if you make me go to school, that means Nana will be all alone."

Mom hauls my stiff body to her and kisses my temple. "While you're working Nana over, I'll see what I can do about hiring someone to sit with her. It may take a few days, so we'll just have to trust Winnie to look out for her until I get things worked out." Mom offers me her hand. "Deal?" No wonder Mom's clients loved her. She's slick.

"I don't mind staying home with her, really."

"You need to give this new school a chance."

"For you?"

"So, *you* won't end up a lonely old woman. I want you to have friends."

"Nana's my friend."

"Friends your age."

"If I don't make friends, will you homeschool me?"

Mom doesn't jump in with her usual, come-on-kid-look-on-the-bright-side pep talk. Instead, she rubs her chin and studies me as if she's trying to peel away the layers of my brain and get to the bottom of why I'm making everything so difficult. I brace for her you're-better-than-this lecture.

"I think you're selling yourself short, but...okay. I'll make you a bet."

"What kind of bet?"

"If you don't make friends by Christmas, we'll reassess and go from there."

"And if I do make friends…which I won't…but if I do?"

"You'll try to get happy in Addisonville. Deal?"

It's not the answer I was hoping for, but it's not a no. "Deal."

She starts to leave then stops at the door. "And while you're scouring the internet for miracles cures for Alzheimer's, why don't you pick out a new bedspread. Preferably something from this century."

"Does it have to last forever?"

Her smile is a mixture of pleasure and sadness. "Nothing last forever, sweetheart. Not even feeling way in over your head."

Chapter 22

CHARLOTTE

I take a deep breath despite the pressure on my chest and open the door to Benjamin's clinic. Across the lobby, Corina Miller is talking on the phone. If Itty was willing to give me his personal number, maybe he'd be okay with me slipping in and out of his office without having to face my sister's old nemesis?

Corina hangs up the phone. "Danged insurance companies."

I take a pen from the can and sign the log-in chart. "Hi, Corina."

She sizes me up for a second, then says, "Ember loves choir." It wasn't a compliment.

"Your daughter has a great voice."

Corina gives a half-shrug. "It's her brother who can really sing."

Then why doesn't he? "So, I've heard."

"He givin' you trouble?" Her interest feels more like she's picking a fight than offering to step in and help me encourage her

185

son to reach his full potential.

I drop the pen in the can. "Not a lick."

She leans forward. "You never have had a believable poker face." She falls back in her chair, a pleased smile on her face. "Ben said to send you on back. I put your chart on the door of exam room one."

Shaking inside, I waver between the lesser of two evils: forgetting about asking Itty for help or going back to school. Corina Miller already has an inside scoop into my classroom, I don't want to give her access to health concerns that are probably nothing more than my overactive imagination.

I'm in the process of quietly skipping out on my appointment when Benjamin appears in the lobby. "Hey, Charlotte," he calls. "Come on back."

"Hi, Doc." I force a smile and slip through the lobby door that leads to all three exam rooms.

Benjamin waves me toward an open door. He ushers me in with a smile, indicates I should take a seat on the exam table and says, "Tell me what's going on with your mother."

I close the door, then hoist myself upon the table's crackly paper. "If she was speaking to me, I might be better able to answer that question."

He sits on a rolling stool and wheels to within a couple of feet of my dangling legs. "How long has she been uncommunicative?"

"Since LaVera died."

"I can adjust her meds." His understanding smile makes my chest hurt worse. He notices my sneaky attempt to press my palm against the pain. "Something tells me this isn't about your mom."

"I think I'm having a heart attack, Itty."

He leaps to his feet. "Maybe you should have led with that." He whips the stethoscope from around his neck.

"It's probably nothing."

"Describe what's going on." He rubs his palm against the stethoscope's bell then nods at the buttons on my shirt.

Unable to make eye contact with him I undo the first two buttons. "Feels like an elephant is sitting on my chest."

He slides the bell over my heart. "When did the pain start?"

"When I moved home."

He fights a smile then moves the bell around and directs me to breathe. After several careful placements and what seems like forever, he sits on the stool, loops the stethoscope around his neck, and slides back a step. "I don't think you're having a myocardial infarction."

"Why can't I breathe?"

"Stress."

Anger building, I button my shirt. "So, it's in my head?"

"I didn't say that. Stress often presents in physical symptoms."

"You know most women who die of a heart attack had a cocky

male doctor tell them it was all in their heads, right?"

He's not amused. "Have you checked into any of the support resources on that list I gave you?"

"Between burying my mom's best friend, starting a new job, and trying to keep my daughter from facing truancy charges, I've had plenty of time for extra reading and sappy group meetings."

"No wonder your body's giving you heck."

"Look, if it's not my heart, maybe you can give me something that will help me…you know…cope."

"This time you have with your mother is a gift, Charlotte."

"So that's a no?"

"For now." He sees straight through me and it's a bit disconcerting. "A chance to heal old wounds. With a little bit of support, I think you'll be glad you did this."

"You sound like Aria."

"Your daughter's a smart kid."

"She's Googled home treatments for memory loss. Started Momma on a regimen of fresh veggies, fruits, crazy herbs, and memory exercise flash cards."

"Is it working?"

"Not really. More and more things are turning up in unusual places. Last week I found Momma's wristwatch in the sugar bowl."

"If you can learn to see the humor in a situation, you might discover the salvation as well."

"I came for a pill, not a sermon."

He nods. "You're not the first caregiver to become overwhelmed by the strain of caring for an aging parent." He rolls over to his little desk and takes out a prescription pad. "Untreated stress can lead to illness, sleep deprivation, depression, and premature aging." He scribbles on the pad, rips off the paper and hands it to me. "Take this medicine twice a week and I guarantee you'll feel better."

My relief is an audible sigh. "Thank you, Itty." I glance down at the script.

Band practice. First Baptist Church. 7:00 pm. Thursdays.

Chapter 23

CHARLOTTE

Nana, you're not even trying." Aria clicks off the Memory Multiplier DVD she'd order from a TV infomercial. She jams her fists on her hips and lowers herself until her gaze is even with Momma's. "Don't cry to me when you're stuck riding shotgun on Aunt Winnie's mail route for the rest of your life."

Aria's frustrated tone snaps my head up from the mess Momma's made of her checkbook. After two hours of sorting through a growing stack of my mother's unpaid bills and unreconciled bank statements, I, too, am on the verge of resorting to a little shaming. Momma's engagement with life isn't the only thing that's rapidly disappearing. Her finances are a mess. None of the numbers add up. She's written checks to causes I've never heard of and ignored monthly bills she's paid on time for years.

Momma's never been a quitter. Tragedy only sharpens her

resolve. She's always been a put-your-head-down-and-press-on kind of woman. But it's like LaVera's death has dulled her steely will…or is this what Alzheimer's looks like?

From the small desk in the corner of the living room, I hold my breath, watching Momma for some sort of reaction to Aria's challenge. I'm secretly willing her to dig deep and find the spunk that has served her so well all these years. But within seconds, her forehead crumples like the discarded index cards she's thrown around the room. It pains me to see my mother slipping away, but it's my daughter's Aria's growing despair that I can hardly stomach. Every day the girl insists we rush home from school. After she checks on her grandmother, she hurries through her homework and piano practice so she can make flashcards and math worksheets that will stimulate her grandmother. So far, Aria's valiant efforts haven't made a dent in the shell of the sour-faced old woman pushed so deep inside herself she might as well be a turtle.

Aria waves her hand in front of Momma's vacant stare. "Nana, can you hear me?"

"Why don't you two take a little break?"

"Maybe she's hungry." Aria steps over the scattered flash cards. "Come on, Nana. Let's get a snack." She takes her grandmother's hand and leads her toward the kitchen.

I bury my nose in my mother's finances once again. Although it feels like I'm pawing through her underwear drawer, it has to be done. Last week, right when I was trying to enter choir grades into my school laptop, the electricity went out. When I asked Momma if she'd paid the electric bill she simply shrugged. When I called the electric company, she hadn't paid for two months.

Trying to make heads or tails out of what's she paid and what is still outstanding forces me to compare the stack of notices with her checkbook. I'm taken aback by Momma's handwriting. On the most recent check stub entries, her third-grade perfect cursive is nearly illegible. Letters lean downhill, fall off the line, and tumble into a tangled mess with the line below. I flip back several pages in the check stubs. The dates and amounts are precise, neat, and correspond to the exact amount on the invoice. Just a few months ago, Momma was handling her affairs.

Had I misunderstood Benjamin, or is my mother's descent into darkness happening faster than predicted?

The talk I've been dreading can no longer be put off. I gather the checkbook and trudge into the kitchen. "Ari, I'll sit with Nana while you take your shower."

Aria's eyes dart from the papers in my hand to her grandmother. "Why is it okay for you to keep secrets?" She picks up her glass of milk.

"This could get…sensitive. I don't want Nana embarrassed."

"Whatever." She kisses Momma's forehead. "Night, Nana."

"Night." Momma's acknowledgment sounds rusty, but it's

appropriate. I take it as a sign she might still comprehend some of what I'm about to say. Her gaze follows Aria out of the room then whips around on me. "Why are you going through my checkbook?"

"Well, that's what I need to talk to you about."

"You've no right to poke around in my money."

I clear my throat. "You've not been yourself lately and a few things have begun to slide."

"What things?"

"Your hygiene for one."

Momma tugs her ratty robe closed. "Winnie doesn't care what I wear."

"No, but I'm sure she'd appreciate it if you bathed every day. Her VW doesn't have air conditioning."

"It smells like cats in that tin can of hers, so what does it matter how I smell?"

"See, this reaction right here is exactly what I'm talking about." I wave a hand over Momma's disheveled appearance. "The Sara Slocum I know would *never* go anywhere without dressing, combing her hair, and putting on her lipstick."

"The mailboxes we stuff full of junk mail don't care if I'm wearing lipstick."

I start to say *well I do* when it suddenly dawns on me that Momma is not only speaking, she's arguing...like Momma.

"What are you grinning about?" Momma gathers the dangling

ties of her robe and whips them into a knot at her waist.

"You."

"Me?"

"Yes, it's good to have you back among us."

"I'm glad I could give you something to smile about because you've come home every day for the past two weeks absolutely a bear." Momma smooths her hair. "I told you Wilma Rayburn was a sadist, but you wouldn't listen."

I don't know how long this window into lucidity will remain open. This may be my last chance to convince her to hand over the checkbook.

"Wilma is pretty demanding." I motion toward the kitchen table. "Can we sit? I could use your advice."

"On what?"

"A senior in my choir class. The boy has a bunch of potential but little motivation to use his talent."

"Evan Miller?"

"How did you know?"

"I'm physic."

"Momma."

"Aria told me. Says the boy slouches in late, sits at the back, and won't open his mouth unless he believes you're not watching."

"Crazy thing is, the moment he does start to sing I can hear him because his incredible voice cannot be hidden."

"He's a Miller. They may not be very likeable but they're all very talented."

"Ember's a Miller but she's nothing like her brother. She's totally involved and from what I can tell, a really great kid."

"That's a relief."

"Why?"

"Ember's name is in nearly every sentence that rolls out of Aria's mouth. I wouldn't be surprised if she doesn't invite the girl over to play those silly brain games with me."

"Ember's been really kind to Ari." Folding my hands over the checkbook, I can't help but hope this break in Momma's silence means I can shelve the issue sure to chip off another piece of her dignity. At least for now. "Any advice on how to motivate Evan Miller to use his gift?"

"I seem to remember trying to motivate you to use yours and failing miserably."

If I close my eyes, I can still see Momma pacing in front of the piano and ranting about my decision to switch majors. "Momma, I love teaching music. You were right. There I said it. Music is what I was meant to do. But I don't regret becoming a very good lawyer. I don't regret living in the heartbeat of this nation. Believe it or not, I don't even regret James. Without James I would never have had Ari. And without Ari, I might not be sitting here tonight."

Momma's head cocks as if the idea is one she's never

considered. And then she does a very strange thing. She looks me dead in the eye, reaches for my hand, and lovingly gives it a squeeze. "Sometimes, the worst path leads us right back to where we belong."

I squeeze back. "If teaching is where I truly belong, then I need to take advantage of your experience and ask you again, how can I motivate this student?"

"When Evan was in third-grade, he was shy and awkward."

"He acts like he owns the joint now."

"We never really change who we are at our core...but we can learn to compensate." Momma rubs her chin like she trying to conjure her recollections. "Evan is much like his mother, full of bluster and unfocused energy. But, as I discovered in Corina, outward swagger can often be a smoke screen to cover up the internal fear of looking like a fool in front of others. The scrutiny of the stage terrifies this type of child. In Evan's case, he couldn't even read his science report to the class." A conspiratorial twinkle lights her eyes. "You know how I can't stand to see a student fail."

"What did you do?"

"I rented one of those video camera things, had the little fellow stay after school, then recorded him giving his report to an empty classroom." Pride at her cutting-edge brilliance brightens Momma's face. "Corina gave me an ear-full when her son missed his bus home, but when I showed Evan's video at parent night, every person in that room, including Corina, knew immediately that the camera loves Evan Miller…and that boy *loves* the camera."

Now I'm impressed as well. "So, you're saying I should offer to record his six-week solo?"

"I'm saying it pays to get to know your students."

Possibilities surge through me. "Evan Miller will be singing his heart out by Christmas."

Momma thumps the checkbook. "Now, what is it you really want to talk about?"

My mother's astute calm gives me courage. "I've been going over your finances and maybe it's time for me to take this burden off of you."

Any earlier good will that had flowed between us quick freezes to ice. "If you want my money, just say so, Charlotte Ann."

"I'm not trying to take your money."

"My teacher's pension is nothing to scoff at."

"Your teacher's pension is barely enough to pay the bills. And it's certainly *not* enough for me to hoodwink you into bankruptcy."

"I worked forty years for that money and I'm not going to simply turn it over."

"Nobody says you have to turn over complete control of your finances. You can still use your checkbook…buy whatever you want. I'm offering to keep up with the bills as they come in. I can even take on the payment of most of them once James and I settle

197

our divorce."

"Oh, I see what's driving this nasty maneuver…little Jimmy McCandless is taking his mommy's money and going elsewhere."

"Momma, this isn't about James. This is about *you* forgetting to pay the light bill. Letting the water bill fall behind. Not filing for any of the senior citizen property tax exemptions. It'll take me a week to sort out what you owe in back taxes. Your records are a mess."

"First you call me a mess and now you claim my money is a mess." Momma pushes back from the table and rises to her full height. "I've been running this ranch since before you were born, Caroline."

"I'm Charlotte."

She studies me hard. "Yes, you are. Caroline would never do this to me."

The sting hangs in the air. Neither of us speak.

"I'm not trying to push you in a corner, Momma. I'm just saying that if you'll let me help you manage your money, we can make it go a lot farther. There are all kinds of breaks on everything from utilities to taxes for seniors."

"I'll not let you rob me blind."

"I've never stolen from you and I never would."

"That's what Cora Jenkins' kids said to her right before they slapped her into the nursing home, sold her house, and skipped out of town."

"Cora raised her five kids in a little rental on Second Street after her husband left her. Cora didn't have a pot to pee in. What was there for her children to steal?"

"Get out!" Momma grabs the checkbook and hugs it to her chest. "And don't come back!"

"You know what?" I grab my purse and the keys to the Escort. "That's the most lucid idea you've had in weeks."

"Mom!" Horror paints the face of my daughter standing in the doorway.

"Come on, Ari." I sling the purse strap over my shoulder. "Let's go."

"No." She rushes to her grandmother and wraps her arm around the old woman's waist. "She didn't mean it, did you, Nana?"

Momma squeezes the checkbook tighter. Fight flickers then dies in her eyes. "Mean what?"

Chapter 24

CHARLOTTE

A couple of hours later, I gun the gas pedal and the Escort bounces over the cattle guard at the end of Momma's lane. Speeding away from my mother isn't going to slow her mental decline, but I'm hoping putting a few minutes of distance between us will keep me sane. The sedative I gave her only keeps her in bed for a couple of hours. Which means, I can't go far.

When I was younger and needed breathing space, I'd either take off for the river or ride my bike to LaVera's. The river's not been my sanctuary in a long time. And now that LaVera's dead...I gaze down the road. Lights beckon from her windows.

Winnie.

I fish my cell phone out of my purse and text Aria in case she wakes up and panics when she can't find me. *Have gone to Winnie's. Call if you or Nana need me.*

Five minutes later, I'm standing on LaVera's porch. The heavy front door is open. Romantic music and laughter drift through the screen. What was I thinking dropping in on newlyweds unannounced?

I turn to leave when Winnie emerges from the kitchen. "C?" The hall light silhouettes her lithe body beneath her thin cotton gown. She sees me staring at her through the screen. "What's going on?"

"I can't take it anymore…" Try as I might, not another word can push past the ball of emotions lodged in my throat.

Winnie pads down the hall, eases the screen open, and I fall into her outstretched arms. "Come on, let's get you something to drink."

Bo appears in the hallway, jeans and a bare chest. "Winifred?"

I don't know if it's the concerned way he says her name, the sparks that pass between them, the easy way they work together to lead me to the kitchen, or if it's simply that LaVera's not here, but something sends tears tumbling down my cheeks. I'm blubbering like an idiot by the time Winnie has me settled at the small metal table in the breakfast nook.

"Do you have any wine?" I sob.

Winnie nods to Bo. While he slips into the pantry, Winnie floats to the china cabinet and fetches one LaVera's elegant pieces of stemware. A large tabby cat curls its tail around my leg as an added gesture of comfort. Swiping my cheeks, I glance around the room where I've spent some of the best parts of my childhood. LaVera used to joke that she only had a kitchen because it came with the house. She hated to cook, but she always had a sweet treat ready to serve. Even though Caroline and I used to gag on her dried angel food cake and awful cookies, we couldn't devour enough of her laughter and unconditional love.

Bo pours red liquid into the goblet. "Do I need to go check on Aria and your mother?"

I shake my head. "They were both sleeping when I left."

Winnie gently touches Bo's arm. "I think Charlotte and I need a little girlfriend time."

Bo's gaze falls upon my blotchy face. "Nice night to sit on the porch."

"Great idea." Winnie takes my elbow and slides her fingers under the fragile bowl of the wine glass. "Let's get some fresh air, C."

Light spills through the screen door and puddles on the glossy porch planks. I trudge to the dark end of the porch and sink onto the big wooden swing. Winnie hands me the glass, sits beside me, and sets us in motion with one push of her foot.

Gliding back and forth in silence allows the familiar sounds of the country to break through my pounding headache. Cicadas sing in the trees. River frogs croak. Somewhere in the darkness, the hoot of an owl joins the symphony. I'm too tired to fight the comfort.

My tears slow. My breath returns and brings with it the courage to say what I should have said weeks ago. "I've not been a very good friend since I moved back. I'm sorry, Win."

"When will you learn that love is not earned?" Winnie squeezes my hand. "Let's hear it."

"It's all so petty and ugly."

"And eating you alive."

I drag my hand across my runny nose. "I miss my sister."

"You've missed Caroline for twenty-five years." Winnie gives my hand another squeeze. "But you've coped. Who picked the scab off your grief tonight?"

"Who do you think?"

"Your mother."

"She threw me out."

"She's talking again?"

"Like a loose-lipped lush," I say.

"That's progress, right?"

"Hurtful," I admit with a one-shoulder shrug. "Clamming up is her way of punishing me. She's done it for years. I don't know why I'm surprised that she'd punish me for LaVera's death."

"Sara may be talking, but you know she's not thinking straight, right?" Winnie gives the swing a gentle push. "And probably won't ever think logically again...no matter how many brain tests Aria makes her take."

"It's not fair." I take a big gulp of wine. "My mother can't remember what she had for lunch, but she's got the memory of an elephant when it comes to arguments she intends to win."

"What were you fighting about?"

"The checkbook."

"Ah." Winnie lifts the glass from my hand and helps herself to a sip. "When you officially take her car keys you better make sure the shotgun's locked up."

I laugh despite the urge to bang my head against a wall and scream. "I hate being the DD."

"DD?"

"Designated daughter, otherwise known as the unlucky scapegoat chosen to fill the hole Caroline and Daddy's death left in Momma." I relieve Winnie of the glass and throw back another slug. "I hate being the responsible one...the only one making decisions."

"You're wishing Caroline was here to help you because she was better at making decisions?"

I snort. "Caroline never thought through anything in her life. She just did whatever she wanted then laughed in the face of whatever hell came from it."

"Your daddy drank, your mother buried her head in teaching, and your sister did whatever she wanted. Sounds like that left you to take on the family responsibility. You've been the designated daughter your whole life."

"No, I haven't."

"Who gave up a shot at Juilliard because there wasn't enough money?"

"I wasn't good enough for Juilliard."

"Who changed their major and married a rich jerk so she'd always have a ton of money to support her mother?"

"I loved James."

"Telling yourself something doesn't always make it so."

"You know, sometimes I really don't like you, Win."

Her laughter drifts toward the stars. "Ditto, friend."

We swing in silence. Winnie waiting. Me sipping wine like it's going to give me an infusion of strength. Instead, I feel my tongue loosen and the truth tumbles out.

"Watching Momma fall apart, piece by piece, is no picnic. But watching my daughter lose her childhood because she's trying to take as much of this burden off of me as she can is..."

"You all over again?"

Winnie's observation hits me hard.

"I'm so mad that I had to grow up so fast...I can't remember doing one crazy, adolescent thing in college. But watching my thirteen-year-old march around the house with a list of caregiving safety measures we need to implement makes me want to cry."

"Safety measures?"

"Non-skid mats in the tub. Medicines stored under lock and key. Throw rugs removed because they create a fall risk."

"The kid may have a future in elder care."

"This is not the life I wanted to give her."

"You know Beauregard and I are happy to give you a break."

"Momma isn't your problem, friend. She's mine."

"Have you talked to Benjamin?"

"About?"

"Available resources."

Facing up to my inability to handle the pressure is something I'm not quite ready to do. "Momma would never agree to help."

"Like mother like daughter."

"Trying to hire someone to come in and sit with her during the day is almost impossible around here."

"I was thinking more along the lines of taking care of yourself. To be a loving caregiver is the highest form of giving – but you can't give what you don't have."

"I'll try to squeeze in a spa day between taking care of chickens, lesson preps for four different subjects, helping Aria with her homework, and having knock-down-drag-out fights with my demented mother." Why can't I tell her about Benjamin's invitation to join the praise band? "I don't know how you stand spending so much time with my mother."

"She's growing on me."

"If you weren't letting her ride the route with you, she'd just sit in that house all day and brood."

"I think you just hit on a solution."

"Give me a hint, because I'm not feeling it."

"Obviously, Sara's still in grief over losing LaVera. She's lonely, and it's exacerbated when you and Aria leave for the day. She needs friends."

"She doesn't have any."

"But she does."

"Who?"

"Ira and Teeny."

"They live in Austin."

"It's not the moon."

"I don't have time to run Momma back and forth to Austin, and there's no way I'm letting her drive there."

"You're right, it's the full-time companionship she needs."

"Objection. Leading the witness." Anger is the rope I've been hanging on to for a long time. If I let it go, I'll drown in the grief of losing my sister and father...and now, my mother.

"Overruled." Winnie's determined for me to listen. "What if you could offer your mother a compromise?"

"I don't think I like where this is going."

"Hear me out." Before I can put an end to this line of questioning, Winnie swoops in for the kill. "What if you offered your mother a trade?"

"What kind of trade?"

"If she'll agree to letting you manage her finances, you'll let Ira and Teeny visit your ranch for a few days."

"Have you not heard a word I said? I'm drowning here and you want me to pile boulders on my head."

"Think about it. While Ira and Teeny were staying at the ranch, your mother was calm, coherent, and very chipper."

"And I was exhausted."

We ride the swing in silence. While I fume, I can feel Winnie plotting her next line of questioning.

"Here's the truth of it, C. I don't think that the mother who raised you is so far gone that she can't tell the difference between obligation and love."

I plant my foot. The swing jerks to a stop. I leap out and whirl on Winnie. "I uprooted my life for her."

"That's obligation. Not love. What do you think would happen if you surprised her with an outrageous act of love?"

"Don't you get it? After the way she's treated me for the past twenty-some years, she doesn't deserve love."

I recoil at my own bitterness. Winnie doesn't even flinch.

"You think you're the first person who's had to love someone who doesn't deserve it?" Her question heaps burning coals on my head.

Winnie's mother was a beautiful rich housewife who became addicted to oxycodone after surviving the car wreck that killed

Winnie's father. By the time Winnie turned nine, her mom had snorted her way through the money. She dragged Winnie and her little brother from one eviction to the next. It was Winnie's high school art teacher who saw something special in Winnie and convinced her to apply for college scholarships and loans. When Winnie and I met in law school, we were two broken halves desperate to be whole.

"Your mom was sick, Win."

"So's yours." Winnie tucks her legs under her. "By the time I was ready to forgive my mom, it was too late." She spears me with that laser stare I've seen her use in the courtroom. "If you keep putting off opportunities to make your relationships right, there's a real good chance your mother won't be the only one to die alone."

Chapter 25

SARA

It's hard to concentrate on Aria's musical training with Charlotte flitting around the dining room, dust cloth in hand. She's been tidying up all morning and I can't remember whether or not she told me why and I'm not about to ask.

"Momma, why don't you and Aria take a break from the piano?"

Normally, I'd feel bad about the sorry state of my home, but since LaVera died I really have no reason to ever dust or clean a toilet again. "If Aria's going to be ready for her Juilliard audition, she must practice every spare moment."

Aria grabs my wrist. "But it's Saturday, Nana."

I loosen her grip and set her hand upon the keys. "Every spare moment."

Charlotte drags the dust cloth across the top of the piano. "It's nearly noon and you haven't combed your hair or dressed."

"Yeah, Nana, let's stop and get you dressed."

"Sweet Moses. What does it matter what I wear?"

Charlotte reaches over and straightens the sheet music. "LaVera used to say a little lipstick always makes a girl feel better."

Using my friendship with an Avon lady against me is a low blow…even for Charlotte. "I feel fine." It's funny how lies repeated often enough eventually don't feel wrong anymore. "We're busy here, Charlotte Ann." I restart the metronome. "Don't you have papers to grade or something?"

My crankiness deserves a stern look, but Charlotte continues coming at me with an unusual cheeriness I think she's manufacturing to prove I was wrong about her working for Wilma. "It's such a pretty day, I think you and Aria should sit on the porch."

"Nana, please, let's move to the porch and—"

"I'll let both of you know when I'm ready to be relegated to a rocking chair." I hold up a palm to silence their nagging. "From the beginning, Aria."

My granddaughter's shoulders slump with a dramatic huff. "I've been at the piano for over an hour.

"But you've wasted fifteen minutes of it sneaking peeks out the window like you're expecting company." I tap the sheet music with my ruler. "Two pages of this Beethoven sonata *from memory* or I don't participate in another one of those silly brain games."

Aria's glare is more like the pre-teen she should be rather than the mature caretaker she's become. "I think I liked it better when you weren't talking."

I tap the sheet music again. "Play."

Aria straightens into proper form, lifts her hands to the keys, then defiantly takes one more glance out the window. "Someone's here." She jumps up. The piano bench scrapes against the floor. Sheet music flies in the air. "See?"

Determined not to give in to another stall tactic, I busy myself with the task of returning the sheet music to its proper order. "Probably just the mail."

"Winnie sleeps in on Saturdays." Aria's hopping around like she's either about to wet her pants or she has a secret she can no longer keep. "Maybe you should come see who it is."

"Sweet Moses!" I scoot past the piano bench and Aria. "If it'll get you back to the task then…"

Two cars are coming up the drive. A dark sedan and a teal Cadillac.

"It's Ira!" I drop the ruler, wheel in my Dearfoams, and head for the front door. I fling the screen open and scramble onto the porch. Hand tented over my eyes, I try to make out who's in the Cadillac. Ira's daughter is behind Trixie's wheel and Ira's riding shotgun, a huge smile on his face and two small dogs in his lap. In the backseat, a giant of a woman with white hair and a big bow is waving and calling my name through the open window.

"Teeny!" I'm stumbling down the steps as they roll to a stop in front of the house.

Aria grips my arm. "Are you surprised, Nana?" Her grin reaches plum up to her glowing eyes.

"You knew they were coming?"

"Mom and I have been planning it for days."

I turn to the porch where Charlotte is standing on the top step, smiling like the cat who swallowed the canary. "You knew I was having company and let me meet them looking a fright?"

"I tried to talk you into changing, but you're a stubborn one." Charlotte comes down the steps, hands me a tube of lipstick, and holds up a small mirror. "Happy birthday, Momma."

"Birthday? My birthday's not until October."

"So, shoot me. We're celebrating a little early." Charlotte motions to the tube of red clasped in my hand. "It'll take them a second to climb out of the car."

I turn my back on my company. My hands shake with so much excitement I can barely keep the lipstick within the outline of my mouth. I blot my lips together, cap the tube, and hand it back to her. "Thank you, Charlotte." In an effort to communicate my sincere appreciation for this unexpected gift, I let my gaze linger on hers. "Short of bringing Aria back into my life, letting my friends visit is the best gift you've ever given me."

Charlotte swallows hard. "Go on. Enjoy."

213

While Ira unfolds himself from the front seat, I pat my hair into submission. Goodness and Mercy bound across the drive and yap around my legs. I bend to pat their heads and tell Aria, "Better hide your cat."

"I've already put Fig up. Thought we'd introduce them slowly."

I straighten. "Well, I guess you've thought of everything."

"Sara!"

I look up and Ira's arms are open wide. "Ira!" I probably look like a giddy teenager glad to see her beau home from war, but I don't care. I fall into his embrace. He smells of the peanut butter and birdseed he uses to make his corncob critter feeders. That he would leave his feathered friends at The Reserve to come see me stirs tears. "What on earth are you doing here?" I mutter into his ear.

Before he can answer, Teeny taps my shoulder. "Sara, we've come to stay."

I pull back from Ira's hold. "Stay?"

Ira nods. "Got a formal invitation in the mail." Ira pulls an envelope from his shirt pocket. The stationary inside is creamy white. Expensive by the feel of it. Charlotte McCandless, Attorney at Law spans the letterhead.

"Me too." Teeny waves a matching envelope. "Just like his."

A quick scan of Charlotte's letter to Ira makes everything clear. This isn't a birthday lunch invite, but rather an invitation to move in…to make Fossil Ridge their home…permanently.

My jaw goes slack. Disbelief clogs my throat. I can only hold out the letter to my daughter and pray she understands the gesture as my need for further explanation.

"It's true," Charlotte says. "I've asked your friends to move in and Aria's been helping me get ready."

"We've had to be so sneaky." The truth comes spilling out of Aria. "I thought for sure you'd notice the grab bars around the tub. Most falls occur in the bathroom, you know."

"I didn't," I say, my mind still reeling from the shock.

"Winnie kept you out extra-long on the mail route for several days last week so Raymond Leck could install them."

"Raymond?"

"Simmer down, Momma," Charlotte says. "He's been a great help."

"Yeah, he helped us rearrange the bedrooms, rewire some lighting, and remove all of the rugs and runners," Aria says. "The Consumer Product Safety Commission estimates 6,800 elderly people are treated in emergency rooms for injuries related to rugs and runners *every* year."

That I hadn't even noticed these changes to the house I've lived in for forty years rocks me to the core. "Well, sounds like you *really have* thought of everything."

"Dad," Esther walks up accompanied by a handsome young man I'd guess to be in his late teens. "Aren't you forgetting something?"

"Oh," Ira takes my hand. "Sara, this is my oldest grandson. He offered to take off work to help us move in. Brandon this is Mrs. Slocum, her daughter Charlotte, and granddaughter Aria. Ladies, Brandon."

"Nice to meet you, ladies." Brandon definitely inherited his grandfather's charm. "Want me to get your surprise for Mrs. Slocum out of the Caddy, Pops?"

"Please." Ira squeezes my hand. "Close your eyes, Sara."

"I don't know if my heart can take any more surprises."

"Close them tight," Ira insists, tightening his squeeze to my hand for assurance. "You're going to love it."

"Very well." I close my eyes.

All around me are the sounds of excitement. I hear the faint tinkle of a bell, followed by a gasp from Charlotte, and a cheer from Aria.

"Go ahead, Sara," Ira says. "Open them."

My eyelids flutter, then freeze in shock. Brandon stands in front of me, his arms straining beneath the weight of a large bird cage. Inside the cage, a beautiful ringneck parrot sits on a perch and peers at me through the bars.

Ira is pointing to the gift like he's Vanna White and I just bought a vowel. "He's all yours, Sara."

Tears spring from my eyes. "He looks exactly like Polygon."

"He doesn't talk," Ira says.

"Yet." I slowly stick a gnarled finger through the bars. The bird hops off his perch and wraps his claws around me. "But he will."

Chapter 26

CHARLOTTE

Here's your *Austin Statesman*, Ira." I place the newspaper on the kitchen table where Momma, Ira, and Teeny are having breakfast and discussing the pros and cons of frozen lima beans. "I'm afraid your copy is always going to be a day late since they have to mail it."

Momma reaches over her tea cup, snatches up the plastic sleeve, and dumps the paper in her lap. "Ira ordered the paper for Bojangles. He needs his cage liner changed every day."

I nearly choke on my toast. "Bojangles?"

"You don't like his name?" Momma asks.

"He's your bird. You can name him whatever you want. It's just that Bojangles isn't a math term I'm familiar with."

"Ira says this bird can't talk but he sure can dance." Aria rocks back on two legs of her chair and sticks her finger through the bars of the parrot's cage. "Dance, Mr. Bojangles."

The bird tilts his head then hops from foot to foot. I can't help but join the laughter and cheers that follow.

"A dancing bird, two tea-cup poodles, one Siamese cat, a brilliant teenager, three challenging senior citizens—"

"And one beautiful music teacher," Ira says.

"Sounds like we've opened a zoo." Momma's brightened so much since Ira and Teeny's arrival, it's hard to believe she has Alzheimer's.

"I'll be ruined if word of this ever gets back to my colleagues on the Hill." I drop the crust of my toast in the scrap bucket Ira insisted we keep for the chickens.

"Our lips are sealed." Ira drags pinched fingers across his grin. "Mind if I read the obits before we cut up the paper, Sara?"

"Obits?" Momma frowns. "Why the obits?"

"Like to check to make sure my name isn't there." Ira's chuckling as he takes the paper from Momma. "Want me to check for yours?"

I have to admit the old man deserves much of the credit for the fresh air we've all sensed since he arrived. His stories about life on his goat farm have Aria begging for a kid of her own.

"Do you know how to read between the lines?" Momma asks.

"Between the lines?" Ira's as confused as the rest of us by this strange statement. He pats my mother's hand patiently. "Can you

219

explain reading between the lines to me, Sara?"

"*After a long illness* is a phrase used for people like me," Momma says flatly. "People who die a piece at a time. Whether it's better to be betrayed by one's body or one's mind has always been up for grabs."

Silence drops like a shroud over the breakfast table. Even Ira doesn't have a snappy comeback.

Bojangles dings the bell attached to his little swing.

Momma squares her body like a fighter ready for the next round. "*Died unexpectedly* can mean an accident, but as in Martin's case, it meant suicide." Momma doesn't look at me. "That's how Mitty Stringer wrote up Martin's obit. Died unexpectedly. Remember, Charlotte?"

"I don't." I spear her with a warning glare she ignores. "Come on, Ari, we're going to be late." I gather my purse and keys. "Now, Aria."

"Wait." Aria refuses to budge from the table. "Did Nana just say my grandfather killed himself?"

Momma's mouth falls open. She looks to me like she can't believe what's just tumbled out of her mouth and she's horrified. The panic in her eyes begs me to fix it. To somehow put the cat back in the bag.

"How did he die?" Aria asks. "Why'd he do it?"

I've faced powerful senators and cut-throat litigators, but I'm not sure what terrifies me more. That sooner or later I'm going to have to reveal family secrets to my daughter or that my mother no longer has a filter.

"It's a long story, Ari." I sling my purse strap over my shoulder. "One that deserves more time than we have right now."

"Tonight?"

Ira comes to my rescue. "Tonight, we have to plan your birthday party, Aria."

I can see why my mother loves this man. "That's right. Labor Day weekend is coming up fast and we have to decide whether to host the party on Sunday or Monday."

"Who's going to come to a party for me?" Aria pushes back from the table.

Teeny's hand shoots into the air. "I will." She pulls her hand down and begins putting names to fingers. "Teeny. Ira. Winnie. Bo. Sara. Gert from the pharmacy. Dr. Ellis. Your mother." She lifts her head, a big smile on her face. "That's eight. We'll need a big cake."

In the week that Teeny and Ira have been with us, it's as if the country air has unstopped Teeny's voice, but still we marvel when she speaks.

"Ember will come and some of her friends, don't you think?" My effort to keep the conversation steered away from suicide is met with the roll of Aria's eyes.

"Ember only hangs with me because she has a crush on you."

"What?"

"Ember thinks you're the bomb when it comes to music and she wants your help to get on one of those stupid talents shows so she can get the heck out of Addisonville."

"Well, it's good to have dreams."

"Did you give up your dreams because your dad killed himself?"

"Come on, Ari. I offered before-school vocal tutoring for the small ensembles and it would be helpful if I was actually there *before* school. And I can't work on their harmonies if you're not there to accompany them. So, let's get going."

We're not a half-mile away from the house when Aria brings up the subject again. "Did it make you sad when your dad killed himself?"

"Of course."

"Is that why you never go with Nana to put flowers on his grave?"

Is it? I'm pondering all the reasons I don't traipse across the pasture and climb the bluff over the river to forgive Daddy when a huge billboard alongside the road catches my eye.

ELECT SAM SPARKS for COUNTY TAX COMMISSIONER

The punch to my gut takes my breath. "Oh, no."

"Mom? You okay?"

I shake my head. "I've been so busy senior-proofing the house, getting Momma's friends settled, and trying to stay one step ahead of constant lesson planning that I've completely forgotten to deal with Momma's in-arears tax bill."

"Don't try to change the subject." Ari spins toward me in the seat. "Why did my grandfather commit suicide?"

I point to the billboard. "Ari, if Sam Sparks gets elected he'll come after Fossil Ridge so fast you'll be asking me to explain murder."

Chapter 27

CHARLOTTE

I watch the clock at the back of the auditorium, awaiting the arrival of my planning period. My fingers itch to check my phone. The moment the bell rings at the end of third period, I grab my purse and race to the teacher's lounge.

"Win," I whisper the moment she picks up. "Will Sam Sparks be elected?" I can hear gravel pinging off the undercarriage of Winnie's VW. She's out on her mail route, possibly driving past Fossil Ridge as we speak.

"C?" she shouts. "I can't hear you."

Luckily, no one else is in the lounge so I turn my back to the door and repeat my question, this time with the volume raised in my voice.

Winnie responds with a loud, "I'm guessing you saw the campaign billboard in the Wootens' pasture."

"Why didn't you say something?"

"What's it to you if Sam Sparks throws his hat in the political arena?"

I check to make sure no one's slipped into the lounge while I had my back to the door. "Momma's behind on her property taxes."

"Yikes."

"I found a notice in one of her mountainous stacks of bills."

"Why didn't you take care of it?"

"This outrageous love crap has me so distracted I forgot."

"So, deal with it now."

"Win, I need help? I don't know Texas tax law, but I'm guessing Momma qualifies for some senior exemptions or reductions in her tax bill."

"I haven't practiced law since I got hired on at the post office."

"Win, please."

Her sigh blasts my ear. "Come by Bo's station after school and we'll draft a letter."

"No time for letters. We've got to *go* to the county seat *today*."

"The election's not until November."

"Once Sam is Tax Assessor he can have Fossil Ridge revalued at a higher rate. I don't know how long it will take to sort and settle Momma's debts. Sam isn't running because of his public servant nature. He's looking for a way to starve us out."

"Settle down."

"Says the woman who accuses me of putting things off." Ding. I pull the phone from my ear and see that the incoming message is from my husband. "Winnie, I'm getting a text. I'll pick you up at 3:30."

My fingers shake as I hang up then click and read the message from James. "That sorry son of a gun."

I sprint from the teacher's lounge and race to the middle school hall. Through the window in the English classroom door I watch my daughter. She's sitting on the front row, working on this week's vocabulary words. Blonde curls frame her innocent face. I clench my phone and make myself a promise. For as long as possible, mastering synonyms and antonyms is going to be my little girl's only problem.

Chapter 28

ARIA

I wait for the dust from the school bus to settle before I tackle the cattle guard between the rusted cowboys guarding Nana's lane. Careful not to twist an ankle, I step from metal pipe to metal pipe then start walking toward the freshly painted house at the top of the hill. When the afternoon sun hits the warped boards just right, you can still see blue beneath the new white paint. Mom started her teaching job before she could give the boards another coat. She said she was going to hire Raymond Leck to finish the job, but then Nana threw a fit. Said she didn't want that crepe murderer covering up the last traces of her past.

I kick a rock and wonder if Mom really had business in town or if she needed time to slap another layer of paint on the truth about my grandfather. It's been hard to concentrate on anything else today. I'm glad Mom's not here. If Nana has forgotten the lecture Mom gave her, maybe I can get her to tell me what really happened.

Music floats through the screen door as I climb the porch steps.

"Nana!" I call.

"In here, Caroline." Nana responds.

Caroline?

I step into the dining room where Ira and Teeny are seated at the long table, their eyes closed like they're listening to my grandmother play my audition piece flawlessly, but I think they're asleep.

"Nana." I don't want to startle anyone, so I talk just loud enough to be heard over the piano. "I'm home."

My grandmother turns her head toward me. Her fingers freeze on the keys. Her mouth drops open. "Caroline? What are you doing here?"

I look behind me thinking someone must have followed me in, but the hall is empty. "It's me, Nana. Aria."

"Aria who?"

"Your granddaughter."

Nana's eyes squint like she's looking me over good, then she snorts. "Don't be silly, Caroline," she says. "I'm far too young for grandchildren."

"In your dreams." I pull out a dining chair and drop my backpack onto it.

The noise startles Ira awake. "Aria." He smacks his lips and drags his palm over his face and bald head. "Didn't hear your mother drive up."

"She didn't. I rode the bus."

"Of course she rode the bus, Martin." Nana picks up the ruler she uses to point out sections on the sheet music that I've butchered. She points the ruler at me. "Where is Charlotte? I'll tan that girl's hide if she missed the bus because she's daydreaming on that stage again."

My gaze darts from Ira to Teeny, who are stirring to full alert, then back to my grandmother. Her brow is wrinkled. "Nana? You okay?"

She cocks her head back and forth as if she's trying to bring me into focus. "Caroline, answer me. Where is your sister?"

"I don't have a sister, Nana."

"Don't get cheeky with me, young lady."

I turn to Ira. "What's going on?"

The old man pushes back from the table. "Sara's been a little confused today." He comes and sets a calming hand on my shoulder. "After you left this morning, we worked with Bojangles, but Sara couldn't seem to remember what to do. She became more and more agitated. So, in an attempt to settle her, I suggested the piano. She's been playing for hours."

"Wait here." I tear from the room and race upstairs. In the closet my mother and I share, I pull out the tub of games I've made. Unsure which one will work the best, I tote the entire heavy container downstairs. "Game time." I plop the tub upon the table. "Everyone gather round."

"I don't have time for games, Caroline." Nana's in perfect command of the piano. "I must get this piece smoothed out before my audition."

"What audition?" I ask.

"Juilliard." Nana fingers race over the keys. "They have only a five percent acceptance rate and Daddy will not be happy if I'm passed over again."

I look to Ira, panic swimming in my eyes. "What's happened to her?"

He simply shrugs. "You have any number games in that box of tricks?"

"Yeah."

"Maybe if we start a game with numbers, she'll join us."

"Good idea." I dig out my homemade Bingo cards. "Aging doesn't have to mean losing memory, or forgetting the people you love. Research shows that some seniors even get smarter, right?"

"Use it or lose it." Ira spreads out the cards. "Come on, Teeny. Let's show this kid what a few years in the old-folks joint can do for your Bingo skills."

I pass out the playing chips and dump a sandwich baggie filled with slips of paper into a bowl. "We're starting a math game, Nana." My grandmother plays on without even acknowledging me. "We're not waiting on you."

Ira and Teeny take turns drawing then I call out the math problem they've selected. While we carry on a rowdy game of adding and subtracting, my eyes cut to Nana. She's playing the piano, her eyes closed and her head thrown back like she's the only person in the world.

"Aria," Teeny taps the folded piece of paper in my hand. "Call out the next problem."

"Yeah, sure." I look at the paper, but the numbers are blurred. I have to blink away tears. "192 plus 189," I shout over Nana's crescendo.

Nana abruptly stops playing. "Three hundred and eighty-one." She swings her legs around on the bench. "Everyone knows that, Aria."

Teeny plops a chip on a square on her card. "Bingo!"

I flip over the piece of paper. "381." Nana's answer is right on the nose. *Plus,* she knows me.

My Nana is back.

My stomach's turning celebratory cartwheels, but I'm a little reluctant to shoot off fireworks just yet, so I test her. "Nana, if you're not going to play, then please refrain from helping the other gamers."

"Give me one of those cards, Aria." Nana slides off the piano bench and takes the seat between Ira and Teeny.

Ira smiles and pushes a huge stack of chips Nana's way. "Feeling lucky, are you, Sara Slocum?"

Nana taps her temple. "Luck has nothing to do with it, Ira Conner."

I can't tell you how good it is to hear Nana calling people by the right name. We spend the next thirty minutes drawing math problems from the bowl and shaking our heads at Nana's ability to spout the answer before I can even turn the paper over. Now that her brain is limbered up, she's completely shaken free of the cobwebs she'd been tangled up in all day. I decide not to waste this moment and hit her with the question that's been burning a hole in my head all day.

"Nana, is my grandfather buried in that little cemetery by the river?"

Ira and Teeny look up from their Bingo cards. Fear that I've said the wrong thing is written all over their wrinkled faces.

"How do you know about that place?" Nana sounds angry at me, but I don't care. I'm tired of everyone acting like I'm some stupid little girl.

"I saw two headstones under a big tree the day I came to look for you and Mom after you and your friends broke out of that senior citizens home."

Nana studies my face. I can't tell if she's forgotten who I am again or if she's trying to decide whether or not to tell me the truth.

"Yes," she finally says. "Martin wanted to be close to…"

She trails off. I'm not sure who's buried beside my grandfather but I'm guessing it's my mother's sister. "Will you take me to see my grandfather's grave?"

No one speaks. Except for the pounding of my heart and the faint tinkle of Bojangles pecking away at the bell in his cage, it's as quiet as LaVera's bedroom the day I found her lying face down on her vanity.

Nana slowly pushes her stack of chips toward me. "When will your mother be home?"

"I don't know. She said she had to beat the tax man to the punch."

My grandmother's eyes narrow, but they're clear as the Frio that runs under the bridge. "What punch?"

I shrug. "She saw a sign with Sam Sparks' name on it and suddenly she was talking about murder."

"Let's go." Nana stands and offers me her hand. "While I still own enough ground to be buried in."

Chapter 29

CHARLOTTE

Ira wants Momma to buy a couple of goats," I tell Winnie on our way back to Addisonville after a quick trip to the county seat to pay Momma's delinquent tax bill.

"With the amount of senior-tax exemptions I just negotiated with the county assessor, Sara will be able to afford a whole herd of goats."

"I don't need one more thing to feed, water, or put to bed."

Winnie rolls the window down. "They'll keep the weeds in check."

I cast a sideways glance at my take-no-excuses friend strapped into the front seat of my mother's old car. Her hair is swirling around the contentment on her face.

"When did you become such a country girl?"

"I love it here." Winnie inhales the scent of ashe juniper

whipping through the open windows. "This life suits me."

"It's about to kill me."

"I never said you had to ask Ira and Teeny to move in." Instead of trying to tame her hair, Winnie throws her head back and lets the wind sweep it away from her face. "I was thinking more of inviting them to stay for a long weekend visit."

"Go big or go home!" I crank the wheel and put us back on the highway. "It's the Slocum way."

"You had them sign liability waivers, right?"

"Are you going to give me some credit or keep hounding me?"

"Have you forgiven your mother?"

"If Momma's happy. I'm happy."

"Not really." Winnie reaches behind her head, grabs her unruly strands, then nails me with her best courtroom stare. "I don't know what's worse—knowing my suggestion guilted you into becoming a martyr or watching you pretend that adding two strangers to your household makes y'all a family."

"Momma's lost her filter," I confess.

"Did she ever have one?"

"With children, yes." I barrel on down the road. "This morning, she told Aria my dad killed himself."

"Isn't that the truth?"

"Yes, but…"

"But what?"

"But I don't think my daughter's ready to hear the story of my father drinking a bottle of Jack Daniels and jumping off a cliff."

"Aria's smarter than you and your mother put together. Sooner or later she's going to figure all of this out. Wouldn't it be better to tell her yourself?"

"I found pictures."

"Of?"

"The moment the tire swing rope broke and Caroline...you know."

"Your dad was taking pictures?"

I nod. "It must have eaten him alive to know he might have saved her if he hadn't been drunk and so focused on his stupid dreams of capturing the perfect picture."

"Does your mother know about the photo?"

"If she did, I wouldn't have ever seen it. She always protected him. I don't think she would have told me Daddy was drunk if I hadn't caught her on the bluff getting ready to chuck his boots and his last empty Jack Daniels' bottle into the river."

"So, you're worried that if Aria finds out about your father, she's going to want to know about Caroline."

"If I pacify Momma's sudden urge to clear her conscience, my daughter gets hurt. If I protect my daughter's childhood, Momma's mental health will decline a little faster. No matter what I do, someone is going to get hurt."

Winnie clasps a gentle hand on my shoulder. "Balancing everyone's needs is a heavy burden for a woman whose shoulders are already slumped under the weight of her own guilt."

"That day is a bad movie I can't quit watching." We pull up to LaVera's house...I mean Bo and Winnie's house. "I substitute different scenarios into what actually happened."

"But it never changes the outcome does it?"

"No."

"That's because your sister hit her head on the ledge." Winnie unclicks her seat belt and swivels toward me. "I've read the autopsy report. Caroline was dead before she hit the water. It's time to let all of this go, C."

I've read the same report a hundred times and yet I wonder if Caroline could have been saved if I had stayed longer, helped Daddy untangle her, instead of panicking and running for help.

"What about Aria's birthday party?" Winnie shakes my arm. "Charlotte?"

"What?"

"You can't change the past. Why not try focusing on the things you can do something about? Like Aria's birthday. She's turning fourteen in a few days. You're planning a party for her, right?"

"She doesn't want one. Says no one will come."

"Never easy being the new kid."

"Not sure how hard she's trying to fit in or make friends."

"Give her time. She's a strong girl."

"I hope so." My fingers tap the steering wheel. "James texted me today."

"And now we finally get to the bottom of what's really bugging you."

"He's filing for divorce."

Winnie's brows rise. "I assumed you'd already filed."

"I guess I…"

"Hoped it would go away?"

"Things have been a little hectic."

"Girlfriend, this twenty-some year impasse between you and your mother is proof that trouble doesn't just go away. James is forcing you to deal. Let your idea of the perfect life go. Tell Aria the truth. And to protect your own sanity, start living each day as it comes."

"Easier said than done."

Chapter 29

SARA

Ira's palm buffs his bald head as he watches me shed my Dearfoams. "You sure you want to do this without talking to Aria's mother?"

I wrestle a pair of snake-proof rubber boots out from under the bench near the back door. "Charlotte may control my checkbook, but she has no say about when I go, where I go, or with whom I go."

"You're your own woman. And I think your daughter's come around to that..." Ira's pause causes me to lift my head.

"But?"

"But..." he proceeds cautiously, "I do believe Charlotte has the final say over what her daughter is and is *not* told."

"Aren't you supposed to be on my side?"

"This isn't about taking sides, Sara." Ira crowds onto the bench. "Deciding when to tell Aria dark family secrets should be a family

239

decision."

"Ira," I clasp his hand. "I don't know how long it will be before the memories slip away and I can't remember what happened there."

His squeeze is calming. "Why would you want to tell that sweet child things better forgotten?"

My eyes map the folds and crevices of Ira's weathered cheeks. The bulbous shape of his large nose. The sheen on his smooth, tan forehead. How long do I have before I can no longer recall the name of this kind goat farmer from Hillsboro, let alone how much his friendship has come to mean to me?

"Some things are too important to be forgotten." I turn a boot upside down, a habit I developed years ago when I stuck my foot in and got stung by a scorpion. "My daughter and granddaughter have come home. But that hasn't made us family. How can we be a family if we don't really know each other?"

"But telling a little girl about suicide—"

"I thought I knew Martin. But I didn't. Not because he didn't try to tell me, because he did with every bottle of liquor he emptied." I take Ira's hand. "I didn't know how badly Martin was hurting because I didn't want to know."

"Sara, you've had a hard day."

"No, I haven't."

Ira stays my hand. "Most of the day your mind was…well, it wasn't playing fair with you."

"What did I say?"

Ira's too much of a gentleman to rub my nose in the sugar bowl where he found my watch when he fixed my tea. "That don't really matter, does it?"

"It matters to me, Ira."

He lets out a heavy sigh. "You were a little girl trying to please your daddy."

"Sweet Moses! That was a waste of a perfectly good day."

"Sara, Charlotte wouldn't want you doing this alone."

"Then she shouldn't have missed the bus." I cram my feet into the boots. "Aria!" I call.

She rushes onto the porch wearing boots like I'd told her. "I'm ready, Nana."

"Get my clippers. I want to snip a few roses to take to your grandfather."

Ira follows us down the porch steps. "At least let me come with you, Sara."

"It's a free country."

Chapter 30

SARA

It's nearly the end of August and I'm sweating like a glass of iced tea on good furniture as we climb toward the bluff. Rose thorns pierce the glove of my clenched hand. Teeny and Aria flank me. Ira insists on going before us. He looks like Moses with his floppy straw hat and that long stick he's brandishing through the knee-high weeds.

Aria snags my elbow. "Tell me the story of how you and Grandpa found this place." Her genuine interest in my past snags my heart. She clicks something on her phone and turns the camera toward me.

"What's that?"

She lowers her phone and weighs whether or not to tell me the truth. "I want to get your stories down, record them before..."

"Before it's too late?"

She bites her lip and nods. "Please."

The idea that she can capture this lucid moment pleases me. "Good thing I put on some lipstick."

"LaVera would be pleased. Berry Nice suits you." Aria holds up the phone. "Okay, for the record, how did you and Pops end up buying Fossil Ridge."

"Pops?"

She shrugs. "Goes with Nana, don't you think?"

I sigh. "Your *grandfather* and I were young. We had dreams of owning a place in the country. Every weekend, we drove the back roads out of Addisonville searching for land. One day we spotted a fence row posted with a few faded Keep Out signs. That was like shaking a feed bucket for a hungry horse to your grandfather. He talked me into climbing the fence row. We hiked several miles through weeds just like these." I proceed to tell her about climbing to the granite outcropping and being stunned by the beauty of the Frio river canyon. "Right then and there, your grandfather peeled out of his clothes and jumped in."

"Did you?"

"You better bet I did."

I tell her about swimming in the freezing crystal waters, but I leave out the part of how glorious our lovemaking had been under the big oak where Martin rests without me.

As Aria's panning the view, it hits me. I have lied to Ira. I lived

243

with Martin for all those years. We worked side by side. Raised children together. And yet, I didn't really know him. I knew he struggled to find his calling. I knew his dreams never seemed to pan out. But I didn't know the depths of his grief were as deep as mine. That part of himself he hid from me.

Maybe some secrets are memories not meant to be told.

"Keep an eye out for rattlers," I remind Aria. "They're thirsty this time of year."

Ira heeds my warning and bangs his walking stick so hard it scares up a couple of jackrabbits. Teeny jumps. Aria squeals with delight and I laugh, not one of those safe little chuckles I've allowed myself over the years, but a full-on, belly-shaking, joy-filled laugh.

This is how I pictured my life. Long nature walks with my grandchildren, a godly man, and a future as big and cloudless as the Texas sky. I inhale deeply of the scents of the rugged country that has tried to break me for the last forty years. When it's all you can do to survive, it's hard to dream. Harder still to keep living. I've had to let go of so many of my notions about life, children, and even my husband.

"The cemetery is just ahead." I point toward the single large tree that shades the bluff. "Under that live oak."

Aria pans her phone like a movie camera toward the hill. While she records for a few moments, I catch my breath. "Got it." She pokes her phone. "Can we go to the river, too?" She's asking off the record. "I'm dying to see it."

A shudder runs through my bones and shakes some sense into my brain. Three old people have no business taking a child to the river. "No."

"Please, Nana," she begs. "I'm not a baby anymore."

"It's too dangerous."

"I'll be careful."

"No."

Aria sandwiches her phone between her praying hands. "Please, Nana."

"No, Charlotte Ann," I snap. "Don't ask me again."

Aria steps back, her jaw hanging like I've slapped it loose. "I'm not my mother."

My mind can't recall what I've just said. Obviously, it was inappropriate, especially when the resemblance between Aria and Charlotte is undeniable. "Yes, you are!"

I don't know why I haven't seen the similarities between them before. A person would have to be blind to argue otherwise. Aria is a carbon copy of her mother. Always has been. Same lithe body shape. Same long fingers. Same blonde hair and blue eyes they inherited from Martin. Caroline, on the other hand, carried my petite frame and dark features. Until this very moment, it has always seemed to me that Aria favors her Aunt Caroline more. It must be their temperaments. There's no denying that Aria's spunk resembles

Caroline's take-no-prisoners view of the world. But the unusual expression currently radiating from Aria's eyes is so unlike Caroline and so much more like her mother's, my stomach churns.

Charlotte has always been vulnerable to what others think. And Aria, though she wants to disobey me, cares deeply about how I'll view her if she defies me. She's curious, yet frightened, and she needs me to appease her intense desire to know everything. I can see now that I erroneously placed too much weight on Aria's headstrong personality. Seldom do I ever misjudge a child so completely.

"Very well," I clasp her hand firmly. "But you will not take one step beyond what I allow. Understood?"

"If I do fall in, you don't have to worry. I'm a great swimmer."

So was Caroline. "Do you want to hear about your grandfather or not?" The threat won't hold her back forever, but hopefully it will give me time to think. To devise a way to keep her away from that deadly ledge. "Turn that phone off. There will be no filming or recording of any of this."

Aria slips her phone into her pocket. "Thanks, Nana."

I take the lead, despite Ira's objections. Aria and I skirt the cemetery and head for the granite outcropping high above the river. When we reach a point about three feet from the edge I stop. Not out of fear for Aria's safety but out of concern for my own stability. Heavy memories threaten to buckle my knees. I don't trust myself not to topple forward.

"Oh. My. Gosh." Aria gasps. "This. Is. Gorgeous."

Despite my granddaughter's slaughter of the English language, I have to agree with her assessment. Far as the eye can see, the landscape rolls between limestone hills and valleys. Below us, the lazy babble of the Frio belies the hard work it's doing to carve a path through the fossils captured in the canyon walls. The determined current carries me back to the wonderful moments I've spent pondering the enormity of God from this very spot.

"That's close enough." I tug Aria snug to my side. She'd have to take a running leap to fall but coming back here does something to my equilibrium. Upends me by the roots and sets my world to wobbling. Frankly, it's me who needs the steadying.

Ira flanks my other side. "No wonder that developer wants to get his hands on your property. This view is worth more than all the natural gas they've sucked up from my piece of dirt." His grip on my elbow infuses me with courage.

I inhale the refreshing scent of spring-fed water. "Martin always wanted to build a house on this bluff."

Aria snatches up a small stone and sends it sailing. "I wish I could see the swimming hole." She turns to me. "Please."

I nod reluctantly. "Hang on to me."

As we inch forward, terrifying memories ignite. Within a foot of the place where everything changed, I stop. "I can go no further."

"Maybe if you sit and scoot to the edge together." Ira suggests.

"I don't think so." I look to Aria's face, praying the child will give me a pass. But there is a longing to know, to find the pieces missing from the puzzle of her life that I can no longer ignore. "Very well, but don't make me regret this."

"I won't. I promise." Aria helps me lower myself to the ground. Next, she and Ira lower Teeny to a seated position. Ira waves off Aria's offer of help by saying, "Someone better stay upright in case Sara and Teeny need a hand getting back on their feet."

"Good idea." Aria drops beside me.

Teeny pushes her sliding bow back to the top of her head. "This is as close as I'm going."

"I'll stay with her," Ira says. "You girls need to settle this on your own." He pats my shoulder. "I'll only be a shout away."

"Maybe you're right," I tell Ira. "This is a job for her mother."

He shakes his head. "We're here now."

"Please, Nana. I have to know."

Arms linked, Aria and I scoot toward the ledge. The rough limestone sands my house dress as we inch forward. The moment my ankles are suspended in thin air, it's as if I can no longer breathe. Then Aria scoots and I have no choice but to go along. By the time my knees bend over the sharp edge of the ledge, my heart is a thundering waterfall between my ears.

"Oh. Wow!" Aria's voice echoes in the canyon.

My gaze, however, is a stone dropped into the river thirty feet below. The swimming hole is not the dark ugly place of my memory. Instead, I can see every rock and crevice in the unexpected twenty-feet-deep indentation in the riverbed.

Aria hurls a rock into the crystal-clear depths. It sinks almost exactly where Caroline perished. Aria tugs on my arm. "Look, you can see all the way to the bottom."

Beneath the swirling ripples, its Caroline's dark eyes staring up at me. They're wide. Terrified. And pleading for my help, help I failed to render in time. A shudder slices through me. "That's not necessarily a good thing."

"What happened here, Nana?" Aria's question echoes in the canyon.

I swallow the boulder-sized lump in my throat and point to the large branch of the live oak tree hanging over our heads. "There used to be a tire swing here."

"Nooooo!" Charlotte's scream rips across the pasture. "Get away from that ledge, Aria." She's huffing and waving her red heels like an enraged bull. "No, wait. Don't move a muscle until I get there."

"I'm in trouble," Aria whispers as she scrambles to her feet.

"No, I'm the one she's mad at." I motion to Ira. "Can you help me to my feet?"

Charlotte puffs up the bluff. "I told you stay put." The slit at the side of her skirt has ripped to almost her thigh. The sharp grasses have sliced her legs bloody. Her hair clings to the sweat trickling down her angry face. "What's going on?"

Before I can explain, Aria jumps to my defense. "I asked Nana to tell me about my grandfather."

"Momma?" Charlotte's gaze cuts to me.

"It's time she knows."

"That's not your decision." Charlotte points a shiny heel at me. "I'm her mother." Charlotte waves Aria to her with her empty shoe. "Step away from the edge, Ari."

"No." Aria turns and jumps.

"Ari!" Charlotte drops her shoes, plows past me, and dives head first into the hole that's already claimed two Slocums.

Chapter 31

CHARLOTTE

Wind whistles in my ear as I dive toward the small body struggling beneath the water's clear surface. There was a time when diving from this height was second nature to me. Daddy would stand on the bluff, toss a stone into the swimming hole, and expect me to pierce the center of the radiating circles with greater accuracy than most men can nail a target with their hunting bows. But twenty-five years of staying clear of the water has rendered me clumsy and slow. I do my best to adjust my hurtling approach to land within a few feet of where I saw Aria go down.

My clumsy entry into the Frio's icy waters knocks the breath from my lungs. I've forgotten how cold this spring-fed water remains, even in the heat of summer. Denying myself the luxury of a slow adjustment, I force my body deeper. Toward the frantic fingers reaching for salvation.

I'm coming, Aria. Hang on.

Kicking with all my might, I fight the steady current and descend until I've nearly reached the murky cloud caused by Aria's kicking near the bottom of the swimming hole. Where is she? Head whipping right then left, my arms thrash the stirred-up silt for an arm, a leg, a piece of clothing. Anything. Straight ahead, I spot a small hand clawing through the haze like it's looking for ladder rungs.

My hand sweeps back and forth, but I'm too far away to make the connection. Kicking hard, I thrust my body in the direction of where I'd seen those precious long fingers reaching for help. My open hands close on nothing.

No. I can't fail. Not this time.

Lungs screaming for breath, I kick deeper.

Suddenly, a hand breaks through the dirty cloud, wraps my wrist, and pulls me down. I clasp onto Aria's wrist, tug reassuringly, then reposition my body toward the splash of sunlight overhead. Aria understands my meaning and immediately calms. Then, as if she's suddenly remembered that she's an excellent swimmer, she pushes off the bottom and we bullet toward the light.

My head breaks the surface first. I yank hard and Aria pops up beside me, wide-eyed and gasping. We suck in short, precious breaths as we tread water, our grips still firmly locked upon the other's wrist. I pull her toward me. All reprimands dissolve.

Her trembling body presses the cold from my bones. "Got enough left in you to swim for the bank?" I ask.

Her teeth are chattering and her lips are blue, but she manages a small nod.

It's all I can do to let go of her. To trust that she can follow me. But I don't have a choice. We're too spent to stay here. I search the canyon for the point of the bluff, the marker by which I've always made my way to shore.

Standing dangerously close to the razor-sharp edge is my mother. Clenched fists raised like a lighthouse beacon. Terror flashing on her face.

"Come on," I say. "I'll show you how to get out of here."

By the time Aria and I can pull ourselves upright in knee deep water, Momma and Ira have managed to scramble down the canyon's overgrown path. My mother waits on the bank. Although her arms are outstretched, the panic has left deep lines around her eyes. I'm not the only one who has just relived the dark moments of Caroline's death.

Momma wades into the river, water rushing over her rubber boots. She wraps an arm around Aria's waist. "Are you all right?"

"Sorry for scaring you, Nana." Aria allows herself to be smothered in kisses.

"Take hold," Ira has waded in now. He offers Aria the end of his walking stick and she grabs hold with both hands. "Don't let go."

Momma turns her attention to me. She looks like an angel in the shaft of sunlight that encircles her. "Come on. You'll catch your death."

I want to take her hand, but my ability to move has washed downstream along with the last of my adrenaline rush. Waves of what might have happened flood my mind. Violent shudders shake me limb to limb. My knees buckle and I fall into Momma's open arms.

She holds me upright. Her embrace feels the way I remember. Strong. Loving. Safe. We are, in this safe and grateful moment, the way we were before death split our worlds.

Momma pulls back and cups my wet cheeks with her bony hand. "I thought I'd lost you, Caroline."

A cloud drifts over the sun and the spell is broken.

Chapter 32

CHARLOTTE

The eight-foot-long *Happy Birthday, Aria* banner I had expedited from an online sign shop flaps between the porch pillars. Over the sounds of jazz music, mesquite-scented smoke drifts from the grill where Bo's flipping burgers, Ira's telling goat stories, and Itty, dressed in athletic shorts and an old A&M t-shirt, is graciously supervising.

Inviting Momma's doctor to the party was Aria's idea. I think she wants to impress him with the memory regimen she's designed and the improvement it's made in Momma's mental state. Frankly, that river stunt my mother pulled makes me think the opposite is true. However, I have to admit the addition of Itty's pile of jazz LPs and the old portable record player he brought to spin them has certainly given an uplifting air to today's festivities.

Out on the lawn, Momma and Teeny are trying to weight the

tablecloth on the picnic table with paper plates and enough foil-wrapped ears of corn to feed the entire county.

I descend the porch steps. "Need help, Momma?"

"I haven't forgotten how to secure a tablecloth, Charlotte Ann." This is the first time she's gotten my name right since the river incident.

I raise my palms. "Have at it."

"What's so funny?" Momma asks.

"Nothing. It's nice to have your help. That's all."

"I've always wanted to give Aria a birthday party." She turns her back and moves the platter of corn closer to the center.

The implication that I've failed her when she was the one who nearly got my daughter killed aggravates every nerve in my body. I start to defend myself.

Winnie cuts me off with a sharp elbow jab to the ribs. "Let it go."

I step aside, giving my old friend room to re-stock an ice-filled galvanized tub with bottles of soda. "I can't win."

"Looks to me like you're winning." Winnie dries her wet hands on her broom skirt and nods toward the porch where Aria and Ember are dancing around the swing to one of Itty's Coltrane records. "For a kid who claims she doesn't have any friends, seems like this impromptu party has made your girl pretty happy."

"Aria said she just wanted family. I had to work to get her to invite Ember." I lift my phone and snap a pic that captures the joy on Aria's face. Before the river, idyllic moments like these would have barely registered. But now, after nearly losing the most precious thing on earth to me, they're treasures. Snapshots I'd walk over hot coals to keep from losing.

This new appreciation I have for the loss my mother suffered when she had to bury her child and the possibility of forgetting everything she ever knew about Caroline's existence sits heavy on my chest. Since the day I pulled my own daughter from the river, I've struggled to breathe.

"But once this is over, Ari and I have to have the *see-why-I-want-you-to-stay-away-from-the river* conversation and all the points I've earned will probably vanish."

"You went into the water and you both came out okay."

"This time." I slip my phone into my back pocket. "I can't go through that again. No, I take that back. I *won't* go through that again."

My gaze seeks out the source of my mother's laughter. She and Teeny have joined the men at the grill. Itty opens a couple of lawn chairs. He teasingly incites a geriatric argument over the taste of frozen lima beans versus fresh, a subject Momma seems determined to win. How she can remember her view on lima beans when she has no recollection of taking my daughter to the river is a mystery I cannot solve. Itty howls when Momma points out food is meant to be eaten, not used as a cold poultice to reduce swelling.

Winnie's elbow to my ribs snaps me back to the present. "Itty seems to fit right in."

"What?"

"The handsome doctor looks like part of the family."

"He's known us forever. We went to school together," I say, shutting this line of questioning down. "Momma was his third-grade teacher."

"When I asked the good doctor about the records he brought, he said he's hoping the music will remind you of high school jazz ensemble and entice you to join his band."

"Until I'm certain Momma and Aria won't be pulling anymore river escapades, I can't add another responsibility to my plate."

"I think living in fear of what *could* happen is…" Winnie points to the dust cloud speeding up the lane. "Someone's late to the party."

I tent my hand over my eyes. "Everyone we invited is here."

"Daddy!" Aria flies off the porch and runs to the gate.

"James?" My jaw drops and I choke on the dust swirling around the shiny black rental car coming to a stop in Momma's drive. "What the heck?"

Aria rips the gate open. "Daddy!" She has her arms around her father's neck the second he pokes his slick hair and dark glasses out of the car. "You came!"

James jumps out of the vehicle with the ease of a man who prides himself on how good his middle-aged body looks in skinny jeans and a tight, white t-shirt. "Told you I would." He scoops up Aria and swings her around. By the time he sets her on the ground, Aria is beaming.

I start for him, intent on wringing his sorry neck, but Winnie pulls me back. "Let's see what happens."

"I thought you weren't coming, Daddy."

"Wouldn't miss this for the world." He taps her nose. "Brought you something."

"What?"

He reaches into the back seat and pulls out an expensive leather case. "Thought it was time you had your own camera." He drops the strap over Aria's head.

Aria fingers the block dangling against her chest. "Thanks." Disappointment dulls her smile. "I thought you were getting me a new piano."

"You have a piano." He pushes a strand of her hair away from her face. "Back home."

"But I live here now."

"Not for long."

How dare he put our daughter in the middle of this mess. In the time it takes for James to slide his sunglasses up onto his Tom Cruise haircut, I exchange my shock for anger.

I shake loose of Winnie and storm to the gate. "What are you doing here, James?"

A side-winder smile splits his tanned face, confirming my suspicion that he's been hiding on his parents' tropical island until the bad press dies down. "You look good, Charlotte."

I jam my hands on my hips. "Why are you in Texas?"

"I invited him," Aria defends.

"Why?"

"It's *her* birthday." Momma threads her arm through mine. "I told Aria she could invite whomever she pleased to my home."

The mental energy I'm expending to process James's threat is the only thing keeping me from ripping into Momma.

James steps forward and offers my mother his hand. "Sara, you look…"

She doesn't accept. "Better than you expected?"

"I was going to say you look good."

"Well," Momma says. "You look…hungry."

He flashes a smirk at me. "Starving."

Before I can flail my mother for colluding with my daughter, I feel Momma tug me in close, her age-old warning to hold my tongue. "Aria," she says calmly. "Why don't you get your *guest* a plate?"

"Hope you made one of your to-die-for peach pies, Sara." James gives Momma a peck on the cheek.

The stiffening of Momma's spine is imperceptible to the untrained eye. But I can feel every muscle in her compact little body bracing for battle. In an instant, she's once again the same mother bear who told my first-grade teacher that she'd be sorry if she ever tried to make me drink all of my milk again.

"Hummingbird cake is Aria's favorite." Momma's aim is level, steady, purposeful. "I hope you're not disappointed, James."

"Whatever the birthday girl wants, right?"

"Unlike some people, Aria's smart enough to know that we don't always get what we want." Momma's grip holds me stationary as James and Aria saunter over to the food table.

Everyone snaps into gear. Itty snags an empty platter off the table and holds it so Bo can take the meat off the grill. Teeny and Ira scurry to remove plastic wrap from the salads.

"Let me go, Momma," I growl between clenched teeth.

"For once,"—Momma pulls me tighter—"use your head. Not your heart."

"He's here for Aria," I confess.

"Then this family will just have to see to it that he leaves empty-handed."

Chapter 33

CHARLOTTE

Toward sunset, I'm leaning against a porch pillar, my temper simmering just below a boil. The hateful stare I have fixed on James doesn't seem to be affecting his horseshoe game in the least.

"Thought you could use a drink." Itty holds out two icy bottles.

I cut a sideways glance at the awkward giant standing beside me. "Is Coke the strongest thing we've got?"

"Come to band practice tonight and I'll take you to the Sonic for something that has a little more kick."

I nod toward the man my daughter's busy adoring. "I'm married."

"It's an invitation to play some music and have a limeade, Charlotte. Not a proposition to jump in the sack."

Startled by Itty's straightforwardness, my focus whiplashes to him. "Sorry, Itty."

"No apology necessary."

I can feel his gaze trail mine back to James.

We sip our Cokes in silence. James seems to sense our scrutiny and proceeds to make three consecutive ringers on the stake. After the last horseshoe lands with a steel-on-steel clang, Aria cheers then throws her arms around her father's neck. Her reaction to her father succeeding at something so simple reminds me of how much I loved my own father...faults and all. Having my child's father involved in her life is the picture I'd always envisioned. I intended to do things differently than my mother. Work. Marriage. Kids. Everything. Yet, here I am wishing Aria would see the truth for herself.

"James makes the game look easy." Itty takes a swig of his drink.

"It's what initially attracted me to him."

"Horseshoes?"

"No." While I take a long draw from my soda bottle, Itty says nothing. His non-judgmental quiet invites me to reveal my aches and pains on my own time, an invitation I can't resist. "After Caroline and Daddy died, I was tired of life being hard. I wanted easy for a change. James seemed like the solution. Smart, ambitious, successful." I take another sip. "Imagine my disappointment when I learned that nothing with James is ever easy."

Itty ponders my revelation. "Music is a great stress reliever."

I turn and study Itty carefully. He's not movie-star handsome like James. And yet, something about him is very attractive. Perhaps it's the kindness of the smile framed by his red beard. Or the inner peace sparkling in his eyes. I'm not sure. But somewhere along the line, the scrawny boy who struggled beneath the weight of a tuba is now a broad-shouldered man capable of carrying many loads. Mine included, if I weren't a woman hell-bent on doing everything myself.

"Is this the prescription you give everyone dealing with a mentally unstable mother, a rogue husband, and a teenager barreling down heartbreak road?"

"I can only prescribe." Itty's large hand gently pats my shoulder. "Whether or not my patients take the medicine is up to them." He clinks his empty bottle with mine. "Sure you don't want to come to band practice?"

"It'll be late by the time we get this all cleaned up."

"Tomorrow's a holiday. You can sleep in."

"There are no holidays from some ailments, Itty."

He hands me his empty bottle. "We'll keep the doors to the sanctuary open if you change your mind. Thanks for letting me be part of your family today, Charlotte." He descends the porch steps. "Happy birthday, Aria," he calls, his good wishes booming across the lawn.

To my surprise, my daughter leaves her father and rushes over. "Thanks for coming, Doc."

"Always glad for an opportunity to check a patient's progress," he smiles. "You're going to have to bring me up to speed on the latest in brain games so I can prescribe them to my other patients."

Aria's face lights up. "You think they're working?"

"I think your grandmother's doing much better since you moved here. Don't let her give you any grief or slack off."

"I won't." Aria points to the record player still spinning out old jazz. "Don't forget your music."

Benjamin gives her a little shake of his head. "That's for you."

"Really? Your whole collection."

"*And* the record player."

"You sure?"

"Every good musician must expand their repertoire beyond their wheelhouse," he says. "Besides, I don't think this world can have too much music, do you?"

"No, I don't." Aria reaches up, throws her arms around Itty's neck, and gives him a quick hug. "Thanks, Doc." She turns and runs back to her father who's stopped his horseshoe game to watch the exchange. Envy doesn't look good on his perfect face.

Itty ambles to his four-wheel drive pickup, nods to me before he gets in, then drives off. As the dust cloud trailing him disperses so does my hazy thinking.

I stomp down the porch steps. "James."

"C, wait." Winnie flies out the screen door. "You sure you want to do this today?"

"Aren't you the one who said it's time I deal?"

"When you're calm."

"That ship has sailed." I storm toward the horseshoe pit. "Aria, can you help your Nana clean up?"

Aria sizes up my intentions in an instant. "Geez, Mom. If you need to talk to Daddy, just say so."

"Okay, run along so I can talk to your father."

"No."

"Ari."

"Do I need a lawyer?" James's attempt to make light of my tone is gas on my fire.

Feeling Aria's eyes boring into me, I do my best to appear calm. "Only if you're planning to slow up our settlement."

"What settlement?" Aria asks.

He shifts three horseshoes from hand to hand. "Look, Aria. Maybe you *should* go help your grandmother."

I'm done giving him a pass. "Tell her James."

"Tell me what, Daddy?" Aria's eyes cloud with concern. "Are you sick?"

"No, baby. Nothing like that." James tosses the horseshoes aside. "You know how much I love you and your mom, right?"

"But?" Aria's tone tells me her baloney meter has finally been activated. She may not be able to ascertain all the legal ramifications

James and I are facing, but my girl has proven herself astute and resourceful when it comes to relationships. Forcing her to choose a side will only push her from me.

I take a page from Momma's unwillingness to trash my father and decide to stand down. To let Aria see James's manipulation for herself. But unlike Momma, I stay close, ready to pounce if she can't handle this.

James combs his fingers through his hair, a tell of his I picked up on years ago that gives him away whenever he's about to lie. "But sometimes it's best for the family if parents…"

"Are you divorcing Mom?"

He looks to me for help, but when I give him none he nods. "I think it's for your good if your mother and I go our separate ways."

"No!" Aria raises both palms and backs away.

"Listen, Aria," James advances toward her. "I know this is hard, but once everything is settled and you're living with me, I'll see that you get to visit Texas and…"

"You want me to come back to DC?"

"It's your home," James says. "I've talked it over with your grandmother and she's going to move in and help us get you settled."

"Grandmother McCandless?"

"Yes."

"But Nana needs me."

267

"Your Grandmother McCandless can help you prepare for Juilliard and..."

"Nana's helping me."

James plants both hands on Aria's shoulders. "Your Nana almost got you killed."

"That's it." Ignoring my earlier inclination to let Aria handle her father, I step into the ring. "What are you talking about?"

James turns on me. "Aria told me about the river. About how she fell in and nearly drowned."

"Mom, I'm sorry."

I silence her with one brief look. "First of all, she didn't nearly drown."

"This time," James says.

"I was there." I leave out my frantic search in the stirred-up silt. "She's an excellent swimmer."

"Letting Aria live within easy access of a river that's already killed two people in this crazy, mixed-up family is out of the question." He waves his hand in the direction of the odd assortment of rubbernecking party guests. "Look at them! Two certifiable geriatrics. A gas station mechanic. A gypsy. A bat-crazy grandma." He turns and points his finger at me. "Are you running a ranch or a home for misfit toys?"

"Whom I choose to call family is my business."

"Family?" He scoffs. "Is that what you're calling this

menagerie?"

"That's enough," I say.

Disgust comes over his face. "What's happened to the high-powered, put-together lawyer I knew." He waves an accusatory hand over my t-shirt and paint-splattered overalls. "All I see is a backwater music teacher who can't pay her bills. There's not a judge in the country who'll grant you custody when I can give our daughter the world." He grabs Aria's arm. "I'm taking her and there's not a thing you can do about it."

I lunge for him. "Let her go!"

"Whoa!" Winnie floats between us. "There *is* one little thing Charlotte can do, James." She pulls a manila envelope from the pocket of her skirt. "Send you to jail."

"What are you talking about?"

"These are the signed affidavits of several *underaged* models willing to testify in open court of your...C, cover Aria's ears."

My gaze locks with the wide-eyed terror in my daughter's eyes. "Aria's old enough to hear the truth."

"Like her mother, she is wise beyond her years." Winnie's implication is not lost on me. When this is over, Aria deserves the whole story of the river and the valley it has cut between me and Momma.

James releases Aria and rips the envelope from Winnie's hand. "What is this crap?"

"The beginning of an extensive investigation into accusations of your *continued* sexual misconduct."

He scoffs and rolls the envelope into a club. "It's their word against mine."

"True," Winnie smiles. "However, in our country's current politically-correct environment, it's much easier than it used to be to prove you used your power in the modeling industry to destroy the careers of women who refused to give into your lurid desires." Winnie thumps the envelope. "You'll sign whatever custody agreement we send your lawyer. You'll be prompt with your child support. And…"

The distinctive cock of a gun cuts off Winnie's ultimatum. I don't have to turn to know who's brandishing the shiny barrel to my left.

"And you won't ever threaten my family again." Momma levels her aim at James. "Get off our land, you, sorry excuse of a man."

Chapter 34

SARA

In a way, I'm relieved Charlotte has finally agreed to tell Aria about Caroline's accident and Martin's suicide. Now I don't have to. Makes it easier for me to remain Aria's favorite. Unless, of course, Charlotte lays the blame for these tragedies at my feet. Which, truth be known, is where the blame truly belongs. After all, if I'd been truthful with my girls, they would have known about Martin's secret weakness. I could have forbidden them from accompanying their drunken father to the river that day, they would have understood why, and none of this would have happened.

I scoot around the piano bench and inch a little closer to the window. Ira thinks it's wrong of me to eavesdrop on the conversation taking place on the porch swing. But just because Charlotte's decided to be open with her daughter, that doesn't mean she's ready to clear the line of communication with her mother. I need to know where I stand with Charlotte, especially after I pulled a gun on her husband.

"Ember says my dad's hot." Aria's unnaturally giddy voice reminds me of that short-sheeted laugh thing Charlotte does whenever she's worried a conversation will not go well.

"I'm sure he's still steaming." Charlotte's remarkably controlled. "James hates to be one-upped."

"Geez, Mom. Hot doesn't mean mad at you. It means handsome. Good-looking."

Charlotte laughs, freer than she has in years. "I'm not as out of touch as you and your grandmother seem to think."

"Did you tell Nana what Daddy was planning?"

I can hear Charlotte ripping that charm I gave her back and forth on the chain around her neck. I pray it gives her courage.

"No."

It hurts that we've come to this, but I can't blame her for growing weary of trying to scale the wall I built.

"Why didn't you tell me?"

There's a long moment of silence, one I fully understand. Charlotte had only wanted what mothers have wanted since the beginning of time: to spare her child the painful cost of loving someone who does not deserve it. I'd done the same. But in the end, not letting my daughters know of their father's weaknesses had only hurt them more. I pray Charlotte doesn't make my mistakes.

Twenty-five years can spool past faster than the river at flood stage.

"You deserve a beautiful, stress-free childhood, not an ugly custody battle. And that's what it will be if I fight him. Your father will drag our current lifestyle before the court and I'll be forced to drag his past from the shadows." Charlotte exhales slowly. "I don't want you to think less of your father...or me, for that matter."

"You gotta quit treating me like a baby, Mom."

"You're right," Charlotte says. "I know firsthand how scary it is to be kept in the dark. You can start imagining all sorts of reasons why, reasons that just aren't true."

I swipe proud, happy tears from my cheeks, grateful for well-grounded maturity the Lord had accomplished in my daughter's life...in spite of me.

Charlotte clears her throat. "I loved growing up here, Ari." Her appreciation surprises me. "I have so many wonderful memories."

"Did you swim in the river?"

"Nearly every day in the summer."

It's as if Charlotte's willingness to go back in time is freeing up memories fossilized inside my head. My mind skips like a rock across the water and lands on one particularly hot afternoon spent at the river's edge. The girls are probably five and seven. Hand and hand, Caroline, Charlotte, and I wade into the shallows. Tiny minnows dart around our ankles. We're splashing and laughing and having a wonderful time when Martin waves to us from high on the bluff. Stripped to his swimming trunks, he's sporting a rancher's tan—white chest, brown arms and face—even though he's completely given up on ranching.

"This is how you do a back flip, ladies." His teasing shout becomes a rock skipping across the water, a rock that sinks at my feet.

At the exact same instant, Charlotte and I scream, "No!"

Martin's feet leave the bluff.

Frozen by fear and unable to do a thing, we watch his twisting plunge toward the swimming hole. I brace for his body to shatter. But a split second before impact, Martin's hands come together and he enters the water slick as a needle threaded through cloth.

"Teach me, Daddy," Caroline crows when he surfaces twenty yards from us. She splashes to meet him, grabs his hand and says, "I'm going to be just like you," as they scramble up the canyon wall, I know that she already is. Headstrong. Daring. Reckless.

Caroline dives again and again, determined to master her father's flip.

But not Charlotte.

My youngest sticks close to me, nursing a mad as hot as mine. It would be several years before Charlotte's father would entice her to go against my protestations and dive off the bluff.

The first time her lithe body arched in the air and sliced an opening in the river with ease, I knew my baby girl had stopped needing me.

So, after Charlotte's sister died, I told myself she could handle things on her own. But deep down, I knew this was a lie. Charlotte was as lost as I without Caroline. She tried to come close, but I wouldn't let her or Martin anywhere near my broken heart. I hadn't meant to push either of them away, but my grief was a balloon growing bigger and bigger with each labored breath. I prayed for the balloon to pop. To free me from the dark bubble. But it never did.

"Night, Nana." Aria's peck to my cheek jerks me back to the present and the unnerving realization that I'd not heard the end of their conversation. "My birthday was...different."

My mind is swimming. I'd missed Charlotte's take on those horrible events. How much had she told her? What had she said about me? About her father? I start to ask Aria, but I don't have the heart to disturb the peace on her face. "Sorry I pointed a gun at your father."

"I'm glad Mom's gotten rid of all the shotgun shells."

I smile. "Me too." I grab her hand. "You okay?" Her weak shrug gives me no choice but to leave the subject alone. For now. "Tomorrow's a new day."

"You're lucky, Nana."

"Why's that?"

"Every day is a new day for you."

As she trudges up the stairs, I wish she wasn't right. But I know she is. Soon I won't be able to sort the past from the present. Alzheimer's will wash my memories and motivations downstream and far beyond my reach. Asking Charlotte's forgiveness is something I can no longer put off.

I reach for the pencil beside the sheet music Aria and I have been working on for her Juilliard audition.

With a shaky hand, I make myself a note. I jot *Please forgive me, Charlotte* right above the appropriately titled Chopin's Nocturne…nighttime prayers.

Chapter 35

CHARLOTTE

The sky is pinking over the hills. I sip coffee and enjoy the peaceful motion of the porch swing. Everyone else is still in bed. It's been a couple of weeks since Momma, Teeny, and Ira helped me clean up the mess after Aria's birthday party and her father's visit. We're all still worn out, but to my surprise, Winnie was right. Dealing with the past, while there's still time, is the only way to ensure this family's future.

The screen creaks open and Momma steps outside, weak tea sloshing over the edge of the cup in her shaky hand. "Morning, Charlotte."

There is something very special in the conversations I've had with my mother since she stood up for me with James. Momma and I are both going through transitions in our lives. There's a lot on our minds. But she's on my side. She's always been on my side. I know

277

that now. Not that either of us have actually come out and talked about what happened at the birthday party. That would be so unlike the Slocum women. But working to protect Aria from the hurt of my divorce from her father has taught me the fragility of mother-daughter relationships. How easily they can be broken, but also how with a bit of communication and unconditional love, they can be restored. Now, whenever Momma talks, I feel as if she's trying to tell me something. I don't want to push her away by trying to apologize for my part in our stand-off and it's too much to hope that she would ever apologize to me. But I hang on to every word she says. Just in case.

"Morning, Momma." I pat the swing cushion. "Join me."

I hold her cup while she settles. We swing in silence, sipping our drinks. Our deep, untroubled breaths seem to sync up as we savor the sounds and smells of the waking countryside. For the first time in years, I'm enjoying having my mother beside me.

My gaze drifts to the bony hand resting on Momma's thigh. Blue veins snake the swollen knuckles and fingers that I've watch roll out a thousand perfect pie crusts. Nicks and scratches litter her paper-thin skin because she insists she's immune to rose picker's disease.

Momma points to the line of empty bird nests made of mud and chicken feathers tucked beneath the eaves. "We're going to have an early fall."

"How do you know?"

"The swallows have migrated south."

"Are you sure they didn't just give up on their war with me?"

She snorts. "They'll be back."

"How do you know?"

"By summer's end, I usually take a broom to them myself."

"You?"

"I'm not a saint, Charlotte Ann." She nods toward the stained porch planks. "They make a huge mess."

"Don't we all."

The chains of the swing creak as we swing in silence and sip our hot drinks.

Momma releases a heavy breath. "I should have told you Aria invited her father."

My heart misses a beat. "A little heads-up would have been nice," I admit.

"I didn't think he'd come." Momma picks at the lint on her robe. "He's only been here once since you two married."

Wading in with the wrong response could close this door I've waited a long time to have opened. "Can't argue that."

"Aria won't go with him."

"What if she does?" I work to speak around the lump of fear that's growing inside of me. "What if I'm not enough?" I rise from the swing and toss my cold coffee over the porch railing. "James has vacation homes. Money for Juilliard. A grand piano in the library."

"He also has a problem keeping his pants zipped."

I don't know what's scarier, Momma's rapidly disappearing filter or these occasional bursts of nailing the obvious. I laugh but it's only to keep from crying. "What if having her father is more important to Aria than what he's done?"

"I've asked myself that a hundred times a day." Regret weights Momma's small admission.

"Momma, I didn't mean—"

"Charlotte, I did the best I could. Kids don't come with lesson plans. You make your decisions for them as you go along. You do the best you can and pray that one day they'll have a child of their own who is equally as taxing. And when they grow up and start making mistakes of their own, you pray maybe, just maybe they'll be able to forgive yours."

Her empathetic expression spurs me to risk a question. "How did you stand losing them, Momma?"

Sadness sweeps her face. "The loss of a husband and the loss of a child are not the same thing. A child is such a part of you, it's like you're breathing the same air. The way they look at you when you come in the door at night. Wrap their arms around your neck when they've had a bad dream. Or snuggle in close during a long sermon..." her voice trails off.

I'm hungry for more, but Momma's engaged gaze has disappeared behind a window. I can only assume she's slipped into the past. And though I'm curious as to what she sees, I know the day will come when she stays there and never returns to the present.

The old rooster crows and Momma blinks.

She looks at me, and I'm sure it's me she sees. "Finding a place to belong, then sharing a life with those we love…that is the essence of living." The smile spreading slowly across her lips is meant to reassure me. "Aria belongs here, with her family, and she knows it."

Chapter 36

CHARLOTTE

Evan." I capture the Miller boy's elbow as he saunters past the piano at the end of class. "I need to speak to you for a few minutes."

His dark brows furrow, but this kid's too good at maintaining his cool façade to telecast his full concern. "Whatever."

I gather the music sheets spread across the piano until all the students have cleared the auditorium. "Have a seat, Evan."

He picks up a chair, twirls it around, and straddles it with little effort. "What did I do now?"

I pull my laptop out of my bag. "Well, quite a bit actually." I scroll to my video files. "After I reviewed your video solo submission for your six weeks grade, I took the liberty of sending it to a friend in NYU's music department."

He gives me his trademark "whatever" shrug, but his eyes have widened considerably.

"Don't you want to know what she said?"

"Do I have a choice?"

I shake my head. "They're having auditions for music scholarships after the holiday break."

"So?"

"So, if you're willing to work hard, I think we could have you ready."

"I ain't singing in front of anyone."

"That's why I had everyone submit videos for their six-week tests. I really wanted to hear you sing. Your voice is…well…frankly one of the best I've ever heard."

"I don't sing in front of people."

"Not yet." I turn the computer screen to him. I tap on the video that displays his ease in the privacy of his bedroom. "But if we start small, I think I can help you conquer your stage fright."

He shakes his head. "Ain't happenin'."

I fish my charm necklace free and hold it out. "See this?"

"Yeah. So?"

"I had a severe case of stage fright. Totally bombed my first piano recital."

"No way," he scoffs. "You're amazing on the keys, Mrs. M."

"For the longest time, my mother was the only one who knew." I press the charm between my fingers and drag it back and forth. "She gave me this necklace. Said I should squeeze it tight whenever I'm afraid."

"You want me to wear a magic necklace?"

"The necklace didn't give me courage, it was the fact that someone believed in me. Momma's encouragement helped me believe in myself. I started working harder, gaining more confidence in my skill and my gift. One day, Momma told me she'd invited our Avon lady for a little concert. "I can't," I argued."

"I dare you," Momma challenged.

"I took a deep breath, went to the piano, and played for her. Although I never made eye contact with LaVera, I'd managed to make it through the entire piece. Unwilling to accept anything less than complete freedom from my fears, my mother set it up for me to play for her Bible school class the very next Sunday. Then she signed me up for band. With each risk I took, my courage grew." I look him in the eyes. "You sang into a camera. Now, I want you to take one small step and sing just for me."

"Now?"

"Now."

"I'll be late to English."

If I give him a millimeter of wiggle room, he'll take it. So, I set the computer on the piano and slid into position on the bench. "I've already cleared it with your English teacher." I start playing the introduction to the song the choir had just rehearsed in class. "Sing. I dare you."

He lifts his chin. Jaw set. I continue to play. I start singing. By the time I get to the chorus, the music has claimed his soul and set his foot to tapping. He can't help but join me. His tone is pitch perfect.

"Chest voice," I coach as I head toward the second verse.

His diaphragm tightens and sends a sound out of his mouth that surprises us both.

I smile. "Stand." To my joy, he does. "Hang on to the piano."

His knuckles whiten over the edge of the piano but he doesn't stop singing.

I drop my voice at the bridge and let him carry the song on his own. "Look at me."

His face turns toward mine and he rewards me with a small, pleased-at-himself smile. By the time we reach the end of the song, his voice is filling the auditorium.

I lift my hands from the keys. As the music we'd made together slowly dies, I hear Momma's voice. The one that dared me to get to know my students and what made them tick.

"Well, Evan Miller," I smile. "You just sang for your first audience. What do you think?"

He slowly shakes his head and peels his hand from the piano. "I didn't die."

"I'll see you after school." I hand him the excuse note I'd written out ahead of time. "Come prepared to work."

Lynne Gentry

Chapter 37

CHARLOTTE

The once-over I gave the bathroom this week will have to do. There is still a pile of Ira's laundry, a dishwasher to reload after Teeny cleared the table last night, and a long grocery list that needs to be filled to keep all of us fed. I don't mind the extra chores, but it's hard to juggle caring for everyone, coaching Evan, *and* finding the time to give the one-on-one attention Momma and Aria deserve.

"You should wear boots, Caroline." Momma stands on the back porch with a small bouquet of roses she's clipped. "Snakes are bad this time of year."

A brisk breeze hails from the north. Summer is not the only season slipping away. Just when our lives were beginning to merge and mesh, Momma's moments of lucidity have started dropping like the river cypress leaves.

I shake dried grass clippings from a pair of old tennis shoes. "Ari and I have worn a path through the pasture. It's easy to keep an eye out."

Since my talk with Aria, I've enjoyed the weekly treks the two of us have been making to tend the family gravesite. Spending time at the river has been a double blessing. While it's been strangely cathartic, it's also building the relationship bridge with my daughter that I'm beginning to realize I'll probably never fully reconstruct with my mother.

"Rattlers can be hard to spot."

"Momma, it's cooled down enough that I don't think we have to worry about snakes anymore." I slip my feet inside the tennis shoes. "Want to come with us?"

"No."

"Maybe next Saturday then." I call through the screen door. "Ari, let's go."

Aria clomps onto the porch wearing the pair of scuffed cowboy boots Ember gave her for her birthday. "Want to come with us today, Nana?"

"That woman just asked me." Momma points at me like I'm a stranger.

"It's me, Charlotte," I say.

Momma's face clouds. "I've got pies to make."

"Pies?" Aria shoots me a look that screams *she's getting worse, do something*, Mom.

But I'm at a loss. A couple of weeks ago Momma was dispensing sound parenting advice. Making me feel better about my decision to fight James for Aria. She was more herself than she'd been in years. The next day it was like she walked through some sort of transparent door, locked me out, and threw away the key. I've knocked and knocked. It's looking less and less likely that my mother, the woman who had a quick and ready answer for everything, is ever coming out again. I should have said I'm sorry while she could still remember what that means.

I stick my head inside the screen door. Ira and Teeny are sitting at the kitchen table, sipping coffee. "Ira, Momma's a little confused."

Ira pushes back from the table. "We've got this, Charlotte." He steps onto the porch and wraps a gentle arm around her shoulders. "Come on, Sara."

Momma jerks free of his hold. "No."

Ira doesn't let her thorny mood rile him. Instead, he offers his hand and keeps speaking in a soothing voice, "Bojangles is talking trash this morning."

"Give him a slice of pear!" Momma snaps.

"Done tried that," Ira says. "This new bird is more temperamental than you."

"Sweet Moses! Do I have to do everything around here, Martin?" Momma storms past Ira and tromps straight to the bird cage sitting in the kitchen window.

I'm horrified that Momma has taken to calling Ira by my father's name and I tell him so.

He shrugs. "Been called worse." He steps inside, turns and waves through the screen. "You girls be careful out there." His I've-got-this nod is a reassurance I've come to rely upon more and more.

"Thanks, Ira."

Hand in hand, Aria and I set off for the big live oak at the far end of the north pasture. The wind sweeping over the bluff can't blow away the tiny pieces Momma's decline is chiseling from my heart. How I wish my father and sister were here to help shoulder the burden.

River treks from long ago spring to mind. Secrets were hard to hide out in the open spaces of the pasture. It must have been so difficult for Daddy to keep his bottled up.

I start the weekly conversation with Aria by bringing up school. She asks about Evan and I tell her how excited I am to help him prepare for his audition. I also tell her how pleased I am with the friends she's making, especially Ember. Aria answers with just enough information to let me know that what she really wants to talk about is my father. The offense I would have felt before by her teenage need for privacy with her friends is gone. In its place is the trust that comes when there's a healthy bridge, should either of us need to talk.

"Tell me another story about my grandfather," Aria pleads.

"You're a bottomless pit."

"I've got a lot of catching up to do."

I inhale the holiday scent of scrub juniper and begin to tell the story it brings to mind. "One Christmas Eve your grandfather agreed that all of us could camp on the bluff to watch for Santa."

"In December?"

"This is Texas. Chilly, but not freezing."

"Can we do it?"

"No."

"Why not?"

"Because we awoke beneath a tent that had collapsed under the weight of an unexpected snow. We nearly froze to death before Daddy got us back to the house." I let my mind drift back to the smell of cedar popping in the fireplace, old quilts wrapped around my shoulders, and my father passing out hot chocolate while Momma sneaked around and put the presents under the tree. "It was the best Christmas ever." The happy ending to this story is sweet on my tongue. Not because I'm trying to sugar-coat Aria's opinion of my father, but because that's how I truly remember him.

The realization that I remember my father fondly despite learning the truth about him jars me.

Huffing as we climb higher, I ponder the hand my mother had in shaping the image I had of him. I saw my father as a hero, not

291

because he'd done anything particularly deserving of the title, but because that's how my mother saw him. She wanted me to love him, flaws and all, as much as she did.

"Ari," I say after we reach the bluff. "My father wasn't perfect." Hands clasped tightly, we inch our toes to the very edge of the ledge. From this vantage point, we can see the Addisonville water tower and the winding path the river cuts through the hills splashed with the color of red sumac and yellow river cypress. "And neither is yours. But it's okay to still love them."

"I know, but the divorce is going to be final in a few weeks."

Deep water swirls below me. "The only thing that is ever final is death, my sweet. If you want to live with your dad, I'm sure we could renegotiate our settlement agreement."

She shakes her head. "Aunt Winnie is right, he doesn't want me."

"Your dad loves you."

"Yeah, but he loves his freedom more, right?"

"Parents are tricky things. We're imperfect people trying to do the best we can."

"Even Nana?"

Years of happy memories—recollections of my mother holding me close, teaching me piano, and always cheering me on—flood my mind. Memories that had so long been buried under my anger and grief.

"Even Nana."

Aria's grip relaxes within mine. Hand in hand, we stand in silence. I'm taking in the twists and turns of the river canyon when my gaze lands upon the tiny fossils, no bigger than little bits of shell, sparkling along the limestone walls. Like Momma and me, these ancient creatures were minding their own business, happily living out their purpose, when suddenly some unexpected and terrible act of nature trapped them in this valley. Only God knew that what had once seemed so catastrophic would lend beauty to a day far in the future.

I pray He can redeem my past to aid my daughter's future. "Tell you what, Ari. Let's try to give both of them the benefit of the doubt. Okay?"

"Okay."

An angry rattle buzzes on my right. "Don't move," I tighten my grip on Aria's hand. "Snake."

"Where?" she whispers.

"Shhh." My gaze scours the rocks for the viper's location.

Coiled less than a yard from my foot is one of the biggest rattlesnakes I've ever seen. Before I can think of what to do, a jolt of pain ten times worse than a wasp sting pierces my ankle.

Aria screams and the snake wheels and disappears over the rocks. "Mom, did he bite you?"

Vibrations, much like those received from an electrical shock, shoot up my leg. I look down to where Aria is pointing. Two prick marks tattoo my ankle.

"Mom, you're bleeding!"

I power through the fog that has already started descending upon me. "Run. Get Ira. Tell him to bring the tractor with the front-end loader on it."

"He can't see to drive it."

"Well then, you'll have to get Nana to drive."

"I can't leave you here. What if that snake comes back?"

"Your scream sent him packing. Run, Aria. Now!"

Chapter 38

SARA

Ira!" The young girl's scream is followed by the slamming of the screen door. "Help! Ira, where are you?"

I leave the piano and trundle off to the kitchen. "What are you doing in my kitchen?"

The blonde girl ripping through the cupboard drawers is red faced and breathing hard. "Nana, a rattlesnake bit Mom."

Something inside of me shatters like a fragile window pane that's been struck by an unexpected fly ball. Fresh air rushes in and blows away the cobwebs. "Where is she?"

"Sitting under the oak tree on the bluff." Aria holds a clean dishcloth under the faucet. "She wants Ira to get the tractor and come pick her up so that the venom won't pump to her heart.

"That old man can't see a thing. I'll drive."

Ira rushes into the kitchen. "What's going on?"

Aria quickly explains the whole thing again. "We need the tractor."

Ira says, "Let me get my glasses."

"It's my tractor. I'll drive it." I push him aside and hurry to the porch.

Ira tells Teeny to call 9-1-1 while I shove my feet into a pair of boots. We all rush to the barn. For some reason, there's a strange tractor-sized hole on one side of the shed. I don't trust myself to maneuver the tractor through that opening without taking off a few more boards. I rush around to the barn doors, unhook the latch and swing them open. Lucky for me, Charlotte had taken the time to back the tractor in after she'd finished brush-hogging the fence rows.

"Hop on." While Ira and Aria scramble up behind the driver's seat, I study the levers and gauges trying to remember how to make this thing go.

"Turn the key," Ira says. "There, on your right."

"I've been driving this tractor for years, Martin." I press the clutch and turn the key. The old engine sputters, then dies.

"Crank it again," Ira urges.

"I know what I'm doing." I pump the gas and twist the key. When the tractor chugs to life, I can't help but feel a little vindicated. "Hang on." I drop the shifter into gear and release the clutch. We shoot forward with a lurch and putt across the yard.

Aria hops off when we reach the pasture gate and quickly undoes the latch. She waves me through and I stop long enough for her to climb back on. It feels good to be behind the wheel again.

"Hurry, Nana!" Aria's pecking around on her phone. "We've got to get her to a doctor within thirty minutes."

Like me, the hurrying days of this tractor are long past. But I stomp the gas pedal as far as it will go. Black smoke belches from the exhaust pipe. The little bit of speed we pick up is soon lost on the climb toward the bluff. Memories of the horrible things I've seen from the highest vantage point in the county swirl in my mind.

What if I'm too late…again?

"There she is!" Aria points to the live oak. "Mom!"

Charlotte's obviously still conscious because she gives a weak little wave and thanksgiving leaps from my lips. By the time we get to her, the color has drained from Charlotte's face and she's sweating like the temperature has risen to a hundred degrees on this cool fall day. But she's still alive. That's all that matters. My baby is alive.

Ira and Aria are off the tractor before I'm completely stopped. I push in the clutch, shift into neutral, then set the parking break. Unwilling to risk that I might not get the old beast started again, I leave the tractor running and climb down.

"Oh, baby!" I squat beside my daughter and give her a good going over. "Momma's here."

297

"I should have listened to you, Momma," spills out of Charlotte's mouth as Aria places the cool cloth on her mother's forehead. "He got me good."

Charlotte's ankle is swollen and a bruise is beginning to spread beyond the fang marks.

"Well, let's hope your heart is as hard as your head." I take her hand. "Martin, you and that girl there help me load this one into the bucket."

"I think I can walk."

"No," Ira says as he drapes one of Charlotte's arms across his shoulders. "You just try to relax."

It takes some doing, but the three of us work together until Charlotte is laid out in the bucket of the front-end loader.

"Go, Nana!" Aria shouts after she climbs up behind me.

I wheel the tractor around and beeline it to the house. In the driveway, Teeny is standing by the idling Caddy with one hand tented over her eyes, the other holding out my purse. "How is she?"

"In desperate need of a doctor." The shakes are threatening my knees, but I can't give in to the possibility that I could lose another child. "Where's that ambulance?"

"I called," Teeny says. "They said *we* could probably get her to town faster than they could come get her."

"Sweet Moses!" I grab my purse from Teeny. "Let's go, Ira!"

"But Nana, you don't drive on the roads anymore."

"I do today, kiddo."

Chapter 39

CHARLOTTE

After Momma sideswipes the Wootens' mailbox, a surge of nausea forces me to lay my head in Aria's lap and close my eyes.

"Mom!" Aria pats my face roughly. "Wake up!"

"I'm okay, Ari." I mumble, squeezing my eyes tighter as the car swerves again. "Nana's driving is more than I can stomach right now."

"See why I need my learner's permit?"

The throb from my ankle has reached my knees, so I massage my hand and try to focus on Aria's terrified face. "Point taken." Another jerk forces me to close my eyes again.

"You hang on, Charlotte." Ira's knuckles are white on the dash. "Sara and I will get you to the hospital."

"I googled snakebite." Aria shakes me gently. "Mom, I can't monitor your physical or mental state if you fall asleep."

"Aria, use that phone of yours to call Dr. Ellis," Momma shouts from the driver's seat. Her voice is not that of the confused woman I'd spoken to earlier this morning. Instead, it's the voice of a woman who's faced more than her share of tragedy, a woman who's done what had to be done, and intends to get it done again.

It is the voice of my mother.

"I called Dr. Ellis on my way to the house, Nana," Aria says. "He's going to meet us at the hospital."

The next ten miles are the longest of my life. Momma's jerky slowing and accelerating at each of the various curves tosses me around on the back seat. I dare to pry one eye open. Branches of overhanging trees fly by. Just when I think I can't take another minute of watching Aria fight tears, my mother, the woman who can't find her way from her kitchen to her bedroom, somehow drives us right up to the emergency room doors.

Itty is waiting with a gurney and two burly aids when the back door opens. "Let me get her out of the car," he tells Momma. "Ira, I'm counting on you to keep Sara and Aria company while I see what kind of trouble Charlotte's gotten herself into now."

"Trouble?" I say, my tongue fuzzy. "I was ambushed by an angry rattler."

"How big?" Itty scoops me from the back seat and pulls me to his broad chest.

I'm too busy trying to sort the reason for my racing heart to answer.

"Huge!" Aria answers for me. "Maybe five feet long."

"That's good." Benjamin places me on the gurney. "The bigger the better."

"What?" Aria's eyes swell to the size of baseballs.

"Older rattlers are far less likely to waste venom on something they can't eat." Benjamin nods and the aids wheel me inside. "Y'all make yourselves at home in the waiting room, Mrs. Slocum. I'll send someone out to get you after I've assessed my patient."

Itty issues commands once we're in the exam room and two nurses scurry to do his bidding. I try not to flinch when he approaches me with a pair of scissors and proceeds to slit my capris up to my thigh.

"Guess city girls aren't used to watching for snakes." He drops the scissors on a metal tray.

As he gently removes the fabric from my swollen leg, I concentrate on the ceiling tiles. "There are plenty of sidewinders in the city," I say between clenched teeth. "But they wear two-thousand-dollar suits and never rattle before they strike."

"Touché." Itty takes a sharpie out of his pocket and makes a mark on my leg.

I push up on my elbows and stare at the black line. "I'm dying and you're playing connect the dots?"

He places his hand on his heart and feigns hurt. "This is a

cutting-edge medical treatment."

"And if it doesn't work, you can always ask Momma to get the shot gun and put me down."

"Only as a last resort." He smirks.

I fall back on the bed. "I hate small towns."

"Relax. It's an old trick I learned in Boy Scouts." Once he sees that I'm in no mood for teasing, he goes on to explain, "Marking the extent of your swelling upon arrival allows me to monitor the progression of the venom spreading. Monitoring the swelling is the only way for me to know how much venom that old boy pumped into you." He caps the marker. "How long has it been since you sustained the bite?"

"Thirty to forty-five minutes."

"Any numbness or tingling in your arms or face?"

"Maybe a little tingling."

"Okay." He lifts my foot to examine the puncture wounds. "Are you up to date with your tetanus shot?"

"I'm not sure."

"Well, I'll give you another one just to be sure." He lowers my swollen leg. "I'll have the nurse draw some blood and admit you for a night of observation."

"Observation? Aren't you going to give me antivenin?"

"Antivenin has a whole different set of risks." He presses my swollen calf. "Besides, why would you want to pay fifty to a hundred thousand dollars for a treatment insurance rarely covers when you may only need an antibiotic?"

"How will you know?"

"If you die, I'll know I should have gone with the high-dollar treatment."

I don't give him the satisfaction of laughing at his inability to resist tossing in another joke. "Shouldn't you at least make an X with that marker and suck out the poison?"

"You've watched too many old westerns. Forty percent of bites from older snakes are dry." He swabs a little alcohol on the puncture marks. "A night of observation, some antibiotics, then a week of putting no weight on that leg is all you'll need. Probably."

"A week?" I push up on my elbows again. "I can't be off my feet for a week."

"For one whole week, you get to let others take care of you." He types something into an iPad. "Ready for me to let your family come back?"

"If you've done everything you can, might as well let the huddled masses take a crack at saving me."

"Gratitude. One of the many rewards of being a small-town doc." He closes the cover on his iPad. "By the way, why was Sara behind the wheel of a car?"

"Because we were all under the impression that time was of the essence when treating snakebites and my demented mother was the best shot we had of getting me here alive."

"That's scary."

"Ari thought I was dying, but I had to keep my eyes closed because I was praying."

"The primary necessity of being a good caregiver is taking care of yourself."

"Right. I'll just kick back and let everyone wait on me for a change."

Itty's brow raises slightly. I don't know if it's the snake poison talking or the remnants of resentment I've been harboring, but my sarcastic edge is not lost on my old friend. "You want to bounce back from this?"

"I have to."

"Then you're going to have to make certain you're resting enough, regardless of all the obligations you're carrying due to your current living arrangement. Everything you invest into your personal well-being will benefit those who are going to eventually need more and more of your time and assistance." Itty pulls out his phone. "Your mother is a little shaken, so I'm going to call Winnie and see if she can drive your family home."

"Don't bother Win."

"Charlotte, I know you'd rather choke on your pride than swallow a morsel of it, but I can guarantee that a mental breakdown is in your future if you insist on doing this alone."

"You want to help?"

"That's what I've been trying to tell you."

"Fine." I turn my head to the window. "You tell Momma that Winnie's coming."

****

"We don't need that hippie to drive us home!" Momma's protests penetrate the closed door to my room. "I got us here, didn't I, Benjamin? I can get us home."

Bracing for a fight, I push the button on my bed rail elevating my head so that my gaze will be eye level with my infuriated mother.

Momma bursts into the room, her arms waving in frustration. "Tell this furry man that I'm perfectly capable of driving a car, Caroline."

"I'm Charlotte."

The correction throws Momma off long enough for Itty to jump in and change the subject. "Once I release Charlotte, she's going to need a few days of rest. Therefore, I'm going to contact Home Health and see what we can set up."

"I'm more than capable of taking care of my daughter, Benjamin. And I don't appreciate the insinuation that I've failed to take care of her up to now."

Itty holds up two bear-sized palms. "It's not a matter of simply keeping her well-fed. Charlotte needs serious relief from all of the..." he cut a look my way that said he was going out on a limb, but didn't care. "Charlotte needs a little fun in her life."

"Charlotte doesn't do fun anymore," Momma says.

"Well, as her mother, it's your responsibility to see that situation remedied. Have I made myself clear?"

The bluster seeps from Momma's shoulders. "I suppose a few *medicinal* suggestions would be helpful."

"That's the spirit." Itty's face is serious. "First on the list is a little fun. There's a local band that needs a good keyboardist."

"No, Itty," I say.

"Why not?" Momma demands.

"Playing with a band is not something I want to commit to right now."

"His band needs someone on the keys, Charlotte, not someone in the sheets."

"Momma, what's happened to your filter?"

She ignores me and points a ruler-straight finger at Itty. "How often does this band of yours rehearse?"

"One night a week."

"I think Benjamin's right," Momma plops into a chair. "A night of music would do you good." She smiles at Itty. "I'll see that she's there."

I let my head fall back on the pillow with a sigh.

"Great." Itty's eyes do not dart from the visual daggers I'm throwing his way. It's as if he can see right through my flimsy excuses. "We practice Sunday nights at seven."

"Sundays at seven," Momma repeats. "Where?"

"At the church."

"She'll be there," Momma confirms, ignoring my distressed moans. "With bells on."

Obviously pleased at his success, a smile breaks into Itty's beard. "I'll be back in a couple of hours with your tests results, Charlotte." He lightly pats my foot. "Remember, no weight on that leg for a week."

"Then I don't know how you expect me to drive to band practice." My exasperation narrows into a glare meant to burn holes in Itty's hard head. "Guess it'll be a few weeks before I can get there."

"I'll pick you up." Itty gives me a two-fingered salute then leaves the room.

"Is he whistling?" My unanswered question gets swallowed up by the questions Aria, Ira, and Momma are firing at me.

"Will you lose your leg, Mom?"

I cross my arms. "No."

"Are they going to give you antivenin?" Ira asks.

"Not unless the swelling goes past that ugly black line my doctor drew on my leg," I snap.

"I don't know why you're acting so pissy," Momma says.

"You really want to know, Momma?"

"I asked, didn't I?"

"Why did you tell Itty I'd play for his band?"

She gives a noncommittal shrug. "Benjamin's right, you do need more fun in your life."

"There's plenty going on in my life right now."

"Not much of it is fun," Momma mutters.

"Fun is overrated," I argue.

"I don't understand why you're not jumping at the chance to spend more time with Benjamin," Momma says. "He has good teeth and a respectable job."

"Momma, those two phrases don't add up to anything even remotely sensible."

"Sweet Moses, Charlotte Ann." Momma laughs and reaches for my hand. "It doesn't take a head filled with functioning brain cells to solve this equation." She points toward the sound of whistling echoing in the hall. "That man is crazy about you."

Chapter 40

CHARLOTTE

Early Sunday morning Itty appears at the foot of my hospital bed. "Swelling hasn't passed the mark. That's a good thing." He examines my puffy, black and blue ankle. "This hurt?"

I squirm under the pressure. "Feels like my whole leg is melting away."

"That's normal. But as far as I can tell, you're only going to suffer temporary tissue damage." He uncoils the stethoscope around his neck and rubs the bell against his palm. "Let's have another listen to your ticker."

"Knock yourself out." I turn my head to the window but I tense as he moves to my side.

He leans over and places hot metal atop my rapidly beating heart. "Hold your breath." He straightens and drapes the stethoscope around his neck, a pleased twinkle in his eyes. "Looks like you'll live."

I tug my gown into place. "My students will be thrilled."

"And your family."

"Momma probably won't even remember that I've been bitten."

"Oh, I think this one is sticking with her. She's called me five times this morning asking when you can come home."

"She *wants* me home?"

"The sooner the better."

"Are you just trying to make me feel better?"

He pulls out his phone and shows me his call history. Five times within fifteen minutes Fossil Ridge's landline number appears.

I know better than to trust Momma's brief mental reprieve, but for now, her concern for me is better medicine than the antibiotics flowing through my IV. "When can I go?"

"It'll take about an hour to process your discharge papers."

"The sooner the better."

An insolent smirk quirks one corner of his mouth. "No *thanks Itty for saving my life*?"

"Thanks."

"Heartwarming," he says. "Winnie's volunteered to give you a lift home." He hands the phone to me. "You want to call or shall I do that for you?"

"I believe you're the one who declared me an invalid in need of at least a week of hand and foot servitude."

"Touché." Itty scrolls through his contacts, then makes a big production of pressing the number. "Winnie, she's grouchy as a bear in spring, but she'll be ready to blow this joint by the time you get to town."

Two hours later, I'm checked out of the hospital and bumping toward Fossil Ridge in Winnie's little VW bug. I appreciate her willingness to take it slow over the cattleguard. The fence rows are tidy now that I've taken Ira's advice and bought five goats and set them free to frolic in the pasture. Except for the three-story turret that remains unpainted on Momma's big farm house, the scene is almost idyllic.

"Glad to be home?" Winnie asks as she steers around a pothole.

On the porch four people are waving. My smiling mother anchors the group. "Yes." And strangely enough, I mean it.

Winnie parks as close to the steps as she can.

"Mom!" Aria is the first to the passenger door. "We have everything ready, including a bed set up downstairs."

I pass my crutches to Ira. "Y'all didn't need to go to so much trouble."

"No trouble at all." Ira helps me balance until I can get squared away on the crutches. "Wish I could carry you."

"Just a little spotting on my left side is all I need, Ira."

"Hang on to her, Aria." Momma stands at the top of the steps. With a touch of relief, I recognize the old spark in her eyes. She doesn't call me by name, but I can tell from the way she smiles at me that today she knows me. Today, she's the same mother who spoiled me with homemade soup and ice cream after I had my tonsils out. It's all I can do not to run and jump into her arms.

"Will do, Nana."

Despite my clumsy effort, the three of us manage to make it up the steps. Winnie follows behind with the computer printout of Itty's detailed instructions and the bag of meds we picked up at the pharmacy. According to Penny, snakebite survivors can't be too careful.

I hobble past Teeny, who's holding the door with her hip and bobbing her head. "I can do your hair." She nudges her pink hairbow back into place. "You'll look nice with a bow."

"Thanks, Teeny." The aroma of fresh baked pumpkin bread fills me with the hope that my recovery will go better than I anticipated. "Something smells good." I aim for the recliner.

"Nana and I have been cooking all morning." Aria takes my crutches so that I can fall back into the chair. "Hope you're hungry."

"Nana's been in the kitchen?"

Aria leans in and whispers, "Don't worry, I supervised."

"In that case, I'm starving."

"Wait right here." Aria's enthusiasm raises my antennas, especially when she motions to Ira, Teeny and Momma and they all silently turn and scurry off to the kitchen like they have some secret.

313

That Momma can make a plan and remember it is…well…it's…perilous to trust the possibility that she's better.

Winnie sets my bag beside my chair. "Sara seems like her old self."

"For the moment." I pull the lever on the recliner and my feet pop into the air.

Winnie looks up. Seeing my grave expression, she smiles. "I'm just down the road."

"This is not going to go well."

"What's to screw up? You sit and they wait on you like a queen."

A few minutes later, Aria marches into the living room carrying the same tray Momma used when I was a sick child in need of warm soup and crackers.

Two pumpkin muffins are flanked by several strips of crisp bacon and a lovely bowl of chopped fruit. "Who did all of this?" I reach for the cup of steaming hot tea.

"Nana planned the menu and made the muffins," Aria beams. "Teeny and I chopped fruit and Ira fried the bacon."

Blinking back tears, I raise my gaze to my smiling mother. "You remembered my favorite breakfast."

The smile slides from her lips and her head cocks to the side. "I remember you're someone I love."

Chapter 41

CHARLOTTE

I pull the covers over my eyes and pretend I'm on a deserted island. Momma and Aria have been arguing since the alarm went off at six o'clock.

They spent the weekend wrestling over who got to plump my pillows, stuff me with soup and pie, and help me to the bathroom. While I've never enjoyed being the center of attention, I have to admit I could get used to having Momma look at me and see me. Not Caroline. Not some former student. But me. Her youngest daughter.

And I believe my own daughter has enjoyed being needed as much as I've enjoyed having her close. Had I known snakebite had these advantages, I would have traipsed across the pasture the moment I got back to Texas.

"Slocums do not skip school, young lady," Momma shouts.

"Mom." Aria pokes my shoulder. "Mom, tell Nana that I need to stay home."

I lower one corner of the blanket. "Ari, I'll be fine."

"But what if you have to get up?"

Three wrinkled faces peer over their glasses as they await my answer. "I've got plenty of help." I push the recliner to a seated position, careful to keep my leg elevated. I take Aria's hand. "You can help me by checking on my sub. Ask if she needs supplemental activities for the lesson plans I've uploaded."

"Mom, she doesn't even play the piano," Aria sighs. "Ember says Evan is worried he won't be ready for his audition."

"Tell him I can work with him if he can come out here."

"You can't sit at the piano," Momma says.

"Either you or Aria can accompany him." I turn my gaze to Momma. "He's ready for a LaVera-sized audience."

Momma's face scrunches. "Who?"

To be fair, the memory of how I finally conquered stage fright may not have been as meaningful to my mother as it had been to me. "Remember when you had our neighbor come listen to me play?" I coach.

Momma's brow pleats tighter, like she trying to squeeze the memory out. But when nothing comes to her, the lines on her forehead relax and she spews accusation. "Why on earth would I do that?"

Panic flashes across Aria's face. "See, I need to stay."

"Come on, Aria," Ira says. "I'll walk you to the end of the lane to catch the bus." He lifts the big stick in his hand. "There's not a snake in the county that will mess with me."

Why hasn't it dawned on me that the possibility of encountering another snake scared Aria nearly as much as her grandmother's unpredictable behavior? If Momma's good days are coming to an end, I don't want Aria to stand around and watch every heartbreaking detail. It will be hard enough on her when Momma dies.

Tears prick my eyes. Hard on everyone. "Thanks, Ira."

"Always does me good to stretch these old legs," he says, rubbing his bald head. "Give me a minute to get my cap, little lady." On his way past Momma, Ira stops and whispers, "Sara, kettle's whistling. Might want to brew the tea."

Without argument, Momma turns and heads for the kitchen.

Aria holds up her phone. "Promise you'll text if you need me?"

"Try not to grow up too fast, Ari." I kiss her hand. "Or you'll be old a very long time."

Thirty seconds after the front porch screen slams, Teeny appears at my propped feet. She's holding a bowl of warm water, a washcloth, and a Ziploc bag crammed with bows and hairbrushes. "Let's get you ready to face the day."

If I've learned anything from my new post in the recliner,

arguing with this giant of a woman is useless. Besides, right now, I need the help. I sit back and close my eyes. Teeny starts at my forehead and slowly drags the brush along my scalp. Stroke after careful stroke she removes the tangles. She works silently, as if she's allowing me to mentally smooth out the sadness that came over me when Momma failed to recall her best friend. How could Momma forget LaVera? They'd grown up together. They were so close they practically wore each other's underwear. They were more than friends…they were family.

"Here you go." Momma places a tray on my lap. "Tea, hummingbird cake, and a pumpkin muffin."

"Thank you, Teeny." I shift in the chair as Teeny silently gathers her supplies. "I'm going to gain weight if you keep this up, Momma."

"You eat like a bird." Momma takes the cloth napkin and gives it an opening snap. "It won't hurt you to have a little meat on those bones." She drops the napkin onto the arm of the recliner.

"Thank you, Momma."

She leans over and brushes a strand of hair from my forehead. "You scared us all to death."

"I'm sorry."

She perches on the arm of the couch. Her head cocks as she looks me over, starting at my now-not-so-swollen ankle then traveling all the way to my face. "Your father hated snakes."

"I remember."

"He hardly ever darkened the door of the chicken house because one morning he stepped on a rat snake." She smiles. "I heard him hollering. By the time I got to the coop he was dancing a jig." Her eyes drift past me. "That man could dance."

"I loved watching the two of you dance around the kitchen."

Momma reaches over and squeezes my hand. "Those were some of the happiest days of my life." She begins to tell me other stories. Some of them I've heard before. Some are told with new details, information she must have thought I couldn't handle as a child. "My father adored me, in much the same way your father adored you. It broke his heart when I married a dreamer like Martin."

Although I've heard this story before, this time there's something different in her voice. A heartbreak I've never heard before. It's as if she's telling her family's story for the last time and wants me to get every detail straight.

Heart beating rapidly, I listen intently. "Is that why we never saw your parents?"

"No, that was my fault." Sadness tinges her voice. "I think my father would have softened had I not marched into the bank and made a big deal of depositing the first check Martin received for selling a photo." Her eyes water. "Papa pulled down the shade to his office."

This is the first time she's given me a peek into the high cost of

319

loving my father. Alienated from her flesh and blood family, she'd made Martin Slocum her family. And though he never would do anything spectacular enough to earn such enduring love…she'd loved him anyway…unconditionally.

"Someone's coming." Momma leaves me to ponder the weight of unconditional love and goes to the bay windows. I want to pull her to me, beg her to tell me more, but it seems she's completely forgotten what we were discussing.

"Sweet Moses!" Momma presses her nose to the window. "Not that woman." She wheels and marches to the front door. The screen slams behind her.

I tug the big bow from my hair and run my fingers through Teeny's work in an attempt to fluff things up. A familiar voice floats through the screen.

Wilma Rayburn.

Tossing the blanket off my not-nearly-as-swollen leg, I scramble to find the lever on the recliner. "Ira!" I press the foot rest down by sheer will. "Ira! Help!"

The old goat farmer rushes into the living room. "What's wrong?"

I grabbing for my crutches. "Make sure Momma doesn't have a gun."

"What?"

"Wilma Rayburn just pulled up."

"Heaven help us!" Ira leaves me floundering like a turtle on its back and flies from the living room.

By the time I get my crutches under me and hobble toward the door, I'm expecting to hear fireworks, but instead Momma and Wilma are standing on the porch steps and having a lovely exchange about the cooler weather. Wilma has *Get Well* balloons in one hand and a stack of papers in the other. Momma has the expression of a woman meeting a stranger.

"Mrs. Rayburn?" Breathing hard, I push the screen and swing my crutches over the threshold.

"Oh, Charlotte." Wilma recognizes my distress. "I'm sorry my arrival forced you to your feet." She nods toward Momma. "Sara and I are doing just fine here."

"This nice woman has brought balloons." Momma's face scrunches. "Is it my birthday?"

And just like that, Momma is gone again. My injured leg suddenly feels as heavy as my heart. "No, they're *Get Well* balloons."

"Is someone ill?" Momma asks.

My gaze darts to Wilma. She's gives me an understanding smile, but at this very moment, I don't want my boss's understanding or her pity. I want my mother back. I want the woman who was telling me stories with great clarity only minutes before. But that woman is gone.

"Would you like to come in, *Mrs. Rayburn*?" I emphasize the principal's name as if it's a club that can knock loose the frozen cogs in Momma's head.

"Yes, please do come in," Momma says with a cordialness I've not seen her express toward Wilma since I was in elementary school. "Have a slice of hummingbird cake."

"I don't want to put anyone out," Wilma hugs the stack in her arms to her chest.

"No trouble at all," Ira says. "Sara and I will make some tea." Ira gently takes Momma by the elbow. "Come, Sara. Let's put the kettle on."

Silence hangs in the cool air of what's left of the morning.

"Labels and lists," Wilma finally says.

I shift on my crutches. "Excuse me?"

"Before my mother passed, she was having trouble keeping things straight. So, I labeled everything...even made a name badge for me."

"Did it help?"

"For a while."

I lift one crutch and point toward the swing. "I need to get off this leg."

"Of course." Wilma holds the swing steady as I drop onto the seat. "Does the doctor think you'll suffer any permanent damage?"

"From the snake or my mother?" I hold out my hands for the

stack of work.

"This can wait." She sits beside me.

"The distraction is welcome."

She transfers the papers to me. "Only if you promise not to overdo."

We swing back and forth. The creak of the swing grates against every negative opinion Momma's ever voiced against Wilma and the quiet acts of kindness this woman continues to show me. The possibility that my mother has had difficulty sorting the truth for more years than I can count hits me in the gut. No wonder it seems Momma is slipping fast. The clock has actually been ticking for a very long time.

"Wilma, why are you being so good to me?"

My boss takes a slow, deep breath as her gaze seems to soak in the changing colors of fall. "Sara may have forgotten how much I learned from her. How much I owe her." Wilma turns to me. "But I never will."

Chapter 42

CHARLOTTE

Momma plops onto the couch and takes the TV remote from the table beside my recliner. "I'm not going to iron another thing."

I glance over the grades I'm entering into my laptop. "Fair enough."

She's been anxious and increasingly unsettled since the principal's visit. Now that I know Mrs. Rayburn has never been the witch my mother believed, I assign Momma's increasing regression to all the extra work she's undertaken to nurse me back to health, which she's done remarkably well...except for the salt on my cereal. To Momma's credit, I had rearranged the cannisters on the counter a few days before the snakebite incident. Mixing up the two similar-looking ingredients is a mistake anyone could have made.

Momma crosses her arms over her chest. "And I'm never letting anyone put me in that bathtub again."

This second announcement is so unlike my mother, the queen of neat and tidy. But these random statements are not what's not setting well with me. Since I still can't navigate the stairs, I've had to rely on Teeny to oversee Momma's hygiene. Teeny's done a passable job of keeping Momma's face washed and her hair combed. She's even convinced Momma to let her pin her bangs back with a big hairbow. But my mother has worn the same clothes for the last three days. I don't know how long it's been since she's washed her hair. In short, my mother stinks.

"Why don't you want to bathe, Momma?"

"People drown." She turns her face to me. "My daughter drowned. My husband drowned. I'll drown."

There's no readable emotion in Momma's eyes or any distress in her voice, but her mind can't seem to make sense of so many tragedies.

For a second, I want to be Caroline. If I could give my mother a minute with the child she lost so long ago, I would. I know that if I lost Aria, I'd give anything for one more minute.

I can't bear to let the *what-ifs* of that heartbreak anywhere near the scabs on my soul, so I close my computer and change the subject. "Why don't I fix us a cup of tea?"

Momma shakes her head. "That bear-of-a-doctor says you need to rest."

"That doctor is picking me up for band practice tonight." I point at my ankle. "The swelling is almost gone. Maybe I should try putting a little weight on this foot before I let him drag me out of this chair."

"You wait right there, young lady." She jumps up and starts pawing through the throw pillows. "Where is it?"

"What are you looking for?"

"The phone!" Pillows sail past my head. "I need to call LaVera."

"LaVera?"

"My lipstick order should have been here days ago." She lifts the couch cushions and glows victorious when she digs out the remote. "Here it is."

"Momma," I lower the lever on the recliner. "LaVera died, remember?"

"Nonsense." Momma stabs at the buttons on the remote. "She's holding my order up on purpose. Sometimes she waits so long I've no choice but to scrape out dabs of color with a Q-tip." Momma holds the remote to her ear. "Hello! Hello!" She lowers the remote and frantically begins to push buttons again. "Something's wrong with this phone."

Something's wrong with you.

"Momma," It's all I can do to keep my voice steady as I set the computer aside and gather my crutches. "That's the television remote."

"Don't argue with me, Caroline." She thrusts the remote at my face, pointing it like a gun. "I'm telling you something's wrong with this phone."

"Ira! Teeny!" I'm afraid to move. "I need some help in here."

"There's no reason to get your panties in a wad, Caroline." Momma bangs the remote on the coffee table several times. "I'll feed that damn cat of yours when I get good and ready."

"Momma!" Foul language is as foreign to her as I am and yet she's taken to cussing like it's her second language. "Ari feeds her cat, remember?"

"We're out of cat food. We need cat food." She paces the living room jabbing buttons on the remote. "Why can't someone get me some cat food?"

Ira shuffles into the room ahead of Teeny. He quickly assesses Momma's heightened emotions and my frustration. Within a few short steps, he plants himself in her path. "Sara, time to play the piano."

"She's in no condition to play the piano, Ira."

Ira holds up his palm. "It's how we deal with these little episodes while you're away. You'll be surprised how the music calms her down."

"She's done this before?"

"A time or two."

"Why haven't you told me?"

"What good is family if we can't bear one another's burdens, hmmm?"

Nothing I've said or done has worked. I've no choice but to back away and let Ira and Teeny have a go at her. They slowly flank my mother on both sides.

"Sara," Ira's talking soft and slow, his hand carefully extended. "Let's hear some Chopin, shall we, Sara?"

Momma shoves Ira with such force that he falls back into the recliner. "Stay away from me, old man."

Ira's eyes go wide. In the deafening silence, he clouds up and begins to cry. "This is the worst I've seen."

I fish my cell phone out of my pocket. "Itty, I can't make band practice tonight."

Chapter 43

CHARLOTTE

The house is finally quiet, but my spirit is screaming louder than a rabbit caught in a trap.

"Here," Itty stands over me with a steaming cup of tea. "Drink this."

"What is it?"

"Tea."

"With Valium?"

"Straight up chamomile."

The warmth from the cup doesn't melt the cold dread that settled in my bones long before we finally settled Momma for the night. If Teeny hadn't been here to hold Momma's flailing arms while I tried to balance on my crutches and wrestle her out of her soiled clothes and into a gown, I would have had to cut them off of her. Ira was the one who thought of using a piece of hummingbird cake to entice her

329

up the stairs. And if Aria hadn't climbed into Momma's bed and started reading, Itty would have had to give Momma a sedative to knock her out.

I glance up at the red-bearded bear standing guard over me. His face is scrunched like he's checking my medical condition and is not pleased.

Suddenly self-conscious at how poorly my appearance has probably fared in my wrestling match with Momma, I smooth my hair. "I didn't think doctors made house calls anymore."

Itty sinks onto the couch. "*Friends* always make house calls."

"I'm sorry you missed band practice."

"Do you realize you've apologized for everything but the national debt since I walked through the door?"

"I'm sorry." We look at each other and laugh. "I just did it again, didn't I?"

"Keep it up and I'll be adjusting your meds too."

"Do you think a chemical imbalance caused Momma's huge spiral?"

He gives a little shrug. "The mind is a delicate and complicated engine. The older the engine, the greater the plaque buildup. Eventually, all of us get too much gunk under the hood. That's why organs malfunction."

"That's something to look forward to."

"Sara's decline could be caused by something as simple as a

vitamin deficiency, an infection, or it could be the onslaught of full-blown Alzheimer's."

"Is she gone for good?"

"Hard to know." Itty pats my hand and stands. "Bring her to the office tomorrow and we'll take a peek under the hood. I'll draw some blood and order a CT to rule out mini strokes."

"I thought coming home would make things easier."

"For her? Or you?"

"Both."

His eyes pan the cozy little nest my family has made for me around the recliner. Ira reinforced a TV tray so that it would support my computer. Teeny stocked a small cooler with bottled water, healthy snacks, and a selection of hair bows. Aria ordered a surge-protector power strip so that I could keep my computer and phone charger cords handy. Everyone does their best to place the TV remote within my reach—well, everyone but Momma. Ira had to fish it out from under the piano after she threw it across the room when she couldn't get LaVera on the phone.

"Seems to me being here beats worrying about whether or not your mom's burning down the house, eating properly, or taking her meds."

"Or having to catch a red-eye flight from DC to scour the highways after she steals a car and escapes from her retirement home."

"Who needs frequent flier miles anyway?"

"I don't know if I can do this, Itty."

He rests a hand on my shoulder and gives me an encouraging squeeze. "You know your limits, and how far you can stretch."

"That's not what I'm afraid of." I lift teary eyes to Itty. "I don't know if I'll survive losing my mother again."

Chapter 44

CHARLOTTE

I sit in the doctor's waiting room, holding jackets, purses, and the fragile memories that used to be my mother. Her glare burns a hole in my forehead. I deserve her wrath. It was stupid of me to insist that she exchange her beloved Dearfoam slippers for her Easy Spirits. Winning a single battle is not worth the war. Or the guilt I feel over digging my heels in on such a silly issue. How my mother looks in public only matters to me because it used to matter so much to her.

Looking at her now makes me want to cry. Pale skin hangs from her cheekbones. Thin lips, naked of her trademark red lipstick, smack like a goldfish needing air. The back of her hair is tangled into a flattened peak that leans to one side of her head. The blouse she's wearing doesn't match the polyester pants with grass stains on the knees. The woman I knew wouldn't even clean out her chicken coup looking like this, let alone flounce into a crowded doctor's waiting room, order a cheeseburger and French fries at the sign-in window, then rattle off a string of cuss words when Corina said this wasn't a drive-in.

"Charlotte." Corina stands before me. "The doctor will see you now." She nods toward Momma. "Can I help you get her back to the exam room?"

"I better do it. As you know, the least little thing can set her off. Sorry about the cussing out she gave you."

Corina shrugs. "She should have let me have it in third grade. I wasn't an easy student."

"Momma loved a challenge."

"Charlotte," Corina says. "It's not easy for me to say thank you, but I want you to know how much I appreciate all you've done to encourage my son. He's a different boy."

Tears sting my eyes. "He's the same boy, just empowered."

"You're a good woman, Charlotte."

"You are too, Corina."

She nods toward Momma's blank face. "I guess we owe our thanks to this lady here."

"I guess we do." I turn and put a hand under my mother's elbow. "Let's go see Itty, shall we, Momma?"

She shrinks back from my touch. "No."

"Momma!" I tug a little harder. "Come on."

"No!" She jerks her elbow free. "Don't touch me."

"Mrs. Slocum," Corina says firmly. "You're going to be late to class and you know how rowdy we can get whenever you leave the room."

The angst immediately leaves Momma's face. She lifts her chin, stands on her own, straightens her blouse with a tug on the hem, then says, "I will not tolerate unruliness."

"No, you will not." Corina offers her arm. "Now go and reclaim order."

To my amazement, Momma marches into the exam room, clinging tightly to the girl who used to give her so much grief. "Where are the children?"

"First, you must have a talk with the principal." Corina helps Momma into a chair.

"What have I done now?" Momma asks.

"Well, now that's a surprise that I'm not at liberty to share." She picks up Momma's chart, scribbles a few notes, then says, "Dr. Ellis will be right with you."

This time it's me who lays a gentle hand on Corina, only my grip is a combination of gratitude and desperation. "Thank you, Corina."

She slips me a card. "You need me, you call. Day or night."

Within two minutes of Corina's exit, Itty sweeps into the room. His presence is so big there's little room for the terror that has its claws around my throat.

"Good morning, Mrs. Slocum." He kneels before her. "How did you sleep last night?"

"I'm afraid you have me at a disadvantage, young man."

"How so?"

"You obviously know me, but I don't know you."

Only the slight twinge at the corner of Itty's mouth reveals the impact of Momma's rapid descent into her own world. "Well, who do you think I am?"

Momma's head cocks. Her eyes slowly trace the outline of Itty's handsome features. "Since teddy bears don't come to life, I'd say you're a kind young man who needs a shave."

Itty chuckles and strokes his beard. "I can't believe you'd have me do away with ten years of hard work." Itty points at me. "Can you tell me who came with you today?"

Momma's head cocks the opposite direction and she gives my face an investigative once-over as well. I hold my breath and pray she doesn't mention the need to have my lip waxed or something done about the bags under my eyes.

She shakes her head and returns her gaze to Itty. "Sorry, dear. I can't place her."

Chapter 45

CHARLOTTE

Quick, Winnie! He's coming your way." I dive for the rooster and land in a puddle of cold mud.

"I've got him!" Winnie holds the last of Momma's feathered escapees by the leg. His flapping wings are flinging mud all over my friend's face. "Open the gate."

I scramble to my feet and fumble with the latch. "I think I'm going to have to put a combination lock on this gate."

Winnie sets the rooster free inside the wire enclosure. "Are you sure it was Sara who left it open?"

"She's obsessed with letting the chickens out and feeding the cat."

"Sara hates cats."

"I know, but she's convinced that Fig is on the prowl for her chickens."

"Then why does she let them out?"

"It makes no sense, but then nothing she does makes sense anymore."

Winnie helps me toss some corn into the feeders and secure the gate for the night. She points at my mud-soaked clothes. "I think farm life is beginning to agree with you."

"I'm glad something does because Momma argues about everything."

"Caroline!!!" The blood-curdling scream is coming from the front of the house. "Help!"

Winnie and I race toward Momma's cries. I round the corner and stop. My mother's standing on the porch. Her robe is hanging open, exposing her completely naked body. She's pacing and raking her fingers through her thinning hair.

"Momma!" I fly up the steps. "What's wrong? What's happened?"

"Polygon." Her eyes are wide and totally crazed. "I can't find Polygon anywhere."

"You mean Bojangles?"

She scowls at me like I'm the one who's lost my mind. "My. Bird. Is. Gone." She jabs her finger toward the screen. "That girl, the one with the cat, left the cage open. I'm sure that damn cat of hers ate my bird."

"Aria would never let your bird out, Momma." I reach for her robe ties and attempt to help her cover herself. "She loves Bojangles."

Momma slaps my hands away. "She did. I saw her. She must be punished."

"Sara, let's go in and look for your bird, okay?" Winnie comes up the steps slowly. "I'll help."

Momma raises two clenched fists. "Who are you?"

"That's Winnie," I say. "Our mail lady."

"She smells like bird droppings. Did she take my bird?"

"No, Momma. Winnie's been helping me round up your chickens."

"I don't have chickens. I hate chickens." She wheels and runs inside. "Polygon!"

Winnie and I exchange glances. "I'm sorry you had to see this, Win."

"I'm sorry you're having to live this."

We kick off our muddy boots and step inside. Momma is cursing and running back and forth on the path she's worn between the living room and dining room. Her robe flies like a cape behind her leaving every sagging body part subject to examination. Ira and Teeny shuffle after her. But she manages to dodge their attempts to snag her arms. Aria stands at the top of the stairs watching the circus, horror written all over her face. When she sees me come through the front door, she races down the stairs.

"Mom, Nana's gone crazy."

"I know, baby." I cup her face. "It's all right."

"Bojangles is in his cage. I tried to show her. Ira tried to show her. Teeny tried. But it's like she can't see the truth even when it's right in front of her." Aria grabs my hand. "Mom, I'm scared."

"Me too, but it's going to okay." I kiss her forehead. "Let's try an experiment."

"Like what?"

"Let's see what happens if you play some Chopin."

"Right now?"

"Ira says music calms her down."

"This is crazy."

"I know, baby, but I need you to trust me."

Aria nods and dashes to the piano. She stretches her fingers then begins to play.

Momma continues frantically searching the house and screaming obscenities. After the first measure she stops running. By the second measure she has quit yelling. By the third measure she begins to inch toward the piano.

A melancholy melody floats through the air and wraps us all in a blanket of calm. I ease toward my bedraggled mother. "Momma," I dare to touch her elbow. "Want to sit?"

She gives up an exhausted nod. "There." She points to the piano bench where Aria's sitting as her fingers dance over the keys.

"Got room for Nana?" I whisper to Aria.

She nods and continues playing without missing a note as she slides to the far end of the bench. "Play with me, Nana," she encourages. "Please."

Momma lifts her hands to the keys. Her fingers move as if they were young and carefree once again. The melody flowing from her hands carries me away to the sultry summer nights our family trekked to the bluff to sit beneath a canopy of stars. Aria drops back, offering an underscored support of broken-chord, left-handed accompaniment. There are so many different layers of sound in this work, each requiring a variety of touches and Momma nails them all...perfectly *and* with the emotion and clarity of someone in their right mind.

I don't want the music to end, this moment of sanity to slip away. But it does. When the last note fades, the only dry eyes in the room belong to Momma.

She lifts her hands from the keys, turns to Aria and says, "You've improved, but don't think that gives you license to slack off."

None of us can restrain the laughter, the sheer joy of seeing this glimpse of her again. But our outbursts startle her. I can see her drawing into herself again, but right before she goes, she looks at Ira and says, "Martin, how could you lose our daughter?"

Chapter 46

CHARLOTTE

Aria and I walk through the pasture, each of us holding onto one of Momma's arms.

"Maybe we should have put her on the tractor." Aria gently guides her grandmother around a clump of bull thistle.

"Loud noises really seem to terrify her."

We shuffle through the green grasses in silence. The cool spring breeze has given way to the heat of summer. Faded bluebonnets are beginning to seed the hillsides. In the distance, vultures hang in the sky, circling the banks of the river like they have all the time in the world. The dead are, after all, going nowhere. I know that any poor creature who'd succumbed to the extraordinarily difficult winter had not died in vain. His body had simply given in to its new purpose...to nourish the next cycle of life. But as I've watched my mother become a ghost of her former self these past few months, I must admit I'm pained by the inevitable reality all of us will eventually face.

The long, cold days of winter bled into a spring filled with my mother's bouts of vicious anger and terrible tantrums. While this phase of her disease has been difficult, it's her newest phase of apathy that I can't stand. No matter what we do, Momma sits and stares out the window. She won't go to church. She won't interact with Aria's brain games. She no longer knows Ira and Teeny. She sleeps more than usual. She can't follow the simple instructions I have taped to everything, simple things like CLOSE THE FRIDGE DOOR, FLUSH THE TOILET, and HOLD RAIL WHEN YOU STEP DOWN. The old stories she used to tell are locked inside of her, along with even short responses like yes or no.

Sadly, my mother has even given up her beloved piano. According to everything I've read, hearing is the last thing to go. Many doctors, including Itty, contend that music is soothing. Aria and I take turns playing. Sometimes Ira and Teeny dance. But Momma remains lifeless in the recliner.

But the worst, the hardest of all to take, is that she no longer speaks my name. I'd even settle for being confused with Caroline, if she would just speak the name of her children. It's as if neither of us ever existed.

This need to reconnect to her one more time is why I've enlisted Aria's help to get Momma outside. Maybe if she breathes some fresh air, feels the sunshine on her face, and walks the land she loves, maybe then she'll return to us.

Every road I've taken on this journey has been paved with pain and pocked with guilt. Today's plan will probably be no different, but I won't know if I don't try.

Is the long goodbye this hard for other families? Do other caregivers worry that their loved one is lonely inside the little shell they've slipped into? Does she hurt? Is she hungry? Tired? Frightened? I ask her these things several times a day, but she can no longer tell me. On those rare occasions when she does look at me, it's as if she's begging me to make her suffering end.

Several well-meaning people have suggested I put my mother in a nursing home. I'd tried pawning her off once. She was so miserable, she stole a car and escaped with Ira and Teeny. For now, sending her away is not an option. As long as I'm able to bathe her, feed her, and continue to do a decent job teaching my students, I will. But I fear the day is not far off when I may have to rethink this decision. Good decisions are not made in panic. I spend a great deal of time gathering information on the expected progression of this disease and the care facilities within driving distance. None of what I've learned is easy. What I wouldn't give to have one more real conversation with my mother, to ask her advice.

This time, I would listen.

There are so many things I still want to say to Momma, but I'm not sure she'd understand the words. I want to thank her for all the hours we spent together at the piano, for all the pie crusts she helped me roll out, for her belief in me. But the most important thing I want to say I should have said twenty-five years ago. Losing her in the past hurt, losing her forever will tear me apart.

I'm so grateful to have Ira and Teeny's help. They give me a break every chance they get and because I trust them to never take their eyes off Momma, I've not had to miss many days of school. I've learned that people want to help if you're not afraid to ask. Watching Ira and Teeny care for my mother, for Aria, and for me, has taught me that the unconditional love of family is far more than helpful and consoling…it's so liberating.

"Look, Nana." Aria bends, plucks a pale bloom from the weeds, then holds it to Momma's nose. "Bluebonnets."

Momma frowns and knocks the bluebonnet away from her nose.

"Guess she can't remember flowers," I say. "Maybe we should take her back."

Momma grunts and leans toward the bluff, like a thirsty horse who's smelled water and is now tugging against its traces.

Aria wipes her hand on her shorts. "I think she wants to go to the river."

"I doubt she even knows there's a river there anymore."

"What would it hurt if we let her see it?"

"The bluff's too dangerous, Ari."

"What's she gonna do? Jump?"

Momma used to dive with the best of them, but since Caroline's death, she hadn't been in the water either. "She might fall."

"We'll hang on to her," Aria argues.

"No, Ari."

"Mom, the last time Nana talked she was telling me about the day she and Pop skinny dipped in the river. I know she doesn't remember us anymore, but maybe she can remember when she and Pops were young. When she was in love."

"You're right, as usual," I concede. "She was happy there long before she wasn't." I tighten my grip on Momma's elbow. Against my better judgment, I say, "Let's give it a shot."

We take it easy on the climb. Momma doesn't stumble on the rocks. It's as if she knows this path as well as she used to know a keyboard or her multiplication tables. If this place remains in her memory, perhaps somewhere, deep inside of her, I'm still there.

By the time we reach the flat outcropping beneath the live oak tree, all three of us are winded. We stop at the wrought-iron fence Momma had built around the graves of my sister and father. Green shoots poke through the dead weeds reminding me that despite my best efforts to keep up with everything, some things, like tending our family's graveyard, continue to fall through the cracks.

"Want to sit on the bench a moment, Momma?"

She stares at the headstones. Silent and blank-faced. Does she even know what this place is? Or is she imagining how her name will look inscribed upon a slab of granite? I study her a little closer, hoping she'll give me a clue as to what's going on inside her head. A lone tear trickles down her cheek. Tears sting my own eyes. She may not know who is buried here, but she knows she loved them.

I make a mental note to record this moment in the journal Itty gave me.

"Journaling can be comforting for people going through difficult circumstances," he'd said when he handed me the beautiful red leather book one night after band practice.

Yes, I play with the band.

Another good reason to never say never, a lesson you think I would have learned when I said I'd never return to Texas. Or changed my major from education to pre-law. Or signed my final divorce decree. Or sent for the two senior citizens I've grown to love like family and can't bear to part with. Or forgave my mother and myself for the way we poorly handled our grief.

And yet, here I am. Once again doing exactly what I said I never would…playing with a praise band on Sundays.

The music gives me great peace, but it's worshipping with my new friends that carries me through these dark days. Winnie says my involvement with the band has taken a load off her. "Being your only friend nearly put me under," she teases on the nights I'm not too exhausted to sit on the porch and share a glass of wine now that the weather has warmed. "If you'd only agree to have dinner with that gem of a doctor, then Bo and I could finally quit worrying about you."

Sometimes I use the journal Itty gave me to sort my feelings for him. Maybe I should start a different journal for the impossible task of untangling him from his care of my mother. The two of them are emotionally tied and have been since Itty was in her third-grade class. But sometimes I can't help but wonder if those big, gentle hands that have so lovingly cared for Momma could also care for me.

For now, I must learn to be content to use those very private pages to vent my frustrations, cry my tears, and remind myself that I won't have Momma forever. This is not the time to sort out the pros and cons of Benjamin Ellis. Nor is it the time to make the same, grief-laden mistake that I'd made with James McCandless.

Momma drops my hand and takes off for the bluff at a full-speed run.

"Nana!" Aria springs into action much faster than me. "Stop!"

"Momma!" I scramble to catch up, but in my snake boots I'm clumsy and slow.

By the time I reach them, Aria's struggling to maintain her hold on Momma's wrist. "Nana, no."

"Momma," I ease close, working to regain calm in my body language and voice. "That's close enough." I offer my hand. "Grab hold of me, please."

She shakes her head and lunges forward.

"Mom, what should we do?" Aria's boots drag across the limestone as she tugs against the supernatural strength Momma suddenly seems to possess.

"Let me go," Momma says. Plain. Clear. Determined.

The first words she's spoken in three months and I understand her plea for freedom perfectly.

My insides tremble in fear. "You'll get your boots wet."

She lifts one booted foot. "Let. Me. Go."

"Is she trying to kill herself?" Terror swims in Aria's eyes.

"I don't think so."

"Call Ira," Aria begs. "Tell him to bring the tractor."

I shake my head. "Take off her boots."

"No!"

"Do it."

Aria glares at me like I'm crazy, but she obeys without voicing the million questions that must be running through her mind. She squats and gently pulls off her grandmother's rubber boots. "There, Nana."

Momma looks at her yellowed toe nails and then lifts her chin and smiles. She holds out her hand to me. "Let's swim, Martin."

My father's name rolls off her tongue with the same delight as if he'd just come up behind her in the kitchen and grabbed her around the waist and kissed her neck.

I glance over the edge, at the water swirling below. This river has no memory of all it has taken from me...the hours and hours of enjoyment...the bond of a tight-knit family...my peace. I haven't jumped from this ledge since I dove in to save my daughter, and I wouldn't have jumped the day Aria fell in, if I hadn't been scared to death of losing another person I loved. I have no intention of jumping again. Ever.

"More fun?" Momma's eyes are clear. I can't be certain she knows *who* she's asking, but she knows full-well *what* she's asking.

She's asking me to let my fear go. To enjoy this river. To enjoy life. To live again. Fearless and free.

I kick off my boots and take her hand. "We can do this together. Right, Momma?"

She nods.

"Wait for me." Aria sheds her boots in record time and flanks Momma on the other side.

Hand in hand, three generations of Slocum women stand on the edge of letting go of everything that has kept us apart.

"Sweet Moses!" Momma's joyous shout echoes in the canyon.

"Sweet Moses!" Aria and I crow at the top of our lungs.

In tandem, holding tight to each other, the three of us leap.

Feet first, we plunge into the crystal water. The water washes over us, sucking us to the limestone bottom. Momma's grip tightens on my hand. I search for her face. Her lips are stretched in a tight smile. If it weren't for the gray hair fanning around head, I'd swear she's suddenly ten years younger. She closes her eyes as if she's allowing the water to remove everything that's weighed her down. Our feet touch the bottom at the same time and her eyes pop open. With a nod to me and then to Aria, she pushes with a leg strength I did not know she possessed. All three of us shoot toward the light.

When we break the surface, Momma throws back her head and laughs. "Oh, Charlotte Ann. Let's do that again."

TO MY READERS:

Thank you for coming along for the Slocum women's bumpy ride to unconditional love. I hope their story has given you the courage to tackle the hurdles in your relationships. If you somehow missed the first book in this series (FLYING FOSSILS) you can pop over to your favorite digital retailer and pick it up.

Remember **reviews** help an author so much. When readers take the time to leave an honest review, it causes the digital book fairies to give this book the love and attention it needs to be seen and read by others. Please share your love of this story and leave a **review** on the retailer site where you purchased this book. Thank you.

If you don't want to miss my next book, sign up for my newsletter. I promise not to blow up your inbox. You'll only hear from me when I have a special treat, insider tip, or a new book to offer you. Here's the link you'll need to receive your first free gift just for signing up: www.lynnegentry.com

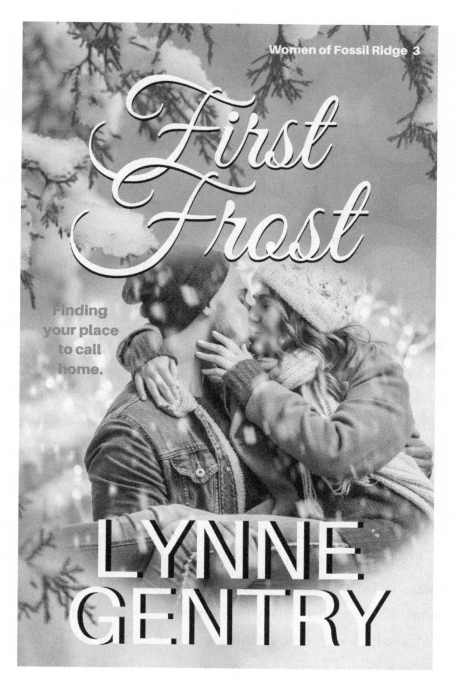

Here's a peek at First Frost:

Chapter 1

Momma died before the bluebonnets went to seed.

I'll admit, my mother's passing came as a relief...at first. Not because I wanted my mother to die. No, quite the opposite. After a twenty-plus-year cold war, we'd finally called a truce. We were in the beginning stages of rebuilding our relationship when the tiny cracks in Momma's cognitive abilities rapidly became uncrossable fissures. As my strong, brilliant, and talented mother transformed into a terrified and helpless child, I became more and more desperate to hang on to her. I searched for the best medical care, signed her up for the latest medications, made drastic changes to her diet, and spent hours trying to stimulate her mind.

Nothing stopped Alzheimer's wicked progression.

My mother's physician, Dr. Benjamin Ellis, an old friend I've always called Itty, reassures me that feeling a sense of relief is a normal reaction after caring for someone who is terminally ill. I don't need a doctor, even if he is also a well-meaning friend, to tell me that watching a loved one struggle to remember who she is, how

354

to eat and, at the end, how to breathe is difficult.

But now that the temporary relief has given way to the grief, I'm the one struggling to catch my breath.

I grip the porch railing. The peeling paint is sticky with mid-August humidity. Overhead, end-of-season baby swallows poke their beaks over the edges of the muddy nests and squeal for their breakfast. I've ignored the poop-splattered porch planks long enough. Now that I'm no longer meeting the demands of Momma's care, I have the time to paint the porch, but I simply don't have the energy.

Losing Momma feels like I'm being held underwater and the air is gone from my lungs. Benjamin assures me that I *will* surface. I'm counting on him to be right. I can't lose my job. My principal, Wilma Rayburn, has graciously allowed me to skip several summer in-service events. Tempting as it is to request a bit more time off, I can't.

This job doesn't pay well. Thankfully, the judge ruled that it's enough to raise my daughter. With Winnie's astute legal representation, James and I reached a divorce settlement. To keep Aria out of a nasty, legal tug-of-war, I agreed to give him custody of our bank account and all of our shared properties. He agreed to give me full custody of Aria.

I definitely got the better deal.

Just how I'm going to pay for an advanced music education on the salary of a country school music teacher remains to be seen. I love my job. Teaching kids has fulfilled my dreams, the ones I had long before I assumed my sister's dreams. Becoming a lawyer was Charlotte's plan. Not mine. My foolish attempt to make up for my failure to save her had nearly killed me and it almost destroyed any chance of ever reconciling with my mother. If Momma taught me anything, it's that I must never forget who I am again.

My gaze drifts to the rose garden. The New Dawn climbers have suffered under my lack of care, but the Butterfly Roses are more beautiful than I've ever seen them. The stunning mix of yellow, pink, and crimson blooms on the same stalk represents the changes that eventually come to all of us, Momma used to say. We're born yellow and bright, full of hope. Then as we mature, life's skirmishes pink us up. It's not until we've bled and learned from our suffering that we turn crimson...the most beautiful rose in the garden.

"Mom?" Aria steps out onto the porch, her Siamese cat Fig tucked under one arm and a cup of steaming Earl Grey in the other hand. The dark circles under my fourteen-year-old daughter's blue eyes are evidence that I'm not the only one having trouble sleeping. "Did you eat?"

I shake my head. "I'll grab a banana from the cafeteria."

"Yeah, but will you eat it?" She hands me the tea. "You're still losing weight." She seems to have matured from thirteen to thirty in a matter of weeks and that adds another layer of guilt to my shoulders.

I had to grow up way too fast after my sister died. I don't want my girl to miss out on what's left of her childhood. "Have I thanked you for helping me take such good care of your Nana?"

"Yeah, like a million times."

I tuck a blonde curl behind her ear. "It's time to let me look out for you now, okay?"

The screen door flies open.

Black and white teacup poodles yap around the feet of my overall-clad boarder, Ira Conner. "Goodness. Mercy. Hush."

The dogs obey the old man who has become such a comfort to me. Ira and his little dogs greet Aria and me every morning and every day after school. The old goat farmer is no longer able to do more than feed the chickens and tend Momma's parrot, but we love having a man around the house. He's both the grandfather Aria never knew and my father the way I always pictured him.

"Mornin', Ira." I shout over the barking dogs.

Ira waves us in. "Hurry." His eyes gleam bright as his bald head. "Bojangles is talking!"

Aria and I have to race to keep up with Ira's spry strides toward the kitchen.

Teeny, my other geriatric boarder, stands at the counter slicing apples. She's dressed in a lime green blouse and sports a giant tangerine bow clipped in her white hair. Rumor has it that I've taken in boarders to help defray expenses at Fossil Ridge. Teeny and Ira do not pay me a dime. They came here after they helped Momma escape from her assisted living facility. They live here because we've made them family.

"Sara was right." Teeny pushes her bow back into place. "This bird has become a regular chatterbox." She hands Aria an apple slice. "Like me, he has to be enticed."

I smile at Teeny's admission. When she and Momma first met at The Reserve, Teeny seldom spoke. Since becoming part of our family, she's talking more and more, a fact that warms my heart as much as it had cheered Momma.

"Go easy now, Aria," Ira coaches.

Aria lowers Fig to the floor then slowly approaches the ringneck parrot's cage. "Here, Bojangles." She eases the apple between the bars and holds it steady. "What does he say?" she asks Ira.

"Hang on," Ira says. "Give him a minute."

We all hold our breath and lean toward the cage.

Bojangles turns his head then inches along his perch bar. "Sweeeet Mo!" He snatches the apple slice and flutters to the opposite side of the cage.

"Did he just say Sweet Moses?" I ask Ira.

"We've been workin' on it for weeks." A grin splits Ira's wrinkled face. "Sara would have loved it."

The memory of Momma standing on the edge of the bluff and

shouting her pet phrase at the top of her lungs brings tears. "Yes, yes she would have." I kiss Ira's cheek. "Thank you." I grab my satchel. "Sweet Moses, Ari. We've got to go. Nana would have had our hides for being late on the first day."

"Sweet Moses," Aria howls.

"Sweet Mo!" Bojangles echoes.

Spirits lifted, Aria and I rush out and climb into Momma's old car. Thanks to my neighbor Bo Tucker and his generous mechanical skills, the Escort is still running, which has saved me from adding a car payment to my slim budget.

"What about Teeny and Ira?" Aria asks as we bounce over the cattle guard.

"What about them?"

"Are you going to send them away?"

The question floors me. Aria knows it was my idea to invite Momma's friends to come live with us. "We couldn't have kept your Nana at home for as long as we did without Teeny and Ira's help." I press the gas and we fly across the bridge that spans the Frio. "They've become so much more than Nana's friends. They're family."

Relief brightened Aria's face. "I was afraid you were planning to change things up since Nana...you know..."

"Died." I reach for her hand. "You can say the word, Ari. Because that's what happened. Nana died."

"I know, but saying it seems so...final."

Loss hangs between us heavy as wet jeans on a clothesline. Tempting as it is to let time dry the weight, I know better. Aria's heartbreak will grow heavier and heavier if I don't address how she's feeling.

I clear the lump in my throat. "When my sister died, my mother refused to use the word. She left my sister's room intact and acted like Charlotte was still away at college. All of that denial and pretense made me very angry." Gravel pings the undercarriage. "It's okay to be sad that your grandmother is dead, Ari."

"Are you sad?"

"Yes, very."

She pondered my admission for a few minutes. "Are you going to sell Fossil Ridge?"

"Why would you think that?"

"Nana said she probably wouldn't even be cooled off good before you put her ranch on the market."

I don't know whether to laugh or cry. I thought Momma and I had cleared up any misperceptions we had about each other's motivations. Apparently not. "Good mothers do what's best for their kids. Education does not come cheap."

"Geez, Mom. How many times do I have to tell you? If you get me a horse, I don't have to go to Juilliard."

"We can't afford another mouth to feed." I crank the wheel and the Escort screeches onto the highway. "I gave up my dreams. I'm not about to let you give up yours."

EXTRA BONUS FOR MY READERS

Have you met my **other** Texas family?

Other Books by Lynne Gentry

Walking Shoes

Shoes to Fill

Dancing Shoes

Baby Shoes

Ghost Heart

Flying Fossils

Here's a peek at WALKING SHOES:

Chapter One

"Living in the parsonage is not for sissies." Leona Harper's husband planted a kiss on the top of her head. "If you want to wear fancy red shoes, wear 'em, darlin'."

"Maybe I'll wait until Christmas."

"It's almost Thanksgiving. Why don't you go ahead and break them in?"

"I was fixin' to, but ..." Leona twisted her ankle in front of the mirror, imagining herself brave enough to wear trendy shoes whenever she wanted. "You don't think they might be a bit much?" She reached for the shipping box. "The bows didn't look this big on my computer screen."

"So what if they are?"

"I wouldn't dare fuel Maxine's fire."

J.D. tucked his Bible under one arm and pulled Leona to him with the other. "If Sister Maxine wants to talk, let's give her somethin' real juicy to say."

Leona loved the way this bear of a man nuzzled her neck every Sunday morning. J.D. Harper was as handsome as the day they met some thirty years ago, even with the silver streaks traipsing across his well-trained waves. Folks often guessed him a successful CEO of some major corporation rather than the pastor of a dying church in a small west Texas town.

"I can hear her now. 'Anyone who can buy new shoes doesn't need a raise.'" Leona pushed J.D. away and undid the ankle straps. "Eighteen years and we haven't even had a cost of living adjustment."

"The church provides our house."

"You know I adore living in this old parsonage, but we're not accruing a dime of equity." She buried the shoes in the box and closed the lid. "How are we ever going to be able to afford to retire?" She stashed the box next to her forgotten dreams.

"We've got equity where it counts—"

"Don't say heaven." Leona rolled her eyes at J.D.'s ability to remain slow to anger. "As long as the Board believes we're living on easy street, I don't know how we're going to make ends meet here on earth."

"The Board? Or Maxine?"

"Same thing."

"Live your life worrying about what Maxine Davis thinks, she wins." He had her, and he knew it. "Is that what you want?"

Ignoring the righteous twinkle in his eye, Leona slipped on the sensible brown flats she'd worn for the past ten years. "I hate it when you preach at me, J.D. Harper." She threaded her hand through the crook in his suit-clad arm.

"So many worries. So little time." He kissed her temple. "If it weren't for guilt trips, you wouldn't go anywhere."

"It's all we can afford." Leona scooped up the Tupperware caddie that contained her famous chicken pot pie. What good did it do to long for exotic cruises or expensive adventures? She'd given up those dreams, along with her dreams of writing, long ago. But she'd never give up on wanting her whole family together, even for just a couple of days. "Let's get the Storys and go."

Sitting on the living room couch were the blue-haired twins and founding members of Mt. Hope Community Church. They waited where they waited every Sunday morning. Today, instead of their regular offering of canned pickles, they each had a large relish tray on their lap.

"Etta May. Nola Gay. I'm fixin' to preach the Word. You girls got your amens ready?" J.D. offered Nola Gay his arm.

Nola Gay blushed, "Reverend Harper, you're such a tease."

"It's my turn to hold his arm, Sister," Etta May complained.

"Lucky for you lovely ladies, I've got two arms."

Arm-in-arm J.D. and his fan club crossed the church parking lot, trailed by the lowly pastor's wife.

J.D. opened the door to the fellowship hall. The familiar aroma of coffee and green bean casseroles assaulted Leona's nose. If only she had a nickel for every meal she'd eaten in this dingy room, maybe they could pay all their bills, save a little for retirement, and even afford the mini vacation J.D. had reluctantly agreed to take when the kids came home for Thanksgiving.

"Y'all need help with those trays?" Leona asked Nola Gay.

"We may be slow, but we can still handle a few pickles," Nola Gay assured her.

"Holler if y'all need me." Leona headed for the kitchen, weaving through the scattered tables. Crock-Pots brimming with roast and carrots or pinto beans and ham lined the counter.

While J.D. checked the overloaded power strip, Leona deposited her contribution for the monthly potluck scheduled to follow the morning service. She glanced at the dessert table. Maxine's coconut cake was not in its usual place. "I'm going to my seat."

"You can't avoid her forever," J.D. whispered.

It wasn't that she was afraid of the sour elder's wife; she just hadn't figured out the best way to address Maxine's latest attack on J.D.'s attempt to make the worship service a little bit more relevant, something that would help an outsider feel welcome.

Truth be known, Maxine and Howard didn't want outsiders to get comfortable on the pews of Mt. Hope Community Church. Especially anyone they considered to be "the less fortunate." With the addition of the highway bypass, the community had experienced an influx of vagrants. Most of them needed help. Howard and Maxine preferred these interlopers to just keep walking.

Why God had seen fit to park a generous man like J.D. Harper at a church where the chairman of the elder board's wife loved only two things—having the last word and adding to her list of complaints against the Harpers—was first in a list of pressing questions Leona intended to ask when she did get to heaven.

"I don't want to start a fight before church," Leona said. "It would ruin my worship and I'll be hanged if I'll let her take that too."

"That's my girl." J.D.'s eyes lighted on something behind her. "Better put your game face on, Maxine's fixin' to test your resolve."

Leona turned to see Maxine prancing through the door with her coconut cake seated on a throne of beautiful cut glass and her heavy purse dangling from the crook of her arm.

"Morning, Leona!" Maxine crowed.

Leona plastered on a smile and maneuvered through the chairs. "Can I give you a hand?"

"I don't think so." Maxine pulled her cake out of reach. "Unlike that Pyrex stuff you bring your little casserole in, this is an extremely expensive piece of antique glass. This pedestal has been in our family for years."

Leona knew all about the Davis glass. Every Christmas, Leona had to practically beg Maxine to let the hospitality committee use the crystal punchbowl the Davis family had donated to the church on the condition the church insure it. The job of washing the slippery thing was one Leona tried to avoid.

Leona nipped the reply coiling on her tongue and offered her best platitude, "Your cake and platter are as beautiful as ever. Oh, I forgot I promised the Storys I'd give them a hand." She smiled and quickly moved on to help the twins fussing over how many dill or sweet pickles they should put on their trays.

Leona regretted that from behind her retreat could leave the impression of her tail securely tucked between her legs. She waited until Maxine exited the fellowship hall before she headed to the sanctuary and her regular front row pew.

J.D. slid in just as Wilma Wilkerson blasted out the first note on the organ. He winked at her and began to sing.

Still stinging from her failure at repairing her relationship with Maxine, Leona inched along the wooden pew that vibrated from the force of her husband's resonant bass. Clutching the worn hymnal, she filled her lungs to capacity, tightened her diaphragm, and joined him in praise. Music always carried her past any earthly troubles.

Behind the large oak pulpit, song leader, Parker Kemp brought the organist and sparse crowd to a synchronized close. Blue from holding on to the last note, Leona glanced across the sanctuary aisle. Maxine Davis eyed her back with her nose wrinkled in disapproval. Leona quickly diverted her gaze.

"And the church said?" Parker flipped to his next selection.

"Amen," the Storys chimed in unison.

"Before the sermon, we'll be singing all five verses of page 156. Please stand, if it's convenient."

Solid oak pews groaned as the congregation lumbered to their feet.

Parker gave a quick nod to the organist, readying his hand for the beat. His expression morphed into that dazzling smile sure to land him the perfect wife someday.

Leona loved the Sundays this radiant young fellow led. Unlike the steady diet of first-and-third-versers, the county extension agent sang every word of every verse. Hymns that once plodded the narrow aisles danced before the Lord under Parker's direction. His ability to stir in a little spirit always gave Leona the distinct feeling rain had fallen upon her parched lawn, offering a smidgen of hope that if this congregation had a shot at resurrection, maybe she did too.

Naturally, Maxine claimed allowing such unrestrained expressions of joy during the song service might lead to who-knows-what in the sanctuary. It had cost J.D. popularity points with the elder board, but in the end none of them had been willing to remove Parker's name from the volunteer rotation. Thank God.

The congregation fidgeted as Wilma Wilkerson attempted to prod some heft into the organ's double row of yellowed keys and squeaky pedals.

Leona used the extra time to beseech the Lord on Parker's

behalf. She'd always hoped their daughter Maddie would one day consider Parker more than an irritation, but Maddie was insisting on going another direction.

Perhaps the recent arrival of Bette Bob's adorable niece was God's plan for Parker. Unlike J.D., who never did anything without praying it through for weeks, she was flexible. To prove it, she made a quick promise to the Lord that she'd do her best to connect Parker and Bette Bob's niece at today's potluck.

J.D. reached for Leona's hand and gave it a squeeze, same as he did every Sunday before he took the pulpit. Some pastors prayed. Most checked their fly. Mt. Hope's preacher always held his wife's hand during the song preceding his sermon.

Relishing her role as coworker in the Kingdom, Leona wiggled closer, her upper thigh pressed tight against her husband's. Nestled securely against J.D.'s charcoal pinstripes, Leona could hear the throaty warble of the Story sisters parked three pews back.

The blue-haired-saint sandwich had a crush on her husband, but to begrudge these seniors a little window shopping bordered on heresy.

The old girls had suffered a series of setbacks the last few months, burying several of their shriveled ranks. What would it hurt if staring at her handsome husband gave them a reason to get out of bed on Sunday mornings? Besides, Widow's Row vacancies were increasing at an alarming rate, and replacing these committed congregants seemed unlikely, given the current trend of their small town's decline.

J.D.'s familiar grip throttled Leona's errant thoughts.

She patted his hand. Her husband felt unusually clammy this chilly fall morning. Was this a new development, or something she'd missed earlier because she'd been in such a twit?

J.D. had been dragging lately. She'd just written off his exhaustion as the discouragement that hounded a man with the weight of a dying congregation on his shoulders.

What if something else was wrong? What if the elders had voted to let them go and J.D. hadn't told her? She felt her keen senses kick into overdrive. Out of the corner of her eye, she checked his coloring.

"Are you okay, J.D.?" Leona whispered.

He kept his eyes on Parker, but Leona knew he wasn't just waiting for his cue to take the stage. He slipped his arm around her trim waist, drawing her close. He whispered, "Who by worrying can add a single hour to her life?" His breath warmed the top of her color-treated head. A tingle raced through her body.

J.D. had promised her he'd take off for the entire week of Thanksgiving. He needed a break and they both needed the time to reconnect their family.

Both kids had finally agreed to come home from their universities. Leona wanted to believe David's and Maddie's hearts were softening, but she knew they'd only consented to a family gathering because it was their father's fiftieth birthday. For him, they would do anything. For her? Well, that was a prayer the Lord had yet to answer.

The song ended, but the glow lighting Parker's dark eyes did not. "You may be seated." He gathered his list and songbook and left the podium.

J.D. ascended the stage steps as if taking some faith mountain.

He removed the sermon notes tucked inside a leather-bound Bible and surveyed the crowd's upturned faces.

Leona recognized the tallying look in her husband's eyes. He would know the dismal attendance count before Deacon Tucker posted the numbers on the wooden board in the back of the sanctuary.

J.D. unbuttoned his coat, ran his hand down his tie. "Mornin', y'all." He greeted his congregation of eighteen years with the same determined expression he had his first Sunday in this pulpit. Filleting the worn pages of his Bible with a satin ribbon, he opened to the day's chosen text.

The rustle of people settling into their favorite pews rippled across the sanctuary.

The Smoots' tiny addition fussed in the back row. Newborn cries were rare here. Leona was grateful the Smoots had decided to stay in Mt. Hope. Other than Parker, most of the young people, including her own children, left after high school and never came back.

The sound of children was something Leona missed. She'd loved the days of diapers, sleepless nights, and planting kisses on the exquisite soft spot right below tiny earlobes.

If only dispensing love could remain that simple and teething remain a mother's biggest worry.

Leona offered a quick prayer for the fertile mother of four. Maybe the Lord would spare that young woman the mistakes of her pastor's wife.

Leona reined in her wandering focus and aimed it on the man standing before the congregation. No matter what became of her relationship with her children, she could always take comfort in the fact that at least she had J.D.

Uneasiness suddenly intruded upon her admiration. Something wasn't right. A shimmering halo circled her husband's head. Surely the unnerving effect was the result of the flickering fluorescent stage lighting. J.D. would surely lampoon her overactive imagination, but Leona couldn't resist scanning the platform.

Four dusty ficus trees and two tall-backed elders' chairs were right where Noah left them when he exited the ark.

Leona smoothed the Peter Pan collar tightening around her neck. Her hand froze at her throat, her breath trapped below her panicked grasp.

Glistening beads of sweat dripped from J.D.'s brow. He

removed a monogrammed handkerchief from his pocket and mopped his notes. With a labored swipe, he dried his forehead and returned the soaked linen to his breast pocket. As he clasped the lip of the pulpit, his knuckles whitened.

Leona stood, ready to call out no matter how inappropriate, but her husband's warning gaze urged her to stay put.

J.D. cleared his throat. "There was one who was willing to die—" the pastor paused—"that you might live." A pleased smile lit his face. He placed a hand over his heart and dropped.

Made in the USA
Middletown, DE
19 August 2024

59402102R00230